TAKEN
Before her very Eyes

Wade Faubert

Cover Designed by, Jessi Nunns

www.heavenlydayphotos.com

ISBN-13: 978-0-9880612-2-4

CONTENTS

Bonus Sample of;
Wampus Springs – Mark of the Wolf

CONTENTS

Bonus Sample of;
Wampus Springs – Mark of the Wolf

PROLOGUE

"What are we doing out here?" Summer sighed, shifting in the front seat and gazing across at Nate's hardened face. "I know we need to patrol the entire County, but there's never anything happening out here. Wouldn't we be more valuable on the city streets?"

Nate's blue eyes met her with a knowing look. "We'll get to those parts of Chatham in due time. But there's a route that's been laid out and we're supposed to follow it."

"How can I forget?" Summer rolled her eyes. "You're so anal. Just because the chief laid out a route doesn't mean you can't deviate from it once in a while. Wouldn't it be nice to spice things up sometimes?"

"Spiced up, huh." Nate sighed, raising his left eyebrow. "Somehow I don't think an old man in the chief's position would like spice. He strikes me as a heartburn, acid reflux and irritable bowel syndrome type of guy."

"I'm just saying," Summer shook her head, "would it kill you to start somewhere different on the route and go

1

backwards once in a while? I'll bet Stephens and Malroy don't follow the same route?"

"I can guarantee they don't. Hell they spend half their time goofing off behind the old grocery store."

"How do you know that?" Summer flipped her blond hair back from her face and leaned closer to Nate, hoping he'd spill the beans.

"Those stupid asses brag about it every night in the change room. I keep telling them that if they wanna screw around on the job, that's fine, but not to go spreading it around the station, cause sooner or later the chief is gonna find out and then there'll be hell to pay." Nate tapped his finger on the dash. "But you'll be able to vouch that we followed protocol the way the chief wanted."

"And what makes you think he'll believe a word we say."

"Not we." Nate grinned. "You. He'll believe you because you're a woman."

Summer felt her cheeks heating up. Nate seldom got to her, but the thought of getting special treatment because of her gender pissed her off. She'd fought long and hard to be treated like an equal all during her training and would never accept anything different now. As far as she was concerned there was no difference between her, Nate, Stephens or Malroy. "That's a sexist remark."

"It sure is, but it's the truth. He knows those other guys would lie to save their asses, but you're the only woman on the force. It's like you're sacred or something." Nate gave her a wink and a big grin. "The truth is, when you strut in that briefing room with your hair all done and those brilliant green eyes scouring the room, half the guys can't stand up for five minutes."

"You're such an ass." Summer turned and stared out the side window at the crumbling silo in the distance. The early morning sunlight was just beginning to brighten the horizon and the shadows of the farmland were coming into view. "I suppose you can't control your hormones either?"

"Oh, I can control them. But if you weren't already married to Dean, I'd be right there with Stephens and Malroy looking for some action."

"I'm sure Dean would be happy to know that all the guys on the force would like to get with me."

"Not all the guys. I'm not so sure that new recruit, Jones, would be interested. He seems a little on the skittish side when he's near you. Could be he's still a virgin—or gay?"

"He is not gay." Summer blew out a deep breath, hoping it'd relieve some of the tension that was building behind her eyes. "He's just a little shy around me."

"So, you wanna bet?"

Summer turned away, refusing to answer. She watched as car lights sparkled to life in the distance to her right and tried to change the subject. "You hear anything new on that drug bust last week?"

"Only what they want us to know. It was headed to Dean's courier company and was slated to be shipped across the country to fake addresses. I'm just glad we were able to intercept it at the transfer yard before it got to his company."

Summer arched her left eyebrow. "He had nothing to do with it."

"Exactly, and confiscating it offsite just makes it all that much easier to prove."

"They don't think he's involved with it, do they?"

"Who the hell knows, but the fact that Gavin Stone is working for your husband doesn't look good." Nate followed Summer's gaze to the speeding car racing down the cross road toward the intersection up ahead.

"Dean only hired Gavin because his parole officer begged Dean to."

"I know, but I still think it was a mistake. You and Gavin have a rocky past. Besides, I don't trust that guy."

"Even though he's served his debt to society?"

"Don't give me that shit. You don't believe it any more than I do." Nate hesitated for a moment, then made eye contact with Summer. "Keep this to yourself and don't breathe a word of it to Dean. The less he knows, the better it'll be."

"What the hell are you talking about? If something's going down then I want to be part of it. I don't care if Dean is my husband. I want in."

"I heard they've got a plain clothed detective. Grimshaw's his name. He's tracing the truck and all the merchandise that the meth was crammed inside."

"And what do they have?"

Nate shrugged his shoulders. "Your guess is as good as mine, but let's hope for the sake of Sabrina and that baby you're trying to have, Dean comes out clean."

Summer remembered how adamant Dean had been about the whole thing. He swore he had nothing to do with the shipment and she had no reason to believe anything to the contrary, but his business has been booming lately and he was finally making a profit. Summer shook her head. It was only a coincidence. Nothing more.

Nate sighed. "You realize that if you get knocked up, we're not skipping the route just so you can hit every drive-thru in the city."

Summer scoffed. "Don't tell me I have to get a doctor's note so you'll allow me food whenever the baby gets hungry?"

"That's not a bad idea," Nate said, his eyes following the approaching car. "I'm sure the chief will go for it."

The car was racing to the intersection ahead, looking to beat them, but little did the driver know he was in for a big surprise if he decided to fly through the stop sign. Nate was waiting, his finger hovering above the switch, hoping the guy runs the stop sign.

Nate smiled. "I'm betting he's gonna run it."

"I'm betting he doesn't know we're cops."

"You think?"

The second the car bounced through the intersection, Nate switched on the roof lights and the countryside was illuminated in a swirl of red and blue, sweeping over the land in a smooth rhythmic arc.

The blue sedan didn't slow at all. It continued on, rounding the bend in the road and disappearing from sight behind the cluster of thick trees.

When Nate slid the cruiser around that same corner, they could only watch as the sedan disappeared around another. Nate pushed the cruiser to its limit, barely holding it on the loose gravel road, determined to catch this guy.

The cruiser slid around the corner then straightened, but the sedan wasn't trying to outrun them anymore. It'd struck a second vehicle at the next intersection, sending them both off the road and into the thick brush beside the woods.

Steam spewed from the front of the sedan's crumpled hood as the driver opened the door and jumped out, dashing toward the thick woods.

Nate slammed on the brakes and slid to a stop beside the two tangled vehicles, then flung open the door and gave chase into the dark unknown, cursing the fugitive like always.

Summer radioed for an ambulance as she raced to the tangled mess. The driver of the van was lying in the long grass beside the vehicle, motionless. His face covered with blood—a lot of blood!

Summer reached into her pocket and withdrew her gloves. After slipping them on, she knelt down beside and searched for the source of all the blood, but couldn't find any cuts or gouges. He seemed to be fine. Covered with blood, but fine.

Pressing her fingers to his neck, she counted the rapid beats of his heart and was about to check his pupils when his eyes snapped open and an evil grin spread across his face. Summer pulled back, letting his head drop to the ground, taken by surprise at his strange reaction. She glanced around, searching for Nate, hoping he'd come back to assist her, when the man's hands shot up, grabbing her arm.

There was a sharp pain in her bicep, followed by a burning sensation that raced up her arm toward her shoulder. Summer glanced down at his blood soaked hands and saw the needle sticking out of her shirt sleeve. She couldn't believe it. He'd stabbed her—and with a dirty needle. And all she was trying to do was save his life.

Summer's head was swimming. Her thoughts were melting into each other as her legs began to buckle beneath. Everything was fading away. The flashing red and blue lights were now sickening pulses behind her closed lids. She felt the cold damp ground beneath, and heard the side door of the van slide open. A second later she was flying, soaring through the air until her face came to rest on the hard steel floor of the cargo van.

She tried to call out for Nate, but no sound would exit her mouth. She could picture him chasing the guy for a mile or more, whatever it took to get his man. The van roared to life and a second later she could feel the vibrations from the tires up through the cold steel floor—then darkness.

CHAPTER 1

Summer Demure sat slouched behind the wheel of the white Volvo, gazing off into the distance down the one-way street. Her unblinking eyes were locked on a single point in the darkness, but her mind was completely blank and she relished the feel of it. The ability to shut down her mind and take a break from the constant barrage of memories was the bliss she'd been searching for.

She couldn't believe how drastic her life had changed these last months and knew the feeling of dread, which coursed through every fibre of her body, was going to be the hardest thing to overcome. She thought of Dean and how he'd tried to comfort her, but a shiver—that same shiver she felt every time he touched her—raced through her body, racking her petite frame with uncontrollable muscle spasms.

It didn't seem to matter how many sessions she spent with the department psychiatrist, the outcome was always the same. She couldn't stand the touch of her own husband.

It devastated Dean when she asked him to move out of the house, and he argued for hours that him leaving wasn't going to solve her problems. Summer knew this was likely true, but like he'd said, this was her problem and she had to find a way to deal with it.

The night Dean left, he said he understood what she needed right now, but she could tell from the look in his eyes that he didn't. Maybe the time apart would do them some good? Maybe after being separated for awhile, she'd overcome her fears and they could once more live as a family, but until then she had to live alone, taking care of Sabrina.

Her fingers strummed nervously against the worn leather steering wheel. Worn smooth by Dean's many miles on the road. He loved this car so much that Summer was floored when he insisted she take it. Sure her old car wasn't reliable, but Dean simply grabbed the keys and drove off, leaving her little choice in the matter. He said he did it for her, but she knew he'd done it for Sabrina.

"Sabrina," she muttered, breaking the trance she was in. If it wasn't for the shared custody, Summer would've sold the house and taken off far from here. Far from Chatham. Far from Southern Ontario. Hell, she would've trekked halfway across the country just to place some distance between herself and the memories of that brutal night five months ago. But even if she had full custody she couldn't. At least not for a few more days. Not until that bastard, John Scott—Summer shivered just thinking about what that madman had done—was locked away for a long time. The mere thought of him sent her body into convulsions. Her muscles twitched and trembled as anxiety and fear gripped her heart, squeezing until she surrendered.

She glanced in the lighted vanity mirror and sighed. Her normally glowing skin had turned pale and sickly. Her face nearly disappeared, hiding behind the veil of white-blond hair. Normally she spent an hour styling it, but lately she couldn't be bothered. Wash and go was all she could muster. Her physical appearance had changed drastically over the last months, that was, except for her bright green eyes. They reminded her that she was still somewhat in control, no matter how lost she felt these days.

She flipped the mirror closed and stared out the window. Summer watched as the painted autumn leaves fluttered along the deserted downtown sidewalk, tumbling and twisting, dancing upon their invisible stage. It was Monday morning and the stores were all in darkness. Not a single sign of life could be seen. The only figures on the sidewalks were the bags of trash set out for the early morning pickup. She glanced at the clock and shook her head at the smothering darkness that not only stole away hours of outdoor activities, but also caused her chest to tighten slightly.

Summer closed her eyes and drew a deep breath.

"Everything's all right. I'm all right." She blew out her breath as she repeated the technique. "Relax. Deep breath. I'm free. Nobody's gonna hurt me."

Slowly Summer opened her eyes. She did feel better. The restriction in her chest was subsiding. After all, this was her home, where she'd grown up and raised her child. This was a safe city. It wasn't Toronto with its murderous gangs and random drive-by shootings. This was sleepy old Chatham, Ontario. Nothing bad happened here, except… The image of John Scott flashed in her mind and she quickly blocked it out.

She turned her attention to the large elephant-ear leaf tumbling, end over end down the sidewalk to her left. She watched as the wind quickened its journey toward her. A few drops of rain landed on the window, slowly striving to the bottom. Summer scanned the empty street for a matching tree, but nothing fit. It was all alone. Running—no, escaping the city at night.

"What is this, a sign?" Summer glanced to the heavens. "Run, while I can?"

These last few months had been trying. She felt oversensitive, like everything held a secret meaning, a hidden message for her. Maybe it was just paranoia, but as she watched the leaf make its great run, she could see herself chasing right behind.

The radio powered off, sending the car into deafening silence. Summer quickly jostled the keys, cranking them back and rejoining the song in play. The green glow of the clock illuminated the car once again. 6:05. He was late.

When she glanced back to the leaf, she gasped as a hand shot from a garbage pile near the corner of the building. It reached out, snatching the large leaf in mid bounce.

Summer wrapped her arms tightly around her body, holding the shutters to a minimum. After settling her nerves, she leaned to the window, watching as the dark hand gripped the leaf by the stem, rotating it slowly between its blackened fingers. Side over side it spun, suspended in midair, prevented from continuing on its journey. She swallowed hard, trying to dislodge the lump which was blocking her throat.

"That's... my life." Summer swallowed again. "Caught... spinning... controlled."

She watched as the black fingers manipulated the leaf and wondered why a vagrant was living on this street. As hard as she tried, she couldn't recall ever seeing a homeless person living on this side of Chatham. Sure there were a few rundown areas in the city where homeless people migrated, but never downtown. The police made sure of it.

As Summer concentrated on the dirt covered sleeve, she realized that nothing stays the same. Everything changes, and if you refuse to change with it, it'll destroy you. She only had to look at her trembling hands to know this was true.

His blackened fingers slowly worked their way up the stem, delicately sliding onto the crisp dry membrane of the leaf, carefully feeling each vein as they thinned toward the tips.

Maybe he needed help, Summer thought, realizing she needed to change her direction in life. She reached for her purse. Maybe a few dollars for a hot meal?

After removing a twenty from her wallet, she reached for the door handle, but froze when his dark hand clamped down, crushing the brittle leaf within. Quickly she checked the door lock then returned her attention to the hand. It was kneading, crushing, disintegrating the leaf within. The hand shook. The arm shook. It was as if he was laughing, uncontrollably, as he crumbled the beautiful form.

The dirty fingernails rolled beneath his thumb as he continued to grind the leaf into obliteration. It wasn't until the next gust of wind came erupting down the empty sidewalk that his fingers slowly opened, releasing the fine powder upon the breeze, sending it sailing into the darkness.

Summer felt a chill move through her body. She reached out, twisted the keys and the engine roared to life. The urge to escape flooded her body. Suddenly she didn't know why she was sitting there on this street, what she was waiting for, only that she needed to get away—and fast.

As she stepped on the brake and placed the car in gear, a red Mercedes came screeching to a halt in front, nearly clipping the front corner of her slowly moving car.

"Shit!" Summer slammed the wheel. She didn't know if she was angrier at the driver's reckless behaviour, or at her own irrational thinking.

The man threw open the door and leapt quickly to his feet. Summer's heart caught for a moment. Her mind flashed back to that night five months ago. She knew she was overreacting. After all, John Scott was sitting behind bars under heavy guard waiting for her to ID him.

"Summer," Dean yelled, racing up the sidewalk. His dark curly hair, which was always a little too long, caught in the wind and obscured his chocolate brown eyes. Hastily he brushed it back, holding it against the wind with one hand. He smiled as he reached the window, his perfect white teeth gleaming against the dark growth of stubble on his face. "I know I'm late, but it wasn't my fault."

"Don't give me that look!"

His smile faded.

"It's never your fault, now is it?" Summer listened to him jingle his car keys, an old habit that drove her nuts on a good day. But today wasn't even close.

"Dean, if you don't stop shaking those damn keys, I'll—"

"Sorry." He clamped his other hand over top. "Hard habit to break." He pointed to the red Mercedes where Sabrina had propped herself in the back window. Although she had Summer's petite build, she would never be her spitting image. Dean's chromosomes had fought the battle and won. Sabrina had emerged into this world with dirty blond hair and eyes the colour of weak tea. The only evidence that Sabrina was her daughter, were those commanding eyes, which had absorbed enough green to almost glow. They were the first thing people noticed and the last thing they remembered.

"Do you like it? Sabrina helped me pick it out."

She smiled at Sabrina and felt the tension begin to fade. She noticed the trembling in her limbs had subsided. "It's nice. Expensive, but nice."

"Since I gave up the house and my Volvo," Dean stepped closer to the window, "I needed something to drive."

"What about my old car? What's wrong with it?"

"No offence, but it was a piece of shit. They actually wanted me to pay them to take it in for a trade."

"You traded my car for that?"

"Your old car wouldn't even pay for the licence plates, let alone a fraction of the cost."

"But it was my car. You had no right selling it."

"I gave you this car. You should be happy." Dean's mouth tightened into a fine line as he started jingling the keys again. "It's a hundred times better than that piece of shit you've been driving around in."

"This," Summer pointed her twitching finger at the jingling keys, "is exactly why we're separated."

The rain began falling harder, driven by a gusting north wind. Dean abandoned his hair and flipped up his coat collar. "We're not separated. We're just taking a break," he turned to check on Sabrina and muttered, "because of you."

Summer glanced in the rearview mirror and saw her face growing red with anger. Her crimson cheeks stood out like stop lights against her shoulder length blond hair. She took a deep breath and decided to change the subject.

"Why do you do this?" Summer forced a smile for her daughter then turned to Dean. "I was perfectly clear. You could have Sabrina for forty-eight hours, then bring her back."

Dean scuffed his white running shoe along the sidewalk. She knew he was taking a minute to calm himself down and when he looked up again, he ran his hand up his forehead, slicking his hair back, then motioned to Sabrina. "I know you're gonna say no," he tipped his head slightly, "but

Sabrina really wants to stay for another night. I can drop her off tomorrow morning instead."

Summer caught the little signal. She turned and Sabrina popped up higher in the back window, clasping her hands together in a mock plea. Although it was a staged act, she felt her heart ache over her daughter being torn between them. She wanted what was best for her, but if she gave in today, he'd ask every time he had custody.

"No, and how dare you put her up to this!" she said through a gritted smile. "You're lower than low using Sabrina against me."

"I'm not using her. She really wants to stay." Dean reached through the window and touched her arm.

Summer jerked away and sat staring at her arm as if Dean had somehow harmed her. As hard as she tried, she just couldn't stop her body from reacting like that. It was an involuntary reaction and one that had fuelled many fights. John Scott was the real reason they were here squabbling over custody times. He was the reason they were separated. He was the reason she couldn't tolerate her husband's touch anymore. Sure they promised to stay together until death, but after what John Scott had done, she felt like part of her had truly died.

"Sabrina's devastated that we're not a family anymore." Dean scrubbed the stubble on his face. "She doesn't understand why we can't live together at home. I tried to explain it, but—"

"What, that her mother doesn't want her father around anymore?" Tears filled her eyes. "That I don't want you around!"

"No." Dean shook his head. He reached toward her arm again, but left his hand hovering inches above, unwilling to chance rejection once again. "I'd never poison her mind. That's not fair—"

Summer's cell phone rang. Glad for a distraction, she rummaged through the centre console until she found it. She quickly flipped it open and glanced at the display. "You're a piece of shit! *This*," she shoved the phone before his eyes, "isn't playing fair."

Dean glanced from the caller ID on the cell phone, to the back window of his car. "I swear I never told her to call you. She's been playing with that thing all day. She actually called my contact in Detroit. Luckily he wasn't there—"

"Hi Sweetie." Summer waved. "Yes, I can see you, too. Why don't you climb out and see how fast you can get inside this car?"

The image of the vagrant destroying the leaf flashed like a warning shot. Maybe she was overreacting? Maybe she needed to up her dosage of medication? Hell, maybe she didn't really know what the hell she needed.

"Actually, maybe you should wait…" She leaned forward, looking past Dean, eyes darting to the pile of trash where she'd last seen him, but his hand wasn't protruding anymore. He probably covered up because of the rain.

"Daddy took me to try on cars yesterday." Summer turned to see Sabrina bouncing on the seat. She had the biggest smile on her face and Summer couldn't remember the last time she'd seen her daughter so exited. "Do you like the one I picked out?"

"Did you pick the colour, or did Daddy?"

"It's red," she waved the back of her hand across the window, "like my nails. You done a good job, Mommy. The man at the car store, he liked them. He said they were pretty like me."

"Well, he was wrong." Summer felt the warmth of tears building in her eyes. She relished the feeling Sabrina brought to her world. The feeling that only her own flesh and blood could bring. Summer dropped a hand to her stomach, feeling the slight bulge below her jacket and sighed. "They're not pretty. They're beautiful."

She giggled and flopped out of sight. "Daddy told the man that, too."

Summer glanced at her husband, realizing how much he truly loved Sabrina. He'd always been able to make her laugh and smile. He always knew exactly how to brighten her saddest days. Even after the incident with John Scott, when Summer had confined herself to the bedroom, unwilling to face Dean and the entire world, he'd brought happiness to Sabrina. Maybe she'd been too hasty with the separation? Maybe she needed to face her demons head on? She thought of the small fetus growing in her belly and realized that in four months she'd have to do exactly that.

"Yes, I know you had a lot of fun with Daddy this weekend, but you have school today." Summer glanced back to the trash pile. A white sneaker protruded from the rubbish. The movement brought relief. At least she knew exactly where the vagrant was.

"I can be sick of school." She peeked over the back seat. "Daddy said he'd take me to the zoo instead."

"The zoo?" Summer caught the brief sight of Sabrina before she disappeared again, then turned her attention back to the trash pile. "I think school is more important than looking at animals."

Dean turned his head, following Summer's gaze. He took five steps onto the sidewalk and stooped over, gazing at the white sneaker sticking out of the trash.

"Please, Mommy."

"Um, no. You have school. Besides, it's too cold. The animals will all be hibernating."

Dean took two more steps, blocking Summer's line of vision. What was he doing? Why is he even getting near that man? Sure he always gave to charity and would never refuse a request for loose change, but this vagrant was dangerous, she could feel it in her bones.

Summer leaned out the window, narrowing her eyes at Dean's back. A low hushed voice caught on the wind, drifting to her ears. The vagrant was talking to Dean. Probably asking for a handout.

"Dean… Dean! What are you doing?" The fear that the vagrant had instilled moments ago was replaced with a fear for Dean's safety. Why was he ignoring her call? Was he doing this just to punish her for refusing to let Sabrina stay for another night?

"What? Yes Sabrina, Mommy's still here." The phone beeped, sounding the low battery warning. "Darling, Mommy has to go now. Hang up and wait in the car for Daddy to get you." The phone beeped again and Summer flipped the cover closed, disconnecting her tie to Sabrina, then dropped it into the console.

"Dean! Get back here right—" She paused, seeing the streetlight reflect off the gold chain around the vagrant's neck. It was the only thing visible as his face remained hidden in the shadows. The image was wrong. A bum would've hawked the chain for a bottle of booze. So why did this bum still have it?

The vagrant shifted and disappeared back into the dark shadows. Dean leaned closer, bending over the vagrant, listening to his conversation. He listened for a few seconds before turning his head in Summer's direction. His face looked different. Pale, shiny, scared. She'd never seen him afraid before.

It happened so fast, but at the same time like in slow motion. The shiny blade slid from the dirty shirt sleeve. Streetlight reflected off as it arched up, straight toward Dean's mid section. Summer watched the polished blade and swore she could see her frightened reflection screaming out a warning to Dean, but in reality she sat, dumbstruck, unable to voice a single word, let alone one syllable.

The blade plunged through the fabric of Dean's light jacket, vanishing within his abdomen. The muscles on the vagrant's forearm bulged as he maintained the death grip on the handle.

Summer's eyes darted from the knife handle to Dean's face. The vagrant seemed to be holding the knife deep inside, adding insult to the attack. Dean's eyes bulged wide as a look of pure terror swept over his face, realizing the blade was still inside—still capable of doing more damage.

Summer winced, sympathy pain shooting through her body. She knew exactly what he was going through, knew the pain of a blade slicing through her skin, flesh and even coming to a jarring halt as it slammed into bone. In a flash, her mind retreated to that bright summer day when she looked from the frightened face of a teenager, to the handle protruding from her body. It didn't matter if it was close to a vital organ or not, because when the blade disappeared inside your body, you thought about death—your own death.

Dean's wide eyes locked onto Summer as the vagrant ripped the blade from his stomach with the speed of a professional hit man. Dean took an awkward step backwards, instinctively pulling his hands to his stomach as the car keys fell from his outstretched fingers, tumbling in the streetlight to the wet sidewalk.

As the vagrant sat fully upright, he held the knife before his face, twisting it—almost admiring the way the blood trickled down the razor sharp edge.

Summer heard muffled screams fill the night. They were unmistakeably those of her child. She broke the trance with Dean, and fighting a new level of nervous spasms, she dared to glance to the car ahead where Sabrina had been watching the whole time. Summer's stomach fell. She wished for Sabrina's sake that she wouldn't have seen this act of violence. God knows she's been through a lifetime's worth in the last five months.

Sabrina's face was red, her mouth wide open airing a high-pitched scream into the night. Tears were streaming down her cheeks as she bounced wildly in the back seat. Even at six years old she seemed to know exactly what had happened to her father.

"Sabrina needs me. She needs her mother," Summer muttered, shaking helplessly behind the steering wheel, unable to gather her usual strength and deal with the situation. Normally she would've jumped out and subdued the perpetrator. After all, she is a cop—a cop who's on stress leave for the last five months because she can't control her stupid emotions in situations… situations like this.

In slow motion, with every muscle jerking uncontrollably, Summer turned back to watch Dean. Her body was rebelling. It seemed to be fighting her every move. Frustration was building as she had to battle her own mind for control of her muscles. Dean had fallen to his knees, one hand clamped to the hole in his flesh, squeezing with everything he had, trying to keep his soul from escaping. His other hand was inches from his face, fingers rubbing the thick blood as he no doubt tried to comprehend what had just happened.

The vagrant drew the blade across his shirt sleeve, wiping the blood off before sliding it back into his pocket. He dug in the bag beside, pulled out a black object and slipped it on his head.

A ski mask.

He yanked it down, adjusted the holes, then slowly climbed to his feet as if nothing had happened. Summer watched as he stood, realizing that he wasn't actually a homeless person, but a killer waiting to strike.

He glanced over. Holding Summer's gaze, he bent to the ground before Dean and carefully plucked the keys from a shallow puddle. Straightening, he flipped the keys up, catching them in midair and gave her a wide smile. A grin of arrogance. A grin of superiority.

Her head flipped from the keys, to the red Mercedes. The red Mercedes, which held her only daughter.

"No," Summer gasped as the attacker walked slowly toward the Mercedes. He acted as if nothing had happened. Nobody was bleeding to death behind. Nobody was watching as he prepared to steal the car. He even seemed to have a slight bounce in his step as he headed straight for the door of the Mercedes.

Hands shaking uncontrollably, Summer cursed while stabbing for the door handle. How she wished she had her control back. After a few tries, she finally managed to grasp it and pull the handle. She pushed against the door with all her might and it swung wide open, causing the attacker to stop with his fingers on the door handle of the Mercedes. He glanced back and Summer saw the smirk through the mouth hole in the mask.

"No!" she screamed, convulsions taking over. "Leave… her… alone!" Reaching out a shaking hand, she gripped the window sash then pulled her trembling body from the car. She watched helplessly as he jumped behind the wheel and started the Mercedes.

Sabrina screamed so loud that nothing came out as she cowered into the farthest corner of the back seat, clutching her hands protectively before her. Summer lurched toward the car, fighting her nerves every inch. She could see the terror in Sabrina's face.

He was waiting. Daring Summer to come closer.

She lunged forward, reaching out to the car.

Sabrina found her voice and started screaming hysterically.

Something snagged Summer's pant leg.

She jerked her leg free.

The engine revved.

Another high-pitched scream erupted.

It was back, gripping her leg, preventing her from getting closer.

She lunged as the tires spun on the wet pavement. Her outstretched fingers brushed the wet cold metal as the Mercedes tore out of the parking spot and down the road.

Summer glanced down, spotted the bloody hand clenched to her leg and realized that Dean was dying.

"He…" Summer croaked, pointing a trembling finger in the direction of the Mercedes, "took Sabrina."

Tears cascaded down Summer's pale cheeks, falling to the damp concrete below.

"Go!" Dean released her leg. He stared down at the bloodstain spreading from under his hand. "Go, after her."

"I… can't?" She glanced at her shaking hands. "I just… can't!"

"Summer, you have to." Dean's voice was strained. He was going into shock. She'd seen this many times before. She knew how to deal with victims, but she couldn't figure out how to deal with her own fears.

"We'll call the police." Summer glanced up and down the street, searching for anybody to help. "They can stop him. They're good at that."

"I'll call." He snagged her trembling hand and pulled, managing to get to his knees. "But you have to go after him!"

Summer clenched her eyes closed, hoping to make everything disappear. She couldn't imagine giving pursuit in her condition. She could barely manage to fight rush hour traffic. Her head was spinning. She knew Dean was right.

Someone had to go after them. But not her. She couldn't do it.

"You're bleeding." She touched a finger to the dark patch on Dean's jacket. "You… need help."

"Sabrina needs your help. Go! I'll be fine."

"But—"

"Go!" Dean's voice broke. His chocolate-brown eyes were pleading. "He's getting away."

"But, I can't. Not after what happened. I just can't!" Her stomach twisted into knots just thinking about the time with John Scott. How she'd emerged from his care with fears she never imagined possible before. Her chest heaved and a shuttered cry escaped her trembling lips.

Pulling himself to his feet, Dean placed his weight on Summer and, stumbling like a drunk, forced her back to the car door. "Don't tell me you can't. You have to. If *you* don't, then nobody will save our little girl."

Summer staggered at the door, fighting against Dean's weight until he shoved her roughly inside.

"The police—"

"Please, Summer, let the past go. You can't change what happened, but you can change what will happen." Dean reached through the window and touched her shoulder. She realized this was the first time in a long time that his touch hadn't caused her to jerk away. Summer chalked it up to shock and drew a deep breath. The smell of blood filled her nostrils. His blood. The same blood that coursed through Sabrina's body.

Down at the far end of the street, the tail lights of the Mercedes were fading. Either her sense of time was failing her or the attacker was waiting for her to follow.

"Summer… please…" She glanced at Dean and saw tears in his eyes—real tears. He'd never shed a tear as long as she'd know him. "Go… save our baby."

CHAPTER 2

Summer watched as the tears trailed down Dean's sweat covered face. His chocolate eyes were melting and it broke her heart to see the pain within them. He'd only come close to tears when Sabrina was born. The moment the doctor placed the small bundle in his arms he turned and blinked away the emotions. It wasn't like him to admit that he was only human, but as he stood on the sidewalk in the cold rain, bleeding from the knife wound, she was sure that hiding his emotions was the last thing on his mind.

Drawing a deep breath, Summer forced herself to look away. The taillights of the Mercedes were now only faint dots in the darkness. Relax. Settle down, she thought. Sabrina's watching out the back window, waiting for me—Summer glanced at her jittery fingers and almost laughed—to rescue her.

She reached down and shifted the car into gear then tightened her trembling hands on the steering wheel until her knuckles were bright white.

Seeing Dean stagger back from the car, she slowly pulled from the curb, cutting across the empty lane and

gradually accelerating down the road. The Mercedes'
taillights winked once then disappeared out of sight, around
the corner.

The raindrops doubled in size, landing through the
open window like a hundred cold, wet slaps against her face.
After fumbling with the button, the window sliced through
the assault, streaking Dean's blood down the entire window
as it rose. She turned her head, trying not to look as the rain
washed it quickly away. High speed pursuits had always been
so easy, but now it was more than she could bear. Add in the
factors of rain—and finding the fucking switch for the wiper
blades—and this was downright impossible.

She wanted to scream. She wanted to lash out and
strike something—anything! When she approached the
corner, she knew she'd have to trust her instincts. There was
no time to slow down and cautiously manoeuvre around it
like an old person with failing eyesight. Instead she'd need to
push herself—challenge her years of training to overcome
the emotionally crippling disease John Scott had planted in
her mind.

Summer held her breath and turned the corner at a
high speed. She nervously waited, praying that her hands
would obey and prevent the car from crashing into the
buildings across the road. The tires slipped and the car began
going into a full out slide. Her heart pounded so hard she
was amazed it didn't burst.

She let up slightly on the gas until the slide was under
control, then punched the accelerator halfway to the floor
and released her breath. A smile crept onto her face, but she
quickly replaced it with a determined stiff lip. There was a
time to celebrate her returning confidence, but not now. Not
with Sabrina held captive in the car ahead.

After rounding the corner, she spotted the taillights a
quarter mile down the street. He should be farther away than

that. Could he be waiting for her to catch up? She shook her head. But why would he do that? No, maybe he decided to park the car and climb in the backseat to…

"No!" Summer shook her head, refusing to let the notion enter her mind. Maybe he stopped to let Sabrina go?

She'd heard of cases like that. A guy hops into a running car, thinking he'll make a quick buck at the chop shop, then looks in the back seat and realizes that he'd just become a kidnapper instead of a car thief. So what does he do? He stops and abandons the kid on the nearest corner.

Yeah, that's it, Summer thought, but she had a hard time convincing herself. After all, he could've approached her and taken the Volvo, but no, he waited until Dean showed up with Sabrina. The realization hit her like a punch to the gut. The timing was perfect. The motive so simple. She should've seen it coming. How stupid could she be? Why wasn't she more careful? She's the only one who can ID John Scott. She's the only one who'd seen his face, even if it was only for a second and it had been covered with blood.

Summer knew she'd never forget the look on John Scott's face that day. That evil grin as he stuck the needle into her arm was burned into her memory forever.

The taillights grew closer. She'd cut the distance in half.

Drawing a cleansing breath, she pushed the pedal harder and the car raced down the empty street, while her eyes narrowed on the driver's door.

Ram it at full speed and he'll be knocked out cold, but… The earlier image of Sabrina in the back window flooded her mind.

"Why the hell isn't she wearing her seatbelt?" Summer calculated the injuries Sabrina would sustain from the impact. The difference between stopping the kidnapper and chasing him, all came down to a simple little belt. She'd done it many times before, used the cruiser to disable a vehicle and apprehend the felons. Normally it was only a nudge off the road, but tonight she'd have to sacrifice this car—Dean's precious Volvo—for good. A full speed impact into the driver's door would buy her the time to extract Sabrina, but at what cost?

"Damn!" The option disappeared before she had the opportunity to commit either way. Just when Summer closed the gap, the car took off like lightning. The Mercedes easily matched her speed, then quickly began pulling away.

Summer glared at the back window, begging to see Sabrina one more time. She was amazed at how strong her body felt. How alive it really seemed. Although her white knuckles were glued to the wheel, there wasn't any hint of the trembles.

Water sprayed from the wheels of the Mercedes, fanning up in the Volvo's headlights before cascading down on the abandoned sidewalk. In a flash of bright red, the car took a hard left turn, rounding the corner with little slippage. Summer had to admit the Mercedes handled much better than her car.

He was heading out of the city toward the 401, the main artery of Southern Ontario. Summer had expected this. She knew it was easier to hide away in the countryside then in the heart of the city. And if he decided to hop on the 401 with that powerful engine, he'd be long gone before they could organize a response.

Summer cut the corner short, jumping over the inside curb. The car landed in a skid, sliding sideways. Her hands panicked, cranking the wheel against the slide as the Volvo's worn tires continued fighting to grip the waterlogged pavement. Summer removed her foot from the pedal and hit the brakes. The anti-lock system kicked in, but not before the Volvo slammed sideways into a parked car. The whole side of the body crumbled, exploding the side windows and showering her with tiny fragments of glass.

"Shit!" Summer shook off the crash and stomped the pedal all the way to the floor. The tires spun and a moment later the car took off with a gut wrenching squeal of metal on metal. The Mercedes seemed to have slowed, but remained at a safe distance. He was playing with her—like John Scott had played that night.

Realizing she'd never be able to catch him in this car, she decided to call for help. Taking advantage of the straightaway, Summer dug in the console until she found her cell phone. After flipping it open, she quickly punched in 9,1, then her finger froze. Before she could depress the last button and summon help, the phone vibrated, then the classic ring tone played. The car slowed as she glanced at the display. It was Dean's phone—the same one Sabrina had called from only minutes ago.

"Sabrina?" Summer's voice threatened to give way. She swallowed a lump. When only silence answered, she stomped the accelerator hard. "Can you hear me? Is that bad man scaring you?" She leaned forward and peered at the car ahead, praying to catch sight of Sabrina as they raced down Richmond Street with the engine whining in protest.

There was a muffled response and Summer sighed, picturing Sabrina huddled in the back seat, concealing the phone in her arms. She was so proud of her little girl for using her head.

"Don't worry, Mommy's right behind you. Look out the back window." Summer had no idea if Sabrina was obeying, or even if she was capable of obeying, but she allowed her a second. "See, that's me in the car behind. Put on your seatbelt, baby. This might get a little rough."

When a deep throaty laugh filled the line, Summer felt her stomach drop. The sound of his voice crushed all her hope. That's why he'd stopped. To get the phone from Sabrina. She wondered if Sabrina had given it to him willingly, or if she'd been too terrified and clung onto it for dear life until he'd ripped it from her small hands.

The trembling spasms started gripping her stomach and spread throughout her body. "No!" Summer yelled, clenching her muscles tight, battling to control the shakes. The last thing she needed right now was to have her car weaving back and forth across the centre line like a drunk.

"Who… is this?" Summer demanded. She felt her anger searing up.

"Who is this?" His deep voice rattled through her mind as she concentrated on each and every word spoken. She tried to place that voice to anybody from her past. Anybody she'd pissed off. "Come on Officer Demure. Now, that hurts. I think you know exactly who this is. We've spent so much time together. I'm shocked that you don't know."

"Please, stop the car. Give me back my baby."

"Maybe I should've taken you again, but then that would've complicated matters."

"Stop the car. Let Sabrina go. I'll do anything you want."

The phone beeped a low battery warning again. She had known it was getting low and should've plugged it in this morning, but Summer remembered exactly why she hadn't. She'd been too distracted with the news of John Scott's arrest to do anything more than lie on the couch and cry.

There was nothing but silence on the line.

Had the phone finally run out of power and disconnected? Had her tie to her daughter been severed by her lack of planning? Summer clenched her eyes tight for a second and refused to pull the phone from her ear just to glance at the display. When she opened them again, she swore she heard Sabrina snuffling back a sob.

"Officer Demure," he said in a professional tone. "John Scott was an innocent pawn that night. He was simply in the wrong place at the wrong time."

"Bullshit!"

"I was there with you the entire time. Hell, I was right there inside you half the night. Remember how much you liked it." He laughed. "Remember how you begged me for more."

Summer remembered all right. She remembered the claustrophobic feeling she had when she'd come to that night. The black sack on her head made the assault unbearable. The darkness combined with not knowing where she was as he beat and raped her repeatedly was the worst. She could've handled the pain if only she could've seen whose hands were doing the damage. That unknown was what seemed to break her nerves and send her into this unstable condition.

The last thing she remembered was seeing John Scott's face as she searched for the source of the bleeding after the accident. No, not an accident. It'd all been a set up. The whole thing.

Could there have been a second assailant that night? Someone she never saw. Could she be wrong about John Scott being her attacker, or was the kidnapper just messing with her mind?

"Let me make this clear. If you stop your vehicle and return home, I can guarantee your daughter's safety. But if you call the cops, or try to be a hero and stop me—well I can't say how this might turn out."

Summer knew she had to keep him talking and let him think he's in control.

"I'm... sorry," she struggled to keep herself calm, "but I can't let you take her."

"Correction, I've already taken her and I could've been long gone by now, but I thought you might want to play. You do like to play, don't you?"

Play? The word rambled throughout her mind. She'd heard that word many times during her captivity. It was all a sick game to John Scott, but to her it was nothing short of torture.

Summer shook her head. But that was John Scott's line. This bastard was only copying him, or was he? She refused to give it another thought. She'd spent so many nights trying to forget the entire ordeal, and now it was back threatening to rip her mind in two.

"Fuck you!" Summer screamed, her white knuckles gripping the wheel too tightly. She realized this wasn't the way to negotiate with a kidnapper, and was precisely why you can't get personally involved. "Release the hostage and—"

The kidnapper's deep throaty laugh ate away at her sanity. "Awe, there we go. There's a hint of the old Summer Demure. Feisty, full of spunk. And what happened? Oh, right, you got a taste of your own medicine?"

Summer heard another low battery warning and knew her time was running out, but she couldn't hang up. She couldn't lose connection with her daughter. She had to keep the line open. "What are you talking about?"

"Your Medicine!" he screamed, bringing a startled cry from Sabrina. "Locked away. Helpless, but to serve your captor. Like the prisoners you lock away in jail."

"Scum like you deserve to be locked away."

"Scum like me," he mocked. "Scum like me can control shit like you! You like to think you're untouchable, but you're not. I've touched you today in a way you never expected. I've hit you so hard that you're still reeling from the blow. You talk tough, but I know you're full of shit. I've been watching you for the last five months. I know about your shrink visits. I know all your fears. Hell, I even know about your doctor visits. You haven't even told your husband yet, but I know."

Summer felt violated. How on earth did this stranger know every intimate detail of her life? How did he know the reason she'd been to the doctor? How could he possibly know about that? She felt her stomach churn.

"Put..." Summer cleared her throat and forced down the bile that was bubbling up. "Sabrina on the phone."

"Why, so you can tell her how much you love her?" He turned the corner fast, straight through the stoplight and the tires squealed as the Mercedes headed toward the highway. "Tell her that you're gonna stop me and get her back." He laughed. "I don't think so."

Summer hit the corner at full speed, fighting hard to keep the Volvo from sliding into the ditch. The moment she was out of the slide, she gave it everything it had. Wind whipped through the smashed windows making it hard to hear as the car started to close the distance. She was definitely making up some ground, but the highway entrance was coming up. She needed to be close behind in case he decided to take the off ramp and run against the flow of traffic.

"If you have anything to say to her, tell me and I'll—" A phone rang, cutting him off. The line crackled then she heard his muffled voice talking. "Yes, just as planned. She's fine... Actually, the mother's on the other phone right now. But... yes, I understand. I was just having a little fun. Yes, I know this is business."

There was a muffled silence, then the irregular whooping noise of a vacuum.

Did he open the window?

Summer continued to close the gap as the whooping noise increased. A second later, she saw it coming—heading straight for her head. The phone smashed into the windshield, sending a spider crack out in every direction.

"Shit!" Summer jumped and the car swerved. Suddenly she knew what he'd been ordered to do. She regained her composure, forced down her nerves and concentrated on catching the bastard.

Quickly she dialled 911.

Veering from the highway entrance, he cut sharply onto an adjoining dirt road. Summer dropped the phone to the passenger seat as she gripped the wheel with both hands, fighting to make the sharp corner. She heard the operator's voice answer. Not daring to drive one handed on the loose gravel roadway, she chose to shout and hope the operator could make out her call.

"This is Officer Demure, of the Chatham Police. I'm in pursuit of a red 2010 Mercedes S series—" The phone beeped one last time then shut down. "Fuck!" Summer slammed the wheel. It was just her luck. Everything was going to hell. It didn't matter what she did lately it always seemed to turn out wrong.

The Mercedes continued following the dirt road up the hill, toward the bridge. Summer felt a twinge of excitement as he passed the laneway on the right. She knew the dirt road he was following would curve after the bridge and circle back, meeting up with the laneway on the other side of the creek. She could take the narrow shortcut and hope the creek hadn't washed out the roadway, then block the road and stop them.

Watching the Mercedes disappear down the country road, she slowed the car and cautiously made the turn onto the narrow lane. The road was sunken down as if they'd cut a path straight through the rising hills of the countryside. The earth rose up on both sides, towering over the hood of the car. There was only one way in and no room to turn around, except for the small clearing at the bottom of the ravine.

Once the road dipped downward, she lost view of the kidnapper's car. She realized that he could stop and backtrack, but that was a chance she had to take. After all, she'd taken this road a few times during pursuits and always came out ahead. She laughed, thinking about his downfall, then remembered what was at stake—Sabrina.

Her adrenalin surged. She was going to stop him, but then what? He had a knife and she had nothing.

She couldn't worry about that. She'd have to deal with it when it happens. Her real concern was her muscle spasms. They seemed to be subsiding during the chase, but she wondered what would happen when she came face to face with him. Would she find herself crumbling on the ground, battling her own body, or would her training take over and her reflexes kick back in?

"Worry about that later," Summer muttered. "Stop them first, disarm him and get Sabrina back."

The narrow lane dipped suddenly and the farmer's fields gave way to the small saplings that grew uncontested in the shallow ravine. Straggly, bare branches poked up from the water soaked banks of the small stream, which surged over the drain tubes and onto the roadway. Muddy water sprayed from the soaked gravel, splashing up and over the hood. The Volvo slid in the mud, but regained traction as the tires gripped dryer gravel on the other side. Summer hurried and flicked on the wipers, then gunned the engine. The car tore up the hill, rocketing toward the intersecting road.

"Only a few more seconds." She felt great. Back to her old self. Back to her cop self.

She narrowed her eyes, squinting at the long narrow objects on the road ahead.

"Shit!" Suddenly she didn't feel like her old self anymore. She felt like an idiot. How could she fall for this? How could she let herself be caught like this? Summer slammed on the brakes, but she was travelling too fast to stop. Her tires hit the spike belts and all four exploded.

The car lurched from side to side, banging off the raised earth walls. It rode up one side, then fell back only to try to climb the other. She managed to make it fifty feet before coming to a stop. Another twenty and she would've been blocking the intersection, but he'd known that and calculated it perfectly.

The headlights of the Mercedes sliced through the darkness up ahead, illuminating the falling raindrops. Summer watched as the car slowed, passing through the intersection. The Volvo's headlights spotlighted Sabrina's face in the side window. Her red, swollen eyes were pleading for help.

Summer felt raging anger fill her body at being outsmarted. She pushed against the driver's door and it opened six inches then stuck in the wet muck beside. She gripped the door and squeezed halfway out before slipping in the mud and slamming her chin down on the top of the door.

The rain continued to fall, blurring her vision as Sabrina disappeared from sight. Summer lowered her head and her chest heaved as she started to cry.

CHAPTER 3

The smell of exhaust hung in the air, filling Dean's nostrils as he gasped for breath. He stood hunched over, holding tight to his stomach as the warm blood oozed over his clenched fingers. When the white Volvo disappeared into the darkness, he'd glanced around the empty street. Nobody was in sight. The street was deserted thanks to the pouring rain which rinsed the crimson blood from his fingers, pooling it around his feet.

The pain from the wound was subsiding and Dean knew this was not a good sign. He'd lost a lot of blood and if he stood there waiting for help to arrive, by the time someone noticed, he'd be long dead.

"Hel…" He started to call out, but the exertion only reignited the pain. Wiping the rain water from his eyes, Dean spotted the glass enclosed telephone booth down the street. With his cell phone still in the Mercedes, this was his last chance to survive. Slowly he staggered to the first parking meter, eyeing the crutches toward the phone.

Why? Why now? Dean couldn't believe this was really happening. It wasn't supposed to be like this. Two minutes, that's all it was supposed to take. Swoop in and sweet talk Summer into another night with Sabrina then make a quick getaway.

He'd heard about the capture of Summer's attacker— John Scott they said his name was. He was captured last night and Dean knew Summer would be in no condition to take care of Sabrina today. He knew her mind would be reliving those painful memories and Dean couldn't blame her. The moment he'd heard about John Scott's capture he felt the newly intensified mixture of anger, sorrow and pity that he'd felt daily for the last five months. He shook his head and glanced down at his blood covered hand gripping his stomach.

This is all my fault. I should've been more careful. I should never have agreed to take that shipment. But how was I to know they hid drugs inside that shit.

The booth was ten feet away, two parking meters to go before he could call for help, but his head was swimming and his thoughts were sinking in the murkiness. If only he could go back in time and erase the last five months of his life. Everything had been so perfect back then. He and Summer were still so much in love and Summer was so eager to conceive a second child. They'd talked about it for months and were in the midst of a maddingly fevered pace of love making that he thought he'd died and gone to heaven. Everything was perfect... until...

Dean lunged from the last parking meter to the side of the phone booth. His hand slid to the corner and almost slipped off, leaving a bloody smear across the glass. He staggered and rested his body against the corner of the booth and tried to stop the spinning in his mind. A second later he rolled around the corner and burst through the swinging doors, falling inside the booth. The sound of the downpour on the glass walls was almost deafening, but at least he could see now without the cascading water flowing down his face.

Dean reached up, grabbed the metal shelf then raised himself. He knocked the phone from the cradle, letting it bounce off the shelf and rap against the glass wall. Quickly he gathered the last bit of strength and punched in the three numbers then collapsed, sliding down the wall, coming to rest beside the dangling receiver.

He couldn't help but feel that this was all his fault. If it wasn't for his business contacts then Sabrina would be happily on her way home right now instead of… Dean squeezed his eyes tight, refusing to even imagine what was going to happen to his little girl. He'd seen what that fucker, John Scott had done to Summer and his gut churned just thinking what would happen to his little girl.

The wind picked up, whipping in every direction, slamming fat raindrops against the sides of the booth. He was soaked and cold. Every ounce of strength zapped on his journey down to this corner.

The phone twisted and banged off his temple before he managed to trap it against the wall. He listened as it rang through, but his mind drifted to the glass door. It was covered with red smudges—his finger prints illuminated against the streetlights.

"At least he didn't hit the aorta," Dean muttered. "Or I'd be dead by now." He felt the searing pain as he reduced the pressure on the cut and glanced down to see the blood trickle over his fingers, pooling in the crotch of his pants. "But the stupid fucker cut me bad."

A second ring came and went and Dean wondered if he'd dialled the right number. "Three numbers. How the hell could I get that wrong?" Just as he finished muttering, a woman's voice came on the line.

"Nine, one, one, what's your emergency?"

"I've…" Dean cleared his throat. "I've been stabbed."

"What's your location, sir?"

"Um… downtown." Dean glanced at the street sign. "Corner of King and Forsyth. I'm in a—"

"Is the attacker still there?"

"No—No, he kidnapped my daughter."

"Sorry, he did what?"

"He stole my car." Dean swallowed hard. "And… took my daughter."

"Hold on a second," she said, and without waiting she left the line.

Dean heard a muffled conversation and wondered what the hell she was doing "Hey! Didn't you hear me, my dau—"

"Sorry, I was just confirming another call that came in."

"Summer," Dean whispered.

"An off-duty officer is in pursuit of the vehicle, a red Mercedes, as we speak."

Dean felt his stomach drop. He couldn't believe Summer was still chasing him. That she might actually capture him and get Sabrina back.

"Where is she?"

"Sorry, I can't say."

Dean pushed his foot against the opposite glass wall, raising himself closer to the mouthpiece. "She's my wife! Tell me where she is!"

He thought about what would happen if Summer did stop him. She was unarmed. He was sure of it. They'd taken her gun as a precaution—for her own safety. And this maniac had a knife and who knows what else.

"No, really, I can't say. The call was cut off."

Maybe she did catch him? Maybe he overpowered her? Dean thought of how strong she used to be. She'd always been a fighter. Strong, capable, even brutal in her self defence, but something happened to strip all that away. Something bad—bad enough to tame a Pit Bull.

He shook his head, remembering the way she had coward away from him in the hospital after the attack. It was as if his own hands had done the damage. As if somehow he'd been responsible.

"Sir, the operator who took the call said it ended during the pursuit, as if her phone died."

Dean felt relived. Felt temporarily satisfied that Summer was all right. The distant sound of sirens echoed through the empty streets.

"Sir, the ambulance is en route. Please stay where you are and they'll arrive in just one minute." Dean hooked the door with his foot then gave a hard yank, swinging it open and hitting his other leg. Ignoring the pain in his stomach, he struggled out of the booth.

The rain felt good cascading down on his face. Maybe it was from the loss of blood, or maybe it was from the stress, but his entire world was swirling past his eyes. He crawled his way to the sidewalk bench as the red flashing lights illuminated the distant store fronts. Although the ambulance was getting closer, Dean hardly noticed the sirens anymore.

Throwing his free hand up, he clasped onto the back of the bench and hoisted himself to his knees. The pain was subsiding and he felt like he could probably stand and walk down to the oncoming rescue, but as he struggled to his feet, he collapsed down onto the hard metal bench. The impact jarred his ribs, knocking the air from his lungs. Dean fell flat out on his back, arms flaying down, letting the blood run free.

"Fucking asshole cut me deep," he muttered as the bright red light of the ambulance bounced off the phone booth. He heard the shouts of the paramedics as they jumped from their vehicle and ran to his side. He could also hear a few murmured gasps from onlookers who'd decided to come from the warmth and safety of their apartments, stirred from their comfort by the sirens.

Dean saw the faces of the two paramedics floating above. Heard their incoherent voices drifting away. Felt the numb pressure of their hands on his belly. Tasted the acidic rain as it fell from the sky to his partially open mouth. Smelt the blood—his blood as they tried to stop it from spilling. But as everything unfolded, his mind kept returning to the same thing—Sabrina.

CHAPTER 4

Fat raindrops fell straight to the earth, splashing hard against Summer's head, plastering her blond hair flat against her scalp. She didn't know how long she'd been standing there with the car door propped open, but she knew it felt like an eternity.

The tightness in her chest had returned. She tried to breathe deep and relax, but she couldn't. Nothing would take away the pain until she held Sabrina in her trembling arms.

"What have I done? What the hell have I done! I should've protected her more. I should've known someone would target her to get to me." Summer shook her head and slowly slid back inside the car. She picked the phone from the seat and glanced at the black display. "Piece of shit," she muttered, tucking it into her purse.

After climbing over the console, she opened the passenger door, hoping it wouldn't get stuck. As it swung open wide, she climbed out, stepping down into a deep rut. The water raced down the road and pooled in the rut, gushing over her running shoe. She froze only momentarily, fighting to keep the anger inside, refusing to scream in rage.

"It's nothing. Only water." Summer drew a deep breath. "Gotta get to the highway and find help. Gotta get Sabrina back."

When her other shoe started to take on water, she cursed softly and began climbing the hill. She knew the most direct route to help was across the empty field. It'd be tough going with all the mud, but it would save a lot of time over backtracking down the dirt roads. The water squished from her shoes as Summer reluctantly set her foot into the thick mud, feeling it gush over the top of the runner. She took large steps, managing to find a few rocks to step on as she made her way up the hill, but slipped nearing the top of the embankment. Her hand grasped a tangle of weeds, preventing her from falling flat on her face, but her purse slid down her arm and landed with a splat beside.

Summer raised the mud covered accessory to her face. "Great. Just fucking great!" She shook off the mud then slid it up high on her arm. As she reached the top of the hill, she looked out over the dark empty cornfield, seeing only a few headlights slicing through the darkness at the bottom of the slope. Summer spotted the highway and wondered if he'd taken Sabrina on there, because if he had, then she didn't have a hope in hell of finding them.

Staggering on her next step, Summer noticed the glow of lights to her left, in the direction she'd been driving. They were definitely car headlights illuminating the thick of trees. She felt relieved knowing that he hadn't disappeared down the highway, but the relief turned sour when she realized the headlights weren't moving. He'd stopped the car about a mile down the road. But why?

"What the fuck's he doing, playing another game? Catch me if you can." Summer broke into an awkward run across the field as her feet continued to sink deep into the mud. When she hit a low area, her right foot sank below the ankle. She fought, pulling hard against the suction, losing her shoe in the process. She stumbled backwards, working her way around the small depression in the field. Hobbling through the mud, she hardly noticed the missing shoe as she was too busy concentrating on the illuminated forest in the distance.

After glancing back at the Volvo, she realized just how much the mud was slowing her down. Quickly she headed toward the dirt road, sure that she'd make better time on a stable surface. Summer grasped onto a small bush poking up on the hillside and struggled to cross a wet depression. Her feet sank deeper with each step and it took every ounce of her strength to continue. Her legs burned and her back ached, but she forged along, knowing that relief was just ten feet away.

When her hand gripped the bare brittle branches of a gooseberry bush, she placed her left foot close to the roots, getting a sure footing and pulled her right foot free from the mud. It held for a second, then gave way with a loud slurping noise.

Summer smirked remembering how that always made Sabrina giggle, but her reprieve ended when the reality struck hard. Down the slope she ran, her right foot limping over the sticks and rocks until she hit the dirt road and broke into a full out run.

She rounded the corner of her shortcut and followed the direction that the kidnapper had disappeared. She started to slow, the exertion of the mud taking its toll on her, but with the memory of Sabrina's red swollen eyes pleading for help, Summer found a little reserve of energy and pushed ahead.

She continued her awkward one shoed gallop around the bend and spotted the taillights in the distance. They looked like evil red eyes waiting to disembowel the innocent, but Summer shook the thought from her mind and hobbled toward the human monster. As her sock covered foot continued to pound the rough gravel, Summer was glad it was numb. She knew she'd pay for it tomorrow—if there was a tomorrow. The pain would be intense, but like she'd come to understand, pain meant you were still alive.

The red Mercedes was parked in a tiny alcove to the side of the road. It looked like he'd parked it there, hoping to hide it from the road—but with the lights blazing away. As Summer approached, she couldn't see any sign of Sabrina or the kidnapper. She ran through a mental list of her purse's contents, then cursed that there wasn't anything more dangerous than a nail file inside.

That's okay. Her hands were trained to fight. She'd beaten some of the biggest and best at the station, but as she glanced down at her trembling hands, she knew she wasn't the same person she was five months ago. Pushing the thought aside, she approached the car. It was still running. The cloud of exhaust hanging in the cool air.

As she neared the driver's door, she could see it sitting ajar. The interior light had been turned off, but the glow from the headlights on the naked trees was enough to tell he wasn't behind the wheel. She came up cautiously beside the car, reaching to her side for her gun, but it wasn't there.

With no sign of the kidnapper or Sabrina inside the car, Summer turned quickly, scanning the woods for an ambush. Her head whipped from side to side, taking in every hiding spot.

Satisfied that the surrounding area was secure, she opened the door and fumbled to find the interior light. She flicked it on and her heart caught momentarily. She froze in terror at the sight of the dark splotch on the back seat as it triggered her greatest fear. She staggered, then grasped hold of the car for support.

Blood?

Summer leaned in closer and caught the distinct smell of urine in the air. Feeling so relieved, she feared she might pass out. It was only understandable that Sabrina had wet herself. Hell, most people would've in that situation.

As much as Summer didn't want to, she had to search the car for any sign of Sabrina. Fighting the urge to throw up, she bent and pressed the trunk release. It opened with a pop and Summer could see the light illuminating the area behind the car. She had to check—had to know for sure. Summer found it difficult to move. As much as she needed to know, she didn't want to see her baby girl's body sprawled out in the trunk of a car.

Thinking about their trip to the library last week, Summer used the memory to busy her mind from thinking bad thoughts. Slowly Summer staggered along the length of the car, picturing Sabrina reading a page during story time.

Summer kept her eyes focused on the trees in the distance as she slid her fingers along the car roof, but when her fingers touched the raised trunk lid, her good memory was replaced by reality.

"Maybe this is all a dream?" She closed her eyes and stepped around the back of the car. "No, definitely a nightmare!"

After taking a deep breath and counting to five, she forced her eyes open. They were barely more than slits when bile surged up her throat, causing her to gag. Her stomach churned. Her head pounded. She felt like she was going to faint. Unable to keep control any longer, she doubled over and lost her breakfast.

The trunk was empty except for some shipping slips, empty boxes and the emergency kit she'd bought Dean last year. Summer couldn't believe her reaction. She could understand if Sabrina had been inside, but to lose her breakfast from pure nerves was terrible.

The wind blew the shipping slips, sending a few cascading from the trunk, out into the brightening morning. Summer bent and gathered a few from beside the car and noticed the set of fresh tire tracks. He had a getaway car stashed here. He drove slow, enticing her to follow, toying with her the entire way. He knew exactly which way she'd go and planned everything perfectly. But how would he know her moves. How...

Summer stood, her eyes following the tracks around the bushes. She reached inside the trunk and grabbed the flashlight from the kit then followed the trail around the bushes and onto the ancient driveway. It appeared to be the remains of an old farmhouse, completely shrouded in overgrown trees and bushes. There were so many hiding places the kidnapper could be waiting behind, but she was sure he was long gone. Summer stared at the hanging shutters and smashed windows and couldn't believe he'd led her here to this place when he could've easily just taken off and outrun her.

His whole planning process seemed intent to get her here, to this old farmhouse. But why?

Summer navigated the puddles in the yard and headed straight for the weathered front door. She knew there would be nobody living inside. Knew there would be no phone to call for help from, but still she had to enter. She had to know why the kidnapper had led her here. This had, after all, been part of his master plan.

The stairs to the front porch sagged under the weight of her feet, dipping down, threatening to snap in two at any quick movement. She grabbed the handrail, then quickly let go as it tumbled off the side of the stairs. "This house needs to be condemned and burned, so why lead me here?"

Summer turned, glancing back at the Mercedes sitting behind, illuminating the bushes, and wondered if she should go back for help instead. She was about to leave when a glint of metal at the bottom of the door caught her attention. It wasn't the fact that something could still be shiny in this rotting mess, it was the colour that froze her to the spot. The gleam of gold caused the flashlight to shake across the porch. Summer grabbed the light with two hands and steadied it on the shiny metal. She felt her stomach lurch again and understood why she had been brought here.

Slowly as if she was caged in a dream, she climbed the remaining steps and stood before the front door, eyes locked on the object as if it were some rare foreign artifact never seen before in the existence of mankind. But she had seen it before and she could never forget the first time she'd set eyes on it.

Bending down, Summer plucked the badge from the soft bed of rotting wood at the base of the door. She knew it was hers even before she read the name. Knew the kidnapper had placed it there deliberately earlier this morning. But why? Why, unless…

Summer gagged and fought back a dry heave. Could this be the place? Could this really be the hide out that John Scott had taken her to and… and…

A shutter racked her body at the memory of that night. As hard as the cops had searched, they never found where John Scott had held her. She knew she'd been inside a structure. A rotting musty building, smelling of mildew, but she'd been forced to wear that hood, never privileged to even the sight of the place or her captor. Hell, the last thing she'd seen was that evil look on John Scott's face when he'd stuck her with that needle.

After placing the badge in her pocket, Summer reached out and turned the doorknob. The squeal of rusted hinges echoed through the house, sending a flurry of tiny feet running for cover. Summer swept the light across the entrance room and saw the set of fresh footprints in the thick dust on the floor. They headed straight for the stairs and Summer ignored her training and followed them blindly, knowing where they were heading. Half of her didn't want to see where she'd been held captive, but the other half—the cop half—needed to know for sure. She needed to answer one of the many questions from that night. Needed to finally put to rest the nagging mystery of where that bastard, John Scott, had beat and raped her.

These stairs, although squeaking and worn, were in better condition that the ones on the front porch. Summer climbed carefully, placing her foot in the exact spot the kidnapper had taken earlier. The grime covered window in the room straight off the stairs was now glowing red as the early morning sun broke free of the horizon, illuminating the old farm house and taking some of the mystery and seclusion away. An old fashioned cast iron bed sat squarely in the middle of the room with straps of cord still hanging from the head and foot boards, each covered in dried blood.

Summer stood at the threshold of the room, unable to enter as memories flooded her mind. Her throat suddenly felt raw and swollen. She remembered how much she'd screamed and cried that night and even though it seemed like a life time ago, fresh tears were flooding her eyes, spilling down her cheeks at the sight of her cage.

Over in the corner in a pile of chewed blue clothes, a nest of newborn mice were squirming. Summer recognized the city issued blue uniform and knew if she'd rustled the mice from their nest, she'd find her name stitched on the front pocket.

The footprints continued inside the room and ended at the side of the bed, then retreated. A white envelope had been laid out directly in the middle of the bed, on the dried bloodstain. Summer knew it was the ransom note. Knew she had to get it and read his demands, but just the thought of stepping foot inside this room was too much to handle. Her heart was racing, her palms sweating as every muscle in her body began twitching at the thought of getting close to that bed.

One shaky foot entered the room and froze in the kidnapper's footprint as the mice scattered into their hiding places.

"I… can't?" Summer wrapped her arms around her body, squeezing her shaking chest, trying to control the tremors inside. "I…" She saw the white swatch of silk underwear in that mouse nest and concentrated on building her fury at the memory of being dumped naked in the ditch to die. She found a trace of hatred for John Scott, grasped onto that thread and closed her eyes, taking two more steps into the room. One last step and Summer slowly opened her eyes. The white envelope sat on top of the crusted hard bed sheet, with her name printed carefully on the front. It looked so beautifully done, so inviting, like a wedding invitation, but she knew what was inside was anything but a cordial invitation to a party. It was an invitation to her horrid past.

Summer reached out a trembling hand, plucked the envelope from the bed then turned and raced from the room. Feeling lightheaded, she stopped momentarily at the top of the stairs and knew she had to get outside.

With the cool morning air cleansing the musty smell from her lungs, Summer leaned back against the wall and tore open the envelope. The paper inside was thick and expensive. As she slid it out and started to unfold it, she expected to see an amount for the ransom, but there wasn't any. The kidnapper wasn't demanding any money at all. All that was printed was one perfectly scripted line. One simple demand. One that could cost her life.

CHAPTER 5

Summer limped down the front stairs, her right foot aching with every step she took. In the time she'd been inside the farmhouse the weather had changed completely. The rain had ceased and the sky was turning a brilliant rosy glow, chasing away the dark clouds to the east. As the sunshine caused every last raindrop, which clung to the leaves of the overgrown trees to sparkle like gems, Summer marvelled at how everything could look so beautiful when inside she felt like such shit.

Hobbling down the broken driveway, Summer wondered if she'd sliced the bottom of her foot wide open, because it sure as hell felt that way right now. She rounded the car, eyeing the soaked boxes and papers inside the trunk then slammed the lid closed.

Without bothering to wipe the water from the seat, Summer slid behind the wheel and closed the door. She sat there staring through the tiny gaps in the bushes at the old farmhouse.

"Why here? Why did John Scott bring me here?" Summer shook her head. How did he know about this place?

Either he'd grown up around here or someone else had told him about it. And if the kidnapper is working for someone else then who's really behind all this.

After backing the car from the alcove, Summer shifted gears then sat staring out across the farmland at the highway below. She knew the chance of finding Sabrina was slim. He could be long gone in either direction down the 401, or he could be hiding close by to check on his demands before letting Sabrina go, but would he release Sabrina unharmed like he said he would? Summer knew the answer that a cop would think, but she refused to give in. Hell, right now she was a mother, not a cop.

"Don't worry, baby," Summer whispered as she started down the road, heading toward the city. "I'll get you back."

The drive back to Chatham seemed to take forever. Summer expected to see cops crawling all over the place, but then again she had not given her location before the phone had died. She reached into her purse and grabbed the phone. She had half a mind to toss the useless thing out the window and watch it smash into pieces for all the good it'd done. Summer lowered the window then paused, realizing that the kidnapper might try calling this phone, but it's dead. She made a mental note to get it charged as soon as possible.

The morning traffic was starting to build as Summer turned onto Richmond Street. She wondered if anybody had come to Dean's aide, or even if he'd managed to call for help. For all she knew he could be lying dead in a pool of blood right there on the downtown sidewalk. The thought of losing him was too much to handle right now. Sure they were separated, but she needed him now more than ever. He was the last thread to her unravelling life—the only thing that held her from falling into obscurity right now. Without

Dean… Summer swallowed hard, refusing to finish the thought.

Up ahead a police cruiser sat behind the damaged car that she'd slid into during the chase. She glanced at the officer investigating the scene and he returned her stare, then reached for his radio. It was Jones, the newest recruit. Summer considered stopping and sending Jones off on the search for Sabrina, but she needed to check on Dean. Besides, thirty seconds more wouldn't make a difference in finding Sabrina.

As Summer neared the end of the street, she saw the lights of the cruiser snap to life. Jones was giving pursuit, chasing after her. Summer suddenly realized that she was driving the kidnapper's car right now. Maybe Jones was following her, hoping to be of service when she stops downtown. Or, maybe he didn't recognize her and thought she was the kidnapper?

The sirens wailed behind, bouncing off the buildings as they neared the downtown core. The way the cruiser was tearing down the street, racing to catch up, Summer believed she was the one who was wanted right now. There was no way in hell she was going to stop for Jones. He'd have to run her off the road and Summer knew he didn't have the balls for that.

Summer ripped the Mercedes around the last corner, gunned the engine as it straightened out, then slammed on the brakes sending the car sliding sideways down the road toward the barricade of police cars blocking the crime scene.

"Shit!" Summer said, shaking nervously from the adrenaline rush. She jumped from the car as the cruiser came sliding to a stop, inches away. There was a confused look on Jones' face as Summer dashed around the other side of the car, limping down the road toward the crowd of onlookers.

The officers broke free of the crowd, guns drawn in her direction, but seemed to stop as one when they saw who Jones had been chasing.

"Summer?" Nate Long said, holstering his gun and rushing down the rain slicked road toward her. His arms were out, waiting as always to give her support.

Summer met him halfway and allowed herself to be caught in his embrace. His strong arms had never felt so good as he lifted her off her feet with ease. She choked back a sob. The last time he'd held her in his arms, she'd been naked, battered and bruised. Left for dead.

Summer squirmed until Nate set her back onto the ground. He wasn't the type of man to openly express his feeling in public and that's what made Summer so grateful that he was there for her. Just the feeling of his arms around her body was more soothing than a bullet proof vest and she knew she'd never forget that feeling as long as she lived.

"Nate, he spiked my tires then dumped his car." Summer fought to catch her breath. "He's got Sabrina."

"I'm so sorry. I heard the call come in and I... I can't believe it happened. But why? Why Sabrina?"

Summer shook her head as fresh tears filled her eyes.

"He was waiting for us—for Dean to arrive with..." She couldn't do it. She couldn't bring herself to say the name again. It was almost as if saying her name would condemn Sabrina to death.

"Don't worry." Nate raised her chin. "We'll get her back."

"Jones! Put it out on the wire. The kidnapper has switch vehicles."

Officer Kyle Jones looked surprised that of all the cops standing around, he was the one Nate had chosen to make the call. "But what should I tell them to look for?"

"I don't know? Give me a few minutes, but for now, a man with a little girl—every man with a child—boy or girl!"

"Dean?" Summer pulled back and stared up into Nate's blue eyes. Eyes she had looked into many times before. Eyes that seldom showed any signs of fear. Loving eyes that seemed to be looking deep inside. Deep into her soul whenever he spoke. "Where's Dean?"

"He's in the hospital." Nate pulled her close, squeezing tight. "In the OR."

"Is he going—"

"He's lost a lot of blood." Nate shook his head. "Luckily the knife didn't hit anything important. Looks like a few stitches and some rest and he'll be fine."

"Are you sure?"

Nate kissed her head then held her out at arm's length. "I'm not a doctor, but I've seen worse come through." He stared for a moment then ushered her toward the nearest cruiser, noticing her limp. "You're hurt?" He gave her foot a queer glance. "Where's your other shoe?"

"I lost it." Summer glanced down at her muddy sock. "I think I might have cut my foot, too."

Nate scooped her into his arms and headed toward the ambulance on the other side of the crowd. "Change of plans. Let's get the paramedics to look at that foot while you warm up."

Summer felt her face flush. She tucked her head down, refusing to look at the crowd of onlookers as Nate carried her like a bride over the threshold, to the ambulance. Sure he'd been her partner for the last two years and they had been very close. Close enough to spur rumours around the station, but they had only been partners—close partners.

Summer heard the ambulance door open and a second later Nate set her on the stretcher.

"I'm fine," Summer insisted, pushing herself back and sitting up. "It's probably only a scratch or a small cut."

The paramedic donned a pair of gloves then slid off Summer's mud covered sock. "Well, let's have a look."

Nate pulled out his note pad. "Tell me what happened to Dean and Sabrina."

"Sabrina," Summer muttered. Her body began to shiver despite the increased warmth inside the ambulance. "He took her. He was waiting for Dean and he took her."

"Where? Which direction did they go?"

"I chased him down Howard line. He'd set a trap and my car got stuck in the cut through." Summer shook her head. She felt the hot tears burning her eyes. "It was all a setup. He led me to the place... the place John Scott had held me."

Nate's eyes were studying her closely. "How do you know it was the same place?"

Summer dug in her pocket and withdrew her old badge then dropped it into Nate's palm. His nostrils flared and his eyes narrowed as the sight of the badge brought back memories that he'd been hiding away.

"It was the right place." Summer closed her eyes. She could see every step she'd taken inside that place. She could still smell the rot and mildew as if she were lying on that bloodstained bed right now instead of this stretcher. She opened her eyes and saw the angry look of hatred in Nate's eyes. "Trust me. It's the place."

Nate turned to Officer Jones, who was standing just beyond the side of the door. "Take Stevens and Malroy out to the cut through on Howard line. Find Summer's Volvo and secure the scene. I want the entire place searched and the farmhouse down the street processed for evidence."

Jones looked nervously around at the group of officers who weren't busy processing the scene of the attack, then to the detective standing close by. "But what about Detective Grimshaw. Shouldn't he be involved?"

"I'm sure he'll follow along." Nate rolled his eyes. "Won't wanna miss a thing."

When Jones hurried across the street to Stevens and Malroy, Nate turned back to Summer. "Did he leave a ransom note? Anything else."

Summer stared out through the ambulance doors at the plain clothed detective standing near the ambulance. Detective Grimshaw was the one who had captured John Scott last night. He was the reason the kidnapper had taken Sabrina and he was the reason Sabrina was being used as a pawn right now.

"Ow!" Summer squirmed as the paramedic pulled a bloodied thorn from her foot. She opened her purse and withdrew the crumpled sheet of paper as Detective Grimshaw watched her every move through the opening, then handed it to Nate.

After unfolding the sheet, Nate read the demand then glanced over his shoulder at the detective. "He's not gonna like this."

"Well, fuck him!" Summer said, holding her eyes locked on the detective as he walked toward the back of the ambulance. "He's the cause of all this. If he doesn't like it then he can go crying to the chief."

"Are you going to let me in on this, or do I have to wait for a briefing at the station?" Grimshaw said, stepping behind and plucking the crumpled paper from Nate's hand.

"It's the ransom note," Summer choked as the paramedic poured some disinfectant on the gash in her foot. It burned like hell and Summer felt like screaming out, but she held it inside, concentrating on the pain, trying to ignite it into an infernal of anger that would help her get through this day.

Grimshaw withdrew a plastic bag from his pocket and slid the note inside. "Looks like we've picked up the right suspect last night. This kidnapper must be his accomplice." He tucked the bag inside his jacket and stepped closer to the ambulance door. "Officer Demure, I know this is a difficult time, but the sooner you come to the station, the sooner you can ID John Scott and we can—"

"Can what?" Summer grabbed the sides of the stretcher and slid herself to the end, knocking the paramedic back. "Lock John Scott away and allow that monster to hurt my baby!"

"Officer Demure, must I remind you that we do not negotiate over hostages."

Nate jumped down from the ambulance, his large frame knocking Grimshaw back. "This is not the time or place to be discussing the situation. When the time is right, Summer will come to the station and see if she can ID the suspect you've arrested."

"Given the situation, I'd say we've got the right man." Grimshaw lowered his voice as he escorted Nate away from the ambulance. "Don't let this little stunt change her mind. She knows we've got the right guy. He fit the sketch perfectly. I'd bet my life on this being her assailant."

"That may be so, but when an innocent girl's life hangs in the balance," Nate glanced back at Summer, then turned away, "don't be surprised at what might occur."

"Then I suggest you put Officer Demure in your car and talk some sense into her on your way down to the station, because I'm not willing to let this guy walk free."

"But you're willing to let a little girl die?"

"Statistics show that we'll be able to negotiate her release under the circumstances."

"Statistics! You're willing to gamble on statistics?" Nate shoved his finger into the detective's chest, backing him up a few feet. "How many children do you have?"

"That's not relevant."

"Exactly. Only a man with no children would answer that way. Now, I'm gonna give you a piece of advice and you'd better listen hard. Leave Summer alone. She'll come to you if she needs your help, but until then, back off!"

Summer overheard their conversation and knew the detective was right, but sometimes being right doesn't always matter. What John Scott had done to her five months ago didn't seem to matter much right now. What was going to happen to Sabrina was all that she could afford to worry about. Summer watched as the paramedic secured a plastic protective boot over the bandages, then slid off the stretcher.

Without saying a word she limped from the ambulance, past Grimshaw's cold black eyes, toward Nate's cruiser. Nate immediately hurried to her side, grabbing her arm and taking the weight off her bad foot, but in the excitement he lifted so much Summer found it difficult to walk.

"That guy is such an ass," Summer said, pulling free from Nate's aggressive grip. "Who the hell does he think he is to tell me what to do?"

Nate opened the car door. "What *are* you gonna do?"

"Whatever it takes to get Sabrina back."

Nate rushed around the car and slid behind the wheel. "Then I suggest we pay John Scott a little visit."

Summer felt some of the courage that she'd gained slip away at the thought of coming face to face with the man who'd turned her into this quivering mess. She knew it was inevitable, but there was something else she needed to do first.

"I have to stop at the hospital. I need to see Dean and make sure he's all right."

"Sure." Nate gripped her hand and gave it a squeeze. "Maybe he'll have a description of the kidnapper?"

"Maybe he will?" Summer felt her gut wrench remembering the look on Dean's face as the knife slit him open. It was an image she doubted she'd ever forget. "After all, they were practically face to face."

CHAPTER 6

The hospital was abuzz with the news of Dean's attempted murder so every eye was glued to Summer and Nate as they rushed down the second floor hallway, then burst through the recovery room doors. Summer had one thing on her mind, find Dean and make sure he was all right so she could concentrate on getting Sabrina back.

"I'm sorry," the nurse behind the desk said, standing quickly, "but the doctor specifically said no—"

"Visitors. Yeah, yeah. I know the drill," Nate said sarcastically, stopping at the entrance to the nurses' station and blocking their exit. "But we're gonna see Dean Demure and if the doctor doesn't like it then he can deal with me. And right now I'm really not in the mood to listen to his bullshit." Nate leaned in closer to the nearest nurse. "Now, where is Mr. Demure?"

Summer couldn't stand to wait. She left Nate behind, moving through the large recovery ward peeking inside each smaller room before finally finding Dean spread out on the bed, hooked up to a ton of monitors. She scanned the machines and determined that his vitals were good, despite his face being pale—so pale that his mop of dark curls looked oddly out of place.

"Dean?" Summer said softly, leaning on the side of the bed. "Dean, can you hear me?"

A moan escaped his lips as his right eye fluttered open before snapping closed again. He looked totally out of it. Probably still doped up from the surgery.

The nurse making her rounds stepped to the opposite side of the bed and checked his pulse. "You must be Sabrina," she said. "He's been asking for you ever since he came out of surgery." She pulled his charts then stopped and gave Summer a big smile. "He must really love you, cause in all my years of working here I've never heard someone so adamant about seeing somebody."

Summer swallowed hard, but the lump in her throat didn't budge. She reached out and reluctantly placed a shaking hand on his cold cheek. Dean loved Sabrina so much that if anything happened to her, it'd kill him. He'd always been there for her, especially during the last five months when she'd been less than capable of showing her own feelings.

"Summer," Nate said, rushing up behind. "Did he say anything? Is he awake?"

"Sum—mer," Dean muttered. His right eye fluttered open for a second and a big smile filled his face. "I knew you could do it." His eye snapped closed and he took a deep breath. "I knew you'd get Sabrina."

"Dean." Summer stood, holding his face in both hands. "Who took her! Who stabbed you!"

Dean's eyes snapped open and wildly searched the room. Although groggy, he seemed to be taking in every face. "Where's Sabrina?"

"She's gone." Summer's hands were shaking so badly that Dean's face was vibrating. "Tell me who took her. You saw his face. He spoke to you. What did he say? What did he say that made you look at me like that?"

Dean strained to focus his eyes and attempted to sit forward—an act that the nurse quickly restrained—but there was something strange about the way he was looking at her.

"He… he told me you were pregnant. That's why I looked over at you. Then… then he stabbed me." Dean's eyes were boring into her and she could feel him searching for an answer, some sign that he'd been played a fool.

He reached out his hand, placing it on her stomach and Summer felt the stab of guilt rip through her chest as his fingers touched the wet fabric to her skin. She could feel the way his hand was cupping her growing belly and it seemed so wrong—so different from the way he'd touched her belly when Sabrina was inside. That seemed like a different time. Hell, a whole different universe. There were no tears of happiness this time. No excited embrace like before. This felt wrong. Felt like a stranger feeling for a cancerous growth inside.

Summer pulled his hand away, unable to stand his touch anymore. She looked from Dean's questioning eyes and watched as Nate escorted the nurse away from the bedside.

"Why didn't you tell me?" Dean grabbed the bed control and raised the head up, grimacing in pain as it rose. "Unless—"

"It would've only complicated matters. Do you think I want everybody knowing that I might be carrying that sick fucker's child inside me?" Summer stood and wrapped her arms around her body. "Do you know how it makes me feel every time I see this lump? Every time I feel it move inside me." She shook her head. "It sickens me. It actually makes me violently ill knowing I may give birth to his bastard kid."

Dean reached out his hand, but Summer stood out of reach. "It could be mine? It could be ours?" He forced a weak smile. "We were trying, remember? Remember how excited we were to have another baby?"

Summer did remember, but it felt so long ago. Like a blurry dream.

"You wanted a boy to complete the perfect family, but Sabrina wanted a little sister so she could have tea parties with someone other than you or me." Dean leaned forward, fighting the pain and gripped Summer's hand, pulling her close. "Why didn't you run the DNA and find out for sure?"

Summer stared down at their interlocked hands. She remembered the first time he'd held her hand. It was as they were leaving the restaurant on their first date. Dean insisted the wet sidewalk may be slippery for her high heels, a ploy by any standards, but it had worked. There was an instant chemistry when their bodies had touched. A tiny charge of electricity that had jumped from his body to hers, erupting a flood of emotions inside. His touch had always given warmth and excitement every time, but his powers seemed to be gone. Faded away with the passage of time.

Unable to take his touch any longer, Summer pulled free. "Cause if it isn't that sick bastard's child, then it'll be yours. And look at us, we've grown so far apart that I don't even recognize us anymore."

"We haven't grown apart, Summer. I still love you. I'll always love you no matter what happens. No matter whose baby you're carrying. No matter how long it takes for you to get over it." Dean paused, drawing a cleansing breath. "I've never stopped loving you. I only agreed to the separation because I thought it would make it easier for you to accept what had happened. I never wanted to be apart. Never!"

Summer dropped onto the stool beside the bed. "But you never came to my rescue. I prayed so many times that you'd show up and save me from him, but you never came." Summer fought back a sob. "You let me down and that's what hurts so bad. That's why I can't be with you anymore. And that's why I decided to give the baby away without knowing whose it is."

Tears were spilling down Dean's face. "You're being unreasonable. I tried everything I could to find you. I searched everywhere I could think of. Ask Nate. Ask anybody. I never slept. I never ate. I would've killed a thousand people just to get you back. And you did come back. That's the most important thing." Dean reached out a hand to her. "You came back, to me?"

"I have to go." Summer turned her back on Dean and wiped the tears from her face. She couldn't let him see her like this. She couldn't allow herself to break down into his arms. She didn't need him anymore. She had to learn how to be strong again, like she used to be. "I have to go. I have to find Sabrina and get her back."

Summer heard the bed creak, followed by groans from behind. She knew Dean was attempting to get up when the nurses dashed across the room. It didn't matter if Dean wanted to help or not. She'd already made up her mind. She didn't need his help.

"Summer… wait! I can help."

Nate's radio crackled to life and he stepped toward the door to take the call. Summer quickened her pace across the room when she heard Chief Dickson's voice on the other end. He sounded pissed and she figured it was because they had disobeyed his orders and stopped here on the way to the station, but the look on Nate's face proved her wrong.

"John Scott's been attacked during the night."

"By a cop?"

Nate took her arm and hurried her out into the hall. "No, by a guy they brought in last night for assault and battery. Seth Millar's his name and somehow he got into John Scott's cell and nearly killed him."

"It'd serve that bastard right," Summer said, gritting her teeth. "Except I need him alive."

"That's what has the chief so worked up. He wants to know what the hell's going on. The kidnapper wants him freed, but someone else wants him dead." Nate turned to Summer. "I know every cop on the force would be willing to look the other way if something happened to him, and maybe that's what happened. But if he's the key to getting Sabrina back then we'd better get down there and keep him safe."

"This is wrong." Summer shook her head as they entered the elevator. "So wrong."

"I agree, but right now we just have to play along and wait for our chance to roll the dice."

The ride to the station seemed to take forever and a part of Summer was glad for the reprieve. How could she step foot in the same room as that monster? How could she not want to rip his balls off and force feed them down his throat? They would've had to restrain the old Summer Demure from doing just that, but she knew she'd crumble like a shit house the second John Scott looked her way. How could this have happened to her? How could she have been transformed into such a spineless piece of shit at the hands of one man?

Summer twisted in her seat and stared at Nate. It felt good riding in the cruiser beside her old partner. Maybe the best medicine didn't come from a bottle, but from the familiarity of a close friend who was there for you when you needed someone.

Nate was so opposite from Dean. His size was intimidating and his stern hardened face brought instant respect and fear from people. He was the kind of guy you wanted standing at your side when bad shit was going down, and he'd proven it on many occasions during their time together. Summer could remember a dozen times that his bruit strength had come in handy in the line of duty. She had been no slouch and could defend herself in most situations, but where she had to fight a good fight to be the victor, Nate could do the same with one swat of his fist. If she hadn't met Dean before being paired up with Nate, then their rumoured relationship might have been more than a rumour.

"So how do you think the kidnapper and John Scott are connected?" Nate said, stealing a glance. "Are they partners? Work for the same boss? Jail house—"

"I'm putting my money on them having the same boss, cause the kidnapper got a call on his cell phone when he was talking to me."

Nate's lips tightened into slits and his eyes narrowed. "You talked to the kidnapper! When were you gonna tell me?"

"Sorry, I forgot. There's so much happening that I can't think straight."

"Maybe I was wrong to take you to the hospital?" Nate's nostrils were flared and twitching. "Grimshaw was right. I should've taken you to the station and got all the information out of you."

"Grimshaw? Don't tell me you're falling for this guy. He's an arrogant piece of shit who only wants one thing. A conviction on his sheet."

Nate took a deep breath and rounded the corner. "So you think the boss called to check that he got Sabrina?"

"I don't know, but the guy—I assume it was a man—ordered him to toss Dean's phone out the window. The guy seemed ticked that the kidnapper was talking to me." Summer watched out the window as the traffic began to thicken. Everybody was heading to their jobs, unaware of the terrible things that had happened this morning. Ignorance must be bliss, Summer thought. Cops never got a chance to be ignorant even when they wanted to be.

"So if John Scott and the kidnapper both work for the same person, then what John Scott did to me," she fought to control the shiver which raced through her body at the memory, but lost, "wasn't a random act. It was meant as a payback."

"For intercepting the drugs heading to Dean's business? But that wasn't even our doing. It was a joint effort."

"That's the only thing I keep coming up with, too." Summer had run through the long list of calls they'd had leading up to the attack from John Scott, but the only thing that could've pissed someone off bad enough to put that kind of hit on her was the drug bust.

Nate glanced over, his eyes lingering a second too long.

Summer raised an eyebrow. "So everything happened because of Dean's business?"

"Come on, Summer. What else do we have here? There's no other explanation for what had happened. You can't tell me that it was a coincidence that John Scott's van was rear ended during our chase. He knew our schedule. The driver of that car knew we'd be on that road. He knew we'd give chase. And he knew John Scott would be waiting for him to crash into. It was all a setup. The crash. The run through the woods. The dirt bike stashed for the driver's escape. He got away clean that morning," Nate sighed, "but I think he's come back."

Summer felt the hot tears building and turned, staring outside, refusing to let Nate see her cry. "But if it was because of Dean's contacts, then why wouldn't John Scott have said anything. Why not send a message?"

"Because I don't think you were supposed to be able to talk after he was through with you." Nate gave her a reassuring squeeze on the shoulder. "But what about Gavin Stone? You can't tell me he's clean and not somehow using the courier business to his advantage?"

"You've checked him out." Summer wiped the tears away and met Nate's blue eyes. "I know you have. There's no possible way you could just sit back and not stick your nose in it."

"Maybe I have?"

"And you came up empty handed, right?"

Nate nodded.

Summer turned her attention to the outside world, but her eyes caught her reflection in the side mirror. She couldn't believe the way she looked right now, all huddled in the corner of the front seat with shoulders drawn down and her face slack and sad. How could she face the world like this? How could she stand tall and fight back when she couldn't even sit straight? Turning to Nate, she pushed back her shoulders and met him with a fixed gaze.

"Gavin Stone has changed. He's not the same man he was eight years ago."

"And what changed him? Eight years behind bars and three months on probation. Maybe he asked God for forgiveness?"

Summer shook her head.

"Once a criminal," Nate said. "Always a criminal."

"Remind me again why you never went through to become a judge."

"I've seen too many kids make mistakes and they usually continue to make the same mistakes until they die from them. So, I guess we'll have to ask John Scott who he's working for. That is, as long as the boys do their job and keep him safe for us."

Summer glanced at her watch and fidgeted in the seat. "We'd better hurry, Nate. We're running out of time."

"Don't worry," Nate said, flipping on the siren and speeding through a red light. "We'll make it work."

CHAPTER 7

The news of John Scott's arrest last night, combined with Sabrina's kidnapping this morning had the entire police parking lot full of reporters all hoping to get a quick sound bite for the lunch news, but Nate wanted no part of the circus so he bypassed the front entrance and rounded the building, pulling up at the back door of the service bay.

"They're a bunch of vultures," Nate said, pushing through the doorway and entering the back hall. "But we might need their help to get Sabrina back."

"Not if we follow the kidnapper's instructions." Summer hurried to catch up. "He only wants one thing."

Nate stopped and turned to her. "And how do you purpose we do that. Do you think Grimshaw will allow John Scott to walk out of here, because I think the detective will put up quite a stink if we try?"

"Then let's not tell him." Summer tried to smile, but couldn't. "Let it be a surprise."

"Yeah," Nate rolled his eyes and continued walking. "The prisoner? Oh… I think he just stepped out for a cigarette. You know how we hate second hand smoke in the jail cells. Come on, Summer, even if you don't ID him they'll match his DNA to the case and—"

"I won't allow it." Summer shook her head. "I'll say I lied about being raped. I'll say I made the whole thing up. That I went with him willingly."

"No, you're not gonna ruin your name like that. I won't allow it."

"What the hell do I care? Let people think what they want. Let them think I was just screwing around and got caught in some kinky sex scandal." Summer pulled Nate to a stop while they were still alone. "I don't care what happens to me anymore. All I want is to get Sabrina back and hold her in my arms."

Nate nodded. "Give me your cell phone. Someone's gotta have a charger here."

Summer pulled it from her purse and handed it to Nate. "I think there's still one in my desk."

When they reached the end of the hall, Nate tossed the phone to the nearest person and ordered them to retrieve the charger then headed toward the interrogation room where John Scott had been placed, for his own protection.

Chief Harold Dickson was standing guard outside the interrogation room, looking anxiously around at the sight of all the reporters gathered in the parking lot. He'd never been one to willingly step into the spotlight, and nearly always fumbled over his words whenever the cameras were rolling, and Summer knew the idea of addressing the public was eating away inside him.

"Summer," Chief Dickson said, placing both hands on her shoulders. "I'm so sorry about what happened. I've got everyone on the case and I've put it out on the wire all across the area. I hope you don't mind but I used the photo of Sabrina from your desk. We've clamped down the entire area and they've tightened the border. Don't worry. They won't get far."

"Is…" Summer tipped her head to the room beside. "He, in there?"

The chief nodded. He looked worn out, like he'd aged ten years in a single morning. His normally slender physic had transformed over the last year, turning him into an unhealthy specimen. She could see it in his washed out grey eyes. There was something he was hiding. Some reason why he'd dropped so many pounds in such a short period of time. She felt a slight tremble in her shoulders but couldn't decide if it was coming from the chief's hands or her own body, so she shook off his touch and turned to the door.

"Summer," Chief Dickson said. "Let's not be rash about this. I know what you've been through and storming into that room in your condition to face him would be a bad thing."

"My condition!" Summer screamed. "That fucker in there is the reason I have a fucking condition anyways! What does it matter if I go in there? What do you think I'll do, go nuts and gouge his eyeballs out?"

Summer drew a deep breath and glanced around, noticing every eye in the station was frozen on her as flashes from the cameras outside lit up the front glass doors. Great, she could see the front page now. Distraught officer freaks out in cop shop.

She felt Chief Dickson pull her close, turning her so her back was to the crowd outside. "I don't know what you're capable of doing right now, so I'd prefer you come with me into the next room and we'll take a look at his mug shots and you can see him through the one way mirror."

Summer glanced over her shoulder at the crowd of reporters waiting behind the police line like caged lions at the zoo.

"This John Scott fits your description and also the artist's sketch. Detective Grimshaw apprehended him in a small warehouse in the west end of Windsor. He was modifying a shipment of merchandise to allow drugs to be hidden inside. Although the merchandise isn't the same as the stuff we confiscated six months ago, crammed with meth, we think he was working with the same dealers."

"So he is working for someone?"

"That's what it looks like." Chief Dickson opened the door to the adjoining room. "But he's not talking anymore."

Summer gave Nate a questioning look. "Anymore?"

"When Grimshaw brought him in, John Scott mentioned that he was interested in cutting a deal. He wouldn't confess or specify what kind of deal until he had a lawyer present, but still he was willing to name names."

"Let me guess, now that the other inmate tried to kill him, he's not talking anymore?"

Chief Dickson nodded.

Summer kept her eyes trained on her feet as they entered the small room. "What was the other guy brought in for?"

"Assault and battery. Beat the crap out of a convenience store clerk claiming he'd short changed him." Chief Dickson closed the door behind. "Then the guy hung around the neighbourhood for the cops to pick him up. At first it seemed like a lucky break, but now it looks like he was trying to get arrested."

Summer raised her eyes and glanced at the man sitting slouched behind the table. "Like someone hired him to keep an eye on our boy and make sure he doesn't squeal?"

"Looks that way. We've run the other prisoner through the computer and he's clean. This is his first offence. No link to organized crime. Not even a speeding ticket on his record."

"Has he said why he attacked John Scott?" Nate asked, placing an arm around Summer's shoulder.

"Said John Scott told him what he'd done to Summer. Said he remembered Summer's story and it'd just set him off." Chief Dickson picked a picture from the small counter and stared at John Scott's mug shot. "We checked the tapes in the cell, but never heard John Scott speak."

Summer continued to stare at John Scott. "Could he have whispered it too softly that the machine didn't catch it?"

"Anything's possible." Chief Dickson dropped the mug shot and leaned against the wall. "But you know as well as I do what kind of sounds that machine picks up."

The man sitting inside the next room didn't look capable of harming anyone right now. He sat slouched down in the chair with his head hung low. Summer glared at his eyes, but they were nothing more than slits in his swollen face. The beating the other inmate had given him was pretty bad. Bad enough to make IDing him almost impossible. There were similarities between this man and the man who'd been lying possum beside the van, covered with blood, but Summer knew even if she wanted to ID him right now, she couldn't be a hundred percent sure that this was the same man.

She knew if she wanted to be sure, she'd have to wait until the swelling and bruises disappeared before she could send this man away to jail, but with Sabrina's life teetering in her grasp, even if Summer could pick John Scott from a crowd, she didn't think she would.

"His face is so battered and I only saw him briefly at the site of the crash and even then his face was covered with blood." Summer glanced at the mug shot on the counter and felt a gut wrenching pain rip through her stomach. She doubled over, grabbing for the steel counter as she went.

Those eyes. She'd seen those eyes haunting her nights for the last five months. How could she forget them? They were the last thing she'd seen that night before the drugs kicked in and her mind and life swirled out of control.

Chief Dickson ran his hands through the tiny fringe of white hair on the sides of his scalp. "I thought you might have a better chance of recognizing him from that photo— back when he had all his teeth."

Summer drew a deep breath and slowly looked up at Chief Dickson. His shallow cheeks had turned flush and the tiny vein running up his forehead, beneath the translucent aged skin was pulsating right now. She and the chief had become very close over the years and Summer knew it was because she was the only woman on the force. When he needed someone to talk to about his wife's fight with cancer, well he certainly wouldn't have turned to the men. Their answers always involved the same thing, drinking.

Summer knew those talks had lessened the pain of losing his wife and at the same time given the chief a peek at her innermost thoughts and dreams. So when John Scott had taken her away, she knew Chief Dickson was doing everything humanly possible to get her back.

"I know this is hard for you, Summer, but take a minute before you tell me if you can identify this man."

Summer felt Nate's arms lifting her back to her feet. The pain in her stomach lessened knowing that he was standing beside her. Knowing that he would accept either of her decisions without consequences.

Chief Dickson flipped the photo over and touched her shoulder. "I read the ransom note myself. I know what we as police officers are supposed to do in a situation like this, but I also know what is truly at stake here. If you look me in the eye and tell me that's not the man who tortured you that night, then I'll turn him loose right now. But if you can't, then I'll have no choice but to demand a DNA sample be taken and run against the samples in the file. Either way, this decision is yours to make."

Nate pulled her closer, shielding her from the one way mirror. "Chief, give us a few minutes, okay?"

Without another word Chief Dickson left the room, leaving Summer to tremble in Nate's arms. Although his arms were strong, she wished that Dean were here to hold her right now. She'd thought about this day, the day they'd catch her attacker and how she'd want to face him and give him a taste of his own medicine, but never, never had she imagined that things would be so twisted as they were right now. If only Dean were here. His opinion would mean everything. After all, he was in this predicament as much as she was.

"Nate." Summer stepped back and held her hands out, watching as they trembled. "I recognize those eyes. I know it's him. He's the reason my hands are like this. He's the reason I can't stop shaking."

Nate nodded. His eyes were narrow slits and his jaw muscles were vibrating as he glanced into the next room at the catatonic bastard sitting at the desk. Summer knew what was going through his mind right now, and if Sabrina wasn't missing, she'd be more than happy to escort him inside that room and watch him unload his fury on John Scott, but regrettably she couldn't.

"He's working for the same person as the kidnapper," Summer said. "He knows where to find the guy pulling the strings. If we can get that name, then we'll have a bargaining chip."

Nate flexed his clenched fists, then re-clenched them. "Five minutes alone with him and I'll have that name. You keep the chief busy and I'll go in there."

"Thanks, Nate." Summer took his fist in her hands and pried it open. "But I can't let you risk your job."

"Then how the hell do you plan to get that name?"

Summer stepped behind Nate, edging toward the door. "I'm going in there."

"Like hell! That's just what he wants."

"I have no choice. Look at me. I'm a mess. I don't think I'll ever be the same again. The only hope I have is to face my fears and that means John Scott. If he ends up walking out of here, I may never get a chance to tell him what a piece of shit he really is."

"I can't." Nate placed a hand on the door. "I just can't let you go in there by yourself. What if he tries something? What if he hurts you again?"

"He's chained to the desk. How much of a threat can he be?" Summer closed her eyes and drew a deep breath. She held it for ten seconds then let it go. "Do I have to remind you, I am a cop? I know how to handle shit like him."

The look in Nate's eyes told her everything. As much as she wanted to see the same silly smirk on his face and the cocked left eyebrow that he regularly gave her whenever she'd proved him wrong and pulled the impossible from her ass, it wasn't there today. He knew she wouldn't be able to pull this one off and it hurt because she knew he was right.

Nate removed his hand from the door and reached for the handle. "I'm coming in with you."

"No!"

"Yes, I am! And if you don't like it then you can shove it up your ass."

Summer stopped with her hand on the door handle, staring into Nate's hardened face. She felt the anger building inside and realized that her body felt stronger right now then it had in a long time. A smirk crept onto her face and she reached up and patted Nate's cheek.

"You're just trying to piss me off."

"Is it working?"

Summer nodded and pulled the door open. The chief was standing on the other side of the hall, anxiously waiting for them to exit the room. He took a step toward them but stopped when Summer turned suddenly and opened the interrogation room door.

"Summer, you can't—"

"It's okay, Chief. I'll keep an eye on her." Nate followed her inside and softly closed the door behind. "I'll be right over here if you need me. If he so much as whispers an obscene word to you, I'll close those puffy eyes for good."

Summer walked slowly across the room toward the table. The strength that Nate had instilled in her was fading fast and the nervous spasms were threatening to rupture through her control and send her into a jittering mess. She glanced over at the one way mirror and even though she couldn't see him, she knew Chief Dickson was standing behind the mirror watching her reaction.

How could this one man have caused so much pain and suffering? Summer swallowed her fear and prayed that her voice wouldn't give out. "Who are you working for?"

John Scott never moved. He sat there with a bored look on his face, like this was nothing more than an inconvenience. A second later his slitted eyes slowly rose until he was staring directly into Summer's. It was hard to read him with his swollen face like that. She couldn't be sure if he was trying to play it cool and tuff, or if it just hurt too much to move his lips.

"Where's your partner at? Where's he taken my daughter?"

There was a slight change in his expression. His eyes seemed to be taking in her whole face, contemplating who she was and who her daughter might be.

"I know that you and the kidnapper work for the same person. I heard him talking to your boss."

"You're that cop." A half smile crossed his swollen lips. "Officer Demure. I remember you now. I've heard all the stories of how you finally got what was coming to you."

"Don't play innocent. You know exactly what you did to me. I know it was you!"

"I don't know what you're talking about. Last night I'm busy minding my own business, working to make some cash when all of a sudden this cop busts in and drags me down here, then to top it off they put this crazy fucker in my cell and let him pound the shit out of me. When I get out of here, I'm suing. I'm suing that guard who left his station and let that crazy fucker try to kill me."

Summer felt her chest twitch and crossed her arms to quiet the rumble. "You deserve to die. It's bad enough what you did to me, but you left me for dead. You left me to rot in that cold damp ditch, but you underestimated me."

"Woman, you're almost as crazy as that fucker in my cell. I don't know what you guys are trying to pull, but you have no evidence. Nothing to hold me on."

"There's conspiracy to traffic drugs," Nate said from the doorway. "Assault and battery. Attempted murder of a police officer. The list goes on and on. If you think what happened with your friend back in the cell was bad, you wait until the prison guards find out what you're in for. They'll make this beating seem like a kiss from your grandmother."

Without removing his eyes from Summer, John Scott said, "Which one of you guys is the good cop and which one is the bad cop. If you ask me, you're fucking up the whole routine."

"We're asking you for the name of your boss." Nate stepped forward, unable to contain himself. "Tell us who he is and where to find him and we'll make you a deal."

"Deal?" John Scott laughed. "I tried to cut a deal last night and look where it got me."

"And what kind of deal were you looking to cut?" Summer paced to the back of the room unable to stand being so close to him. "Give some names and get out of jail."

John Scott sat there quietly waiting for Summer to make an offer.

"Cause if you cooperate and tell us who you work for and where they took my daughter, then you'll be free to go." She turned and met his gaze. "You have my word on it."

"I still don't know what you're talking about. So I make modifications to merchandise. That's my business. What other people do with the shit isn't my concern. I have a job to do and that all."

"Fine." Nate motioned for Summer to come to the door. "If you're not willing to talk, maybe we'll send in your old cellmate to keep you company."

Nate waited until Summer passed through then let the door slam shut. He glanced at his watch. "I thought he'd be anxious to get out. We're nearing the ransom deadline, but he's acting like he has no clue."

"Well," Chief Dickson said popping out of the adjoining room. "That went about as good as Detective Grimshaw's interrogation. He's still not saying anything, is he?"

Summer shook her head. "We still have over an hour before he needs to be released. There's no sense in letting him go one second before the deadline."

"Are you sure that's what you want to do?" Chief Dickson asked. "I mean, really sure that's the best way to attack this situation."

"I have no choice. I'd love to see him locked away for the rest of his life, but it doesn't matter. Nothing we do now will change what happened in the past. Sure I'm angry and could use some good old fashioned revenge right about now, but for the last five months that's exactly what's been holding me back, preventing me from getting better. I've been counting the days, praying that he'd be caught so I could get some satisfaction out of the system, but I realize now that just being alive is the best thing I've got going on right now. What if I'd died back in that ditch?" Summer turned to face Nate. "What if instead of finding me staggering beside the road, cold, naked and half dead, you had to drag my lifeless body from the cold stagnant water and bury me in the earth. Isn't this better? After all, I'm still alive."

Nate nodded. "You're right. I don't know what I would've done if you weren't alive. It would've ripped me apart, sent me off on a hunting mission for that bastard and probably destroyed the rest of my life."

"Come on, let's go to my office and get you two some coffee." Chief Dickson led the way down the hall, past the curious eyes in the station. "They've got your phone charging in there and we'll take a break and plan our next step."

Chief Dickson paused outside the office door and turned to the nearest officer. "Get the sketch artist over to the hospital right away. I want a composite as soon as Mr. Demure is able."

When he turned and closed the door on the buzz of noise in the main station, the silence seemed to surround Summer, smothering her and crushing her under its weight.

CHAPTER 8

With the effects of the anaesthetic wearing off, and the shot of morphine kicking in, dulling the aching pain in his stomach, Dean slowly climbed from the bed and gathered his clothing from the locker. Everything was there except for his shirt. The paramedics had cut that completely off when he was lying in the ambulance.

After struggling to slip on his pants without falling over, Dean withdrew the IV line from his arm then systematically removed the series of wires from his body while deactivating the alarms that would alert the nurse about his flat lining pulse.

There was no way he could stay in the hospital while Sabrina was still in danger. The doctors had patched him up enough, but now he needed to act, not rest. He knew exactly where to go. He had to pay Gavin Stone a little visit and find out what the hell was going on. All fingers were pointing in Gavin's direction. After all, he was the one with the criminal past. The one most likely to have connections with dangerous people. He might even be the cause of all of this—Or maybe the solution.

Glancing out the door, the hallway was quiet. The nurse on duty had just disappeared into the next room with a tray, so Dean quickly slipped out and headed down the hall in the opposite direction with his hospital gown flowing down over his bloodstained jeans. He dipped into the supply closet at the end of the hall, beside the stairway, and traded his gown for a less noticeable green smock then dashed into the stairwell.

Fifteen seconds later, he was standing in the bright morning sunlight, shivering as the early morning chill hung in the autumn air. Luck seemed to be on his side. A taxi was sitting, waiting at the front of the hospital and he was in need of a lift.

"29 Chestnut Street," Dean said, easing himself into the backseat, suddenly aware of how painful the stab wound was.

"You all right, buddy?" The cab driver was watching Dean's facial expressions in the mirror. "Looks like you should be going to the hospital instead of leaving it."

"Never mind." Dean groaned. "I'll live."

"If you say so?"

The drive across the city was never so painful. They seemed to hit each and every bump on the way and Dean had to bite his lip so hard to keep from screaming out, that he actually drew blood. When the taxi finally came to a stop outside Gavin's home, Dean was never so happy. He slid so slowly across the seat that the driver came around to offer him a hand, but froze when his eyes locked on Dean's bloodstained pants.

"Just a little knife accident." Dean grabbed the side of the door and pulled himself out, fighting to keep from screaming in pain. "Slipped and cut myself. It's nothing serious, just painful."

The driver nodded. "Oh…"

Dean could tell he wasn't buying it so he withdrew his wallet and gave him two twenties. "Keep the change."

Standing on the sidewalk, Dean drew a deep breath and concentrated on walking a straight line to the front door. The last thing he needed right now was to have the cops show up while he was breaking into Gavin's home.

When the taxi was a safe distance down the road, he rang the bell, knowing Gavin would be down at the office working away or off dealing with a customer. Dean had to wonder if one of those customers was behind all this. And the only way to find out was to get inside and search this place.

With no answer, Dean tried the front door. It was locked. He checked the usual hiding spots for a spare key but found none and decided to follow the pathway around the house, into the side yard. With large bushes and shrubs hiding him from view, Dean grabbed a small rock and smashed the lower pane of glass on the side door then reached inside and flipped the lock.

Taking a quick glance back down the pathway, making sure nobody was coming, he slipped through the door and stood in Gavin's kitchen. It wasn't anything fancy. Your run of the mill starter home, but after living in prison for the last eight years, Dean guessed anything was better than a 10x10 cell.

Dean made his way straight to the bathroom medicine cabinet and rummaged through the contents for some painkillers. The morphine shot was beginning to wear off. His whole stomach felt like it was on fire, burning away at the flesh and muscle.

There were plenty of prescription bottles of pills to choose from, more than the average person would have in a life time and Dean wondered if a doctor had prescribed all these narcotics or if Gavin had picked them up off the street corner. Either way Dean was glad for the selection. He plucked a bottle of Percocet from the cabinet and after popping the lid, swallowed two, then pocketed the bottle for later.

Dean headed straight for the work area in the living room. It seemed to be the most logical place that Gavin would keep any secrets about who his business associates were. "There's got to be something here that'll make sense of this whole mess."

Rummaging through the stacks of papers on the desk, Dean came up empty handed. There didn't seem to be anything out of the ordinary. Everything was laid out nice and neat, well organized considering Gavin's office at work. That place was a complete mess and Dean wondered how he found anything in the pile of trash stacked on the desk.

Dean searched through each drawer, feeling for any false bottoms, but came up empty again. He'd given up his search and was replacing the contents of the middle drawer when he felt the coldness of steel on the back of his hand. After removing the drawer, Dean bent down and carefully removed the handgun and magazine from the clip mounted under the desk.

"Gavin, Gavin, Gavin. How many times have they told you, never play with guns?" Dean made sure the chamber was empty then dropped the magazine into his pocket and placed the gun in his waistband at his back.

The sound of a car door closing made Dean jump, which in turn caused the pain in his stomach to re-ignite. Could the taxi driver have called the cops? Dean hoped not, but the other option was even worse.

Quickly he replaced the drawer and hurried as fast as his body would allow across the living room to the big picture window. After pulling the drapes back an inch, he spotted Gavin's car sitting in the driveway.

What's he doing home right now? Dean huddled in the corner of the living room, next to the front door, hoping to make his escape if Gavin headed for the kitchen or the upstairs.

It wasn't until Dean spotted the flashing red control box mounted behind the desk that he realized exactly why Gavin was home. It must be some kind of security alarm, motion sensor by the look of it. How could he have been so stupid? Sure Gavin would have an alarm installed in his house, but why not have it call the cops? Why have it alert only him?

Dean backed further into the corner and felt the bulge of the gun in his back. The cold steel had never felt so good as it did now. Quickly he removed the magazine from his pocket and quietly snapped it into the gun. He knew exactly why Gavin didn't alert the cops. He couldn't afford them finding a gun in his possession and sending him back to prison.

Dean listened as Gavin opened the front door, then watched his shadow move slowly along the far wall as he cautiously entered his own home. Dean prayed that he wasn't armed, because he'd hate to take a bullet so soon after taking a knife to the stomach.

Gavin's shadow was moving closer, getting near the corner of the living room and Dean felt the blood pulsating under the newly stitched hole in his stomach. He had always marvelled at the stories that Summer recounted of being a police officer. How cool and collected she remained during confrontations, but he knew he'd never make a very good cop. The rush of adrenaline was too much for him and he knew he could never get used to it. Some people thrived on the rush, but not him. Especially not right now.

"The police are on their way. I suggest you hurry and get the fuck out of my house before they arrive!" Gavin stuck his shaved head around the corner, scanning the room from the far side, where the desk was located, all the way to the corner where Dean was pointing the gun at his head.

"Then I suggest you call the cops and tell them it's a false alarm, otherwise they'll take your gun and toss your ass in prison."

Gavin let out his breath and closed his dark eyes, allowing the redness in his cheeks to drain away, leaving only the dark glow of his natural bronze colour behind. He actually looked relieved to see Dean hiding in the corner of his living room.

"What the fuck are you doing in here?" Gavin said as the vein on his forehead continued to pulse with each syllable. "And where the fuck did you get that gun?"

"Don't play stupid with me, Gavin. It's your gun." Dean waved him into the room, still training the gun on his head. "You know exactly where it was hidden."

"Will you put that fucking thing away! You know I'm not allowed to have a gun in my possession."

Dean raised an eyebrow. "The cops?"

"They're not coming." Gavin walked across the room and stood before his desk. "How fucking stupid do I look?"

"Stupid enough to have a gun in your house while on probation."

"So, what? I feel better knowing that I have protection against break-ins."

"It's working very well, now isn't it?"

"Dean, will you please put that fucking thing away. Look at you. You're barely able to stand. The last thing I want is for you to accidentally shoot me. Hell, I didn't do eight years of hard time just to get shot by you."

"Sit over there." Dean pointed the gun to the corner chair as he walked to the desk and propped himself on the corner. "Who took Sabrina?"

There was a look of confusion on Gavin's face and Dean didn't think he was acting.

"What are you talking about? Sabrina's probably with Summer, or that old lady she gets to sit for her."

Dean stared long and hard into Gavin's eyes. Although they were the same colour, there was something different. Something untrustworthy about the way they looked through you. "You know as well as I do that Sabrina's been kidnapped!"

"Kidnapped? What the fuck's wrong with you? You think I'd kidnap your daughter. You're totally fucked up! How dare you break into my house then have the balls to accuse me of something like that!"

Dean grimaced as he slid back onto the desk, knocking the stack of books to the floor. "I know you're behind this. You didn't think I'd figure it out."

"Come on, Dean, you're not making sense right now. Look at you, you're bleeding and it looks like your pants were borrowed from some menstruating bitch. What the fuck happened to you?"

"Seth Millar."

Gavin shrugged his shoulders, but couldn't keep from swallowing.

"The cops conveniently picked him up last night, only hours after that fucker, John Scott had been jailed."

"So?"

"So, he's a friend of yours isn't he?"

Gavin nodded. "An acquaintance, that's all."

"And he just happened to get arrested only hours after they pull that piece of shit, John Scott off the streets."

"Coincidences happen."

"So tell me, why would your friend want to harm John Scott?"

Gavin leaned forward, staring down at his clenched hands. His clean shaven cheeks were moving fast as he chewed on the inside of his cheek.

"Listen. I fucking did it for you. Seth Millar owes me everything. I met him when he was a junky and I got him off the shit. He's been waiting to pay me back anyway he could, so when I heard that the cops had picked up Summer's attacker, I gave him a call."

"And what did you tell him?"

"I told him that I owed you a great deal for helping me out after prison, when nobody else would. I told him what that fucker did to Summer and he was more than willing to do it."

"So you did this for Summer? For the person who'd put you behind bars in the first place."

Gavin nodded. "For her and for you. How many times have you said you'd like to kill that fucker?"

"A lot." Dean saw the gun tremble slightly. "But I didn't mean it."

"Didn't you? Cause I know that if it were me, I'd want fucking front row seats for the event. I'd want to watch the fucker snivel and beg for his life before I blew his fucking head right off his shoulders."

Dean shook his head. He thought of Sabrina's kidnapper and knew he would have no trouble pulling the trigger for her.

"Tell me who's behind Sabrina's kidnapping."

"Honestly, I have no fucking clue. Maybe it's John Scott's partner? You said there was someone else involved in that crash. Maybe they're working together?"

Dean glared at Gavin who slid back, settling into the chair. It was almost impossible to tell if Gavin was telling the truth or not. His face seldom gave away anything more than general dislike for most people.

"He was waiting on the street when I dropped Sabrina off." Dean slid back onto the desk and lowered the gun. "Then he stabbed me and took off with my car and Sabrina."

"Then maybe it was just a jacking?" Gavin glanced up and met Dean's gaze. "Maybe he's dropped her somewhere?"

Dean shook his head. He knew by the look in the kidnappers eyes that it had all been well planned out. Everything from the opening line about Summer's pregnancy right down to the way he'd stuck the knife inside his belly. "If only it was just about the car. I could care less what he did to my Mercedes."

"Listen. I'm here for you. Even though you broke into my pad and made a mess out of my living room, I'm still here for you. Whatever you need, just ask. I've already put the hurt on that fucker in jail, but I can ask around and see if anybody's heard about Sabrina."

Dean stood and gave Gavin a questioning look. "You still have connections?"

"After eight years in prison I've got better fucking connections than I had before your wife sent me away."

Dean waved the gun back in Gavin's direction. "It was your own fault that you went to prison, not Summer's."

"I know." Gavin stood and paced the floor. "I was into some pretty messed up shit back then and I guess I got a little sloppy."

"And now?"

There was a slight smirk to Gavin's mouth before he answered. "Let's just say I know how to keep my hands clean."

Dean held the gun up. "This is keeping it clean?"

"Not a single fingerprint of mine is on that gun. But yours are all over it." Gavin walked across the room to the corner bar and set two glasses up, filling them with brandy. "You can borrow it if you want. You never know when it might come in handy."

Dean ran his finger over the trigger. If he'd had this with him this morning, Sabrina would be fine right now. He'd have shot that bastard down and would never have let him leave with Sabrina. Feeling a little more relaxed, he set the gun down on the desk beside him and watched as Gavin carefully carried the two glasses of brandy back to the desk.

"Let's drink a toast."

Dean shook his head. "I don't feel much like drinking. Not right now."

"It'll do you good." Gavin forced the glass into his hand. "Take the edge off that stitch job those butchers did."

Dean reluctantly raised his glass, wondering if he should mix the Percocet and alcohol together.

"To working together to find Sabrina."

Gavin downed his glass while Dean reluctantly sipped from his.

"And to brothers."

CHAPTER 9

The ticking of the clock on the far wall of Chief Dickson's office was beginning to drive Summer mad. She knew with each second that passed they were coming closer to the deadline to release John Scott. It wasn't the fact that she had to release a guilty person and allow him to roam free; it was the fact she had to trust in a perfect stranger to keep his half of the deal and set Sabrina free. But could she just let John Scott wander away into the city without having Sabrina at least within arm's reach. That was the question that kept nagging away at her stomach. She didn't know if she could follow through with the demands.

"So," Chief Dickson said, unplugging Summer's cell phone from the charger and sliding it across the desk. "Have you made your decision?"

After looking Nate in the eyes, Summer nodded. "For the record, it's not him. Not the man who harmed me."

There was definitely sadness in the chief's eyes. Sadness and anger at what they were about to do. "Well, that's good enough reason for me to release him. We'll make it official at nine forty-five and set him free at ten, but don't worry. He won't get far. We've got his mug shots, his fingerprints and a DNA sample thanks to the spilled blood during the fight in his cell."

Nate gave her a reassuring smile. "And I can guarantee he won't get far. Once the kidnapper releases Sabrina, I'll be all over that piece of shit. I only hope that the kidnapper and John Scott are together so I can have twice as much fun."

Chief Dickson leaned forward on the desk and tented his fingers. "Now, Nate. I strictly forbid you from getting involved in the take down of the two suspects—"

"What!" Nate shot out of his chair, sending it flying back across the white tiled floor. "What are you saying? You don't want me there because I might get a little physical with them."

"I know damn well that you'll do everything you can to inflict harm on them both, and not that I disagree with your tactics, I'm thinking about your own welfare. I don't want you stuck behind a desk for a year while the SIU decides if you went past police protocol and nearly killed them. So that's why I'm restricting you to only monitor the situation."

"Monitor. That's bullshit!" Nate slammed his hand on the chief's desk, rattling the family photo and sending the name plate falling face down. "Who's going to be there to stop them, Jones?"

"Jones," Chief Dickson said, righting his name plate and giving Nate a stern glare. "Or whoever is able. But your job is to keep an eye on the situation and if things get bad, then and only then, are you allowed into the mix."

Finally Nate smiled and Summer knew no matter what happened he'd get his licks in the fight. Ever since that night he left her side to chase the hit and run driver into the woods, Nate, although he'd never admit it, felt a hundred percent liable for what had happened to her. Summer could see it in his eyes every time she looked his way. He'd never been the same since the day John Scott had thrown her life into the shitter and for Nate's sake, she hoped he'd get a chance to make things right.

"But the ransom note only specified to release John Scott and hand him my phone at exactly ten o'clock. How will we know that the kidnapper has released Sabrina?" Summer swallowed hard, trying to hold back the tears which were burning to escape. "And how will we know that she's still…"

"She'll be fine." Chief Dickson glanced at his family photo on his desk. "Trust me, she'll—"

"I know what you're up to," Grimshaw said, barging into the office. "And don't think I'm going to let you release my prisoner."

"Your prisoner?" Chief Dickson said. "This is my station and I'm the one calling the shots here."

"Not for long. I've contacted my superior and notified him about the situation here and what I suspect is being planned. Now, I don't know what normally goes on in this little city, but it won't fly with the big boys."

Nate stormed across the room, stopping an inch from Grimshaw's face. "You wanna fly? Hey, I'll take you to the fucking roof myself and we'll see how many times your arms flap before you hit the pavement."

"Officer Long, you never disappoint me." Grimshaw brushed past Nate and stood beside Summer, staring down at Chief Dickson. "I've told Miss Demure that we won't negotiate with the kidnapper. We'll wait for his call and I'll discuss the terms of the girl's release."

"The girl's release!" Summer stood and faced the detective. "Do you even know her name? It's Sabrina. I should know cause I'm her mother." Summer crossed her twitching arms and stared into Grimshaw's beady black eyes.

"*And* if I say that John Scott is innocent, then that should be good enough for you."

"But he's not. The preliminary samples from John Scott match the data in the case file."

Nate came to Summer's side. "Who authorized those tests?"

"I'm the lead officer in this case and I can authorize anything I want. It won't take long before the lab has a definite DNA match to link him securely as the perpetrator of the crime. And when they do, I'll have him locked up for the rest of his life."

"Please," Summer begged, "don't do this detective. I have to let him go. Sabrina's life depends on it. Besides, he won't get far. And once Sabrina's safe, you can put him away for as long as you want because I'm never letting Sabrina out of my arms again."

"That all sound fine and dandy, but what if he gets away? What if he skips the county and we never find him again?"

Summer drew a shaky breath and wiped the tears from her eyes. "That's a chance I'm willing to take."

Grimshaw snatched the cell phone from the desk. "Well, I'm not." He attempted to slip the phone into his pocket, but Nate was too fast. He grabbed the detective's wrist with his large hand, and by the look on Grimshaw's face Nate was squeezing with all his might.

"Officer Long," Grimshaw said, gritting his teeth and fighting to pull his arm free. "You're interfering with a police investigation."

"Correction," Nate began twisting Grimshaw's wrist until his knees buckled and he dropped to the floor. "I'm apprehending a thief right now and if you continue to resist, I will be forced to use alternative measures to subdue you."

"Fine!" Grimshaw opened his hand and let Nate take the phone. "But this is far from over."

"By my calculations," Nate said, grinning from ear to ear. "It should be over in about forty-five minutes."

Grimshaw turned, flexed his right hand repeatedly and fixed Nate with a look of pure hatred before storming to the office door. He trained those beady black eyes on Summer. "If you go ahead with your plan and release John Scott, you'll live to regret it."

"May I remind you, detective," Summer said, getting to her feet and walking halfway across the room. "That it's because of you that my daughter is out there right now in the hands of a madman."

Grimshaw arched an eyebrow, turned and stepped out into the hall, closing the door behind.

"I was hoping that he would've just stayed out of this," Chief Dickson said, rounding the desk and standing next to Nate. "But I'm glad you've still got those vise-like hands."

"Comes in handy for opening bottles, too." Nate walked to Summer's side and placed an arm around her shoulder. "Or for snapping John Scott's neck if need be."

"Those hands could explain why you don't have a girl friend. Women love a tender caress," Summer felt his hand tighten on her shoulder, "not a bone crunching massage."

There was a knock on the door and a second later, Jones stepped inside. His thin face was flushed and his clothing covered in dirt and mud. It looked like he'd just come from a day on the farm.

"Stephens and Malroy sent me back, said I was getting in their way, but I don't think I was. I was only trying to help. They're still busy dusting for prints and searching the farmhouse for clues. Also, we've towed Officer Demure's car and placed it inside the service bay."

"Very good, Jones." Chief Dickson walked to the doorway and glanced out into the station. "And how's the crowd control coming along?"

"It's getting worse. News vans keep pulling in every few minutes. It's like a circus out there."

"Then guess what? I'm appointing you Circus Master, in charge of all three rings."

Jones gave the chief a queer look, then turned to leave. "Oh, I almost forgot. They said the sketch artist went to see Mr. Demure at the hospital, but he wasn't there."

"Wasn't there?" Summer felt the pressure building in her head. "But he has to be there."

"No, they're sure he's not. They said he must've slipped out the back door. The whole hospital is in a panic. They say Mr. Demure isn't in any condition to be out walking around and they want him brought back in as soon as we see him."

"Yeah, good luck with that." Summer felt terrible at the way she'd left Dean back at the hospital and knew she was partly responsible for him taking off. How could she blame him for leaving? After all, she'd have done the same thing if put in his position. Summer prayed that he'd be all right, because the last thing she needed right now was to be worrying over him, too. "Cause if he's got something on his mind then there's nothing you or I can say that will stop him."

Nate raised an eyebrow. "What about the loss of blood?"

Summer rolled her eyes. "We'll just have to hope the doctors did a good job patching him up then, won't we?"

Jones took out his note pad. "But where would he take off to?"

"Probably home or the office." Summer let Nate escort her out into the main area of the station. "Or searching the entire city door by door."

Summer watched as Jones tracked more muddy footprints back across the white floor, toward the front glass doors. He stopped, holding the door open and noticed the mess he'd just made in the station.

"Oh, crap, Chief. I'm sorry. I'll clean that up when I get back."

"Just go." Chief Dickson shook his head. "Someone else will take care of it. You've got a job to do right now."

Jones nodded and disappeared out into the sea of reporters.

"That," Nate said, hitching his thumb at Jones's disappearing act, "is why you've gotta get better and come back to work. I heard the chief talking about partnering me up with him, and you know that'll never work. I'll kill him. Not because I don't like the kid, just because he irritates the hell right out of me."

CHAPTER 10

Chief Dickson stared through the small glass window at the slouching form behind the desk, then turned around and saw every eye in the station was watching him. He had a bad feeling about what he was about to do and would have given anything to wipe this whole mess clean.

After running his fingers through what was left of his short white hair and tugging the tails of his jacket down, Chief Dickson exhaled as he turned the knob and stepped inside the interrogation room.

"Mr. Scott." He paused, waiting for the prisoner to acknowledge him, but like normal, John Scott refused to be even the least bit cooperative. "I have some good news."

John Scott gave a bored sigh and slipped a little lower in the chair.

"You're free to go."

It took John Scott a few seconds before he responded. He cocked his head and slowly lifted his chin until his swollen, slitted eyes were peering at Chief Dickson. He appeared to be waiting for the punch line to be delivered, and why wouldn't he. He knew he was guilty and that they had him dead to rights, but still there must have been something in the way the chief had said those words because a pained toothless smile spread across John Scott's face.

"What the fuck's going on?" He tipped his chin in the chief's direction. "You jerking my chain?"

"No, I wish I was." Chief Dickson felt his stomach churn at the thought of what this man had done to Summer, and who knows what else he was guilty of, and now he was about to be set free. It went against everything he pledged to do for the community, but how could he not? If something happened to Sabrina because of his decision, he didn't know how he'd go on living. This one was for Summer.

"We've made a mistake and you're free to go."

John Scott sat up in the chair and strained to open his blackened, swollen eyelids as wide as possible. "Just like that?" He glanced from Chief Dickson to the open door behind. "I can walk right out that door and nobody's going to stop me?"

Chief Dickson nodded and stood back, making the pathway to the door wider. "There's not enough evidence to hold you on, so we're forced to release you, but please, don't leave the country. We may need to ask you some further questions as the case progresses."

John Scott slid the chair back and his smile widened, splitting his lip and sending a trickle of blood from the crusted corner of his mouth. He raised his hand and waved it around his face. "This is why you're letting me go. You don't want me to report this to anybody."

"Report it if you want," Chief Dickson said. "I've already talked to the guard on duty and steps have been taken to prevent another such incidence."

"Incident. It wasn't an incident and you know it! There were plenty of empty cells, but that guard put that sadistic fucker in with me."

"What can I say? We're not used to getting this many visitors in our jail at one time. Besides, why dirty two holding cells when one is more than adequate?"

John Scott stood and stared out the door into the crowded station. He seemed to be contemplating whether to leave or stay and Chief Dickson couldn't believe that he was still lingering around, considering what he'd done and how much evidence they had against him. If it was him, Chief Dickson would've run as fast as he could and never stopped until he was outside the Chatham line.

"Well, are you ready to go?" Chief Dickson glanced at his watch, noting how close time was running. "We can gather your belongings at the admissions counter and you can be on your way in no time."

John Scott dropped back into his chair. "And what if I don't want to leave?"

Chief Dickson couldn't believe what he was hearing. "What are you talking about? Why wouldn't you want to leave?"

"I'm just saying, what if I want to stick around and press charges against the guard who let this happen to me?"

"That's not going to happen. You go out and find yourself a nice lawyer and then come back and we'll discuss what happened with him. But," Chief Dickson stepped to the side of the table and leaned down, placing his palms on the surface, "this is a limited time offer. You either get up and walk out this door with me right now, or I'll send you away for the rest of your fucking life!"

John Scott leaned back in the chair and crossed his arms. "I thought you didn't have the evidence to keep me?"

"I'll get it one way or the other. I don't care if I have to frame you for the crimes, because I know what you did to my officer and I'll make you pay for that." Chief Dickson stood and walked to the door. "It's now nine forty-five. You have exactly five minutes to come out of this room, gather your shit and get the fuck out of my life, or this door will be closed and you'll only leave when they transfer you to the prison or," Chief Dickson lowered his voice, "cart your lifeless body out in a bag. Do you understand me?"

John Scott seemed to be weighing his options. There was little doubt of his guilt, and he had to have known they would gather enough evidence to put him away for a long time. But still there was a look of trepidation on his face and that look troubled Chief Dickson. There was something he was hiding.

Slowly John Scott rose to his feet, cautiously making his way across the room. He stopped at the doorway, staring out into the sea of reporters gathered in the parking lot and the sight seemed to brighten his day.

Chief Dickson realized at that moment that John Scott was planning on playing the assault to the media, hoping to create such a stir that if they tried to convict him again, a jury would take it into consideration while sentencing him. But somehow Chief Dickson didn't see this guy waiting around to be picked up a second time. That's exactly why they would have to keep him on a short leash and not let him get out of their sights.

The second John Scott stepped out into the main room of the police station, a blinding surge of lights began flashing from every window. Normally Chief Dickson would've ordered the barricades to be backed to the edge of the road, forcing the reporters to work harder for a good shot, but the truth of the matter was he'd never seen this many reporters in one place in all his career.

Chief Dickson glanced over at Summer who was frantically tapping her watch with her finger. He held up a hand to John Scott, stopping him just outside the door of the interrogation room. "Follow me. We'll finalize the paperwork over here. This shouldn't take too long."

Ten more minutes was all he had to stall for then the reporters would do the rest, keeping John Scott busy with all their questions. Chief Dickson knew everything would fall apart if John Scott wasn't close by when the kidnapper called to confirm his release.

They walked across the station, then down the short hall to the admissions counter where Chief Dickson disappeared through the door and met John Scott at the window opening. He knew exactly where John Scott's belongings were, but he fumbled through the filing cabinet, digging through old log sheets and forms, pretending he was searching for his file.

After stalling for a few minutes, he turned back but John Scott wasn't at the window anymore.

"Shit!" He grabbed the small pouch of belongings and ran around the corner and out into the hall, but John Scott was gone.

****

Nate didn't know if he was doing the right thing or not, but he slid open the drawer marked with Summer's name and stared at the newly issued badge and gun. She'd never worn either since the night John Scott had stripped her of her old ones. There was hatred bubbling inside at the mere thought of that fucker laying a hand on Summer and he would never forget the day he found her. The image of her small naked body, battered and bruised, covered with blood, clawing up the side of the weed choked ditch was enough to make him sick.

Summer never did anything to deserve what he'd done to her. The amount of physical damage was so massive that he didn't think she'd survive for a single day. It had only been a matter of twenty-four hours that she'd been stolen away from him, desecrated, then left to die like a wounded animal on the side of the roadway.

Nate reached into the drawer, withdrew Summer's service revolver and clip of ammunition. The cold steel felt good in his hand and he wondered if he should just walk into that interrogation room and sink every bullet into that fucker's skull.

What did he have to lose? His wife left four years ago. Packed up, left in the middle of the night and moved across the country. The last he'd heard, she was shacked up with some other guy, but he didn't care. He couldn't be bothered to waste another thought on someone who'd left without saying goodbye. Besides, he had Summer as a partner. What else could he ask for? She was ten times prettier than Julie, and despite her tough exterior, he saw Summer for what she really was, a beautiful, caring woman who didn't seem to realize just how captivating her appearance was. She knew she was a looker, but he doubted that she really understood exactly how she made him feel.

Even without any chance of a sexual relationship, he still counted himself lucky just to spend time with her.

Nate shook his head and tucked the gun in his ankle holster. He could get in a lot of trouble for this, but hell, he owed Summer so much more. He'd never forget that day he ran off into the woods after the hit and run driver, leaving Summer alone with John Scott. How could he ever forget? How could he have left her alone? Why did he always have to be the hero and capture the criminals? Why couldn't he have stayed at the scene of the accident and let the other cops try to track the runner down?

Nate slammed the drawer shut and pounded his fist on the top of the cabinet. If only he'd stayed at the scene, he and Summer would be out patrolling the city like old times—And she wouldn't be reminded about his failure every time her body shook.

Nate slipped into the adjoining room and opened his locker. He stood staring at the two photos clipped inside and felt the nagging, burning pain in his stomach intensify. He grabbed for the bottle of antacids and popped four in his mouth as his eyes darted between the two photos of Summer. There was one taken at the staff party where Summer looked like a supermodel posing for the camera, then the one taken for evidence, illustrating the massive damage that had been inflicted upon her body. Every time Nate looked at these pictures they reminded him of how much he'd let her down and how stupid he could be when he didn't take the time to think.

Nate could hear the chief's voice echoing down the hall and knew he was busy releasing John Scott while he stood there, reliving the nightmare that the bastard had caused. He glanced in the mirror and saw the puffy bags hanging from his eyes. He knew he looked like shit and owed it all to that guilty bastard. Nate tried to smile, hoping to look less like he was capable of ripping someone limb from limb, but it didn't work. The effort it took to smile right now was just too much, so he let his frown lines live and headed for the door.

If the chief found out he'd retrieved Summer's gun for her, he'd be strapped to the reception desk for the rest of his life, but when Summer asked, he didn't have to think about it, he had no choice in the matter. He owed her a lot. More than he was capable of giving. Besides, a little reprimand would take his mind off the guilty feeling that has been eating at his stomach for the last five months.

Nate slammed the locker door, hearing footsteps out in the hallway. Everybody in the station knew about the pictures in his locker—everyone except Summer. How could he explain why he had those pictures posted in there? The guys let it go, thinking he was secretly in love with her, but how would she react? Nate knew exactly how she'd react. She would fly off the handle and rip them into tiny shreds and request never to be his partner ever again.

Stepping through the doorway, Nate tried to look happy for her sake, but it wasn't Summer coming down the hallway heading toward the back exit. It was the cause of all his pain, heading straight toward him.

Seeing that bastard walking calmly down the hallway with no one else in sight ignited the fury inside. His body quivered with excitement at the thought of putting an end to all Summer's pain. He could try, convict and sentence John Scott right here and now in this hallway and nobody would know what had really happened.

When Nate stepped from the doorway, into the middle of the hallway, blocking John Scott's exit route, he thought he would see fear in the bastard's eyes, but there was none. John Scott stopped in his tracks, waiting for Nate to move out of his way as if he owned the place.

Anything from John Scott would've been better. A scream. An attempt to run in the opposite direction. Hell, Nate had hoped for him to land a free shot to his chin, but there was nothing and that pissed him off even more. John Scott was acting like he was king shit and Nate was his toilet paper.

Nate lunged for his throat, gripped him by his shirt collar and paused a second to see if there was a small bit of regret in those blackened eyes for what he'd done five months ago, but they looked empty. As empty as a vampire's soul.

"You son of a bitch!" Nate unleashed his furry with a blistering series of right hands to John Scott's face. He landed each blow harder and harder, hoping to snap John Scott's neck with each one. It felt so good, like nothing he could've ever imagined. He welcomed the pain in his fist and savoured each impact.

"Stop!" Chief Dickson grabbed his arm and only managed to slow the last blow before restraining Nate.

"He tried to escape," Nate said, feeling his nostrils flaring so much that it was painful. "But I stopped him."

John Scott stepped back and spit the mouthful of blood onto the white ceramic floor. "What the fuck is going on?" He turned to the chief. "You said I was free to go and that's exactly what I was doing until he started pounding on me for no reason!"

"Oh, I've got a reason. A good reason!" Nate glared at John Scott who was standing behind Chief Dickson, just out of reach. "Her name's Summer Demure. Officer Summer Demure."

Chief Dickson wiped the smile from his face and turned to John Scott. "You're not free to leave until the paperwork is completed. So next time you think about sneaking out the back door you'd better think twice, because there may be an angry friend from your past waiting to catch up on old times."

Chief Dickson paused at the far corner and turned back to Nate. "Wait inside until this is over, understand?"

Nodding, Nate waited until they'd disappeared around the corner before he tucked his swollen hand under his other arm and bit back the scream of anger that needed to escape.

CHAPTER 11

Crippling pain exploded in Dean's stomach as he struggled to pull the shirt over his head. He knew Gavin was standing right beside, but would never admit that he needed help getting dressed, even if it was from his own half brother.

"Sorry, man," Gavin said, standing beside the closet, holding a few pairs of pants in his hands. "These are the smallest I've got. I guess you should've eaten all your fucking vegetables like I did."

Dean poked Gavin in the stomach. "Don't tell me that's vegetables."

"It's a little of everything." Gavin sucked in his stomach. "I guess after eight fucking years of eating prison crap I kinda went overboard on the treats."

Dean ripped the top pair from his hands. "Give me the jeans. Even if they're a little baggy, at least they won't attract as much attention as these things."

"That's a fuck load of fucking blood you've spilled on yourself. Are you sure you shouldn't be getting back to the hospital?"

Dean grinned. This was the first time he and Gavin have been this close in a long time. Ever since Gavin got hooked up with the wrong crowd, about ten years ago, their close relationship had slowly deteriorated until they never talked at all. "Now you're starting to sound like mom."

"Fuck you!" Gavin threw the other pair of pants at Dean then headed to the bedroom door and glanced at his watch. "Put your fucking makeup on and let's get you the fuck down to the fucking police station and find out what those stupid fucks have found out." He started down the hall and called back, "And hurry up! I'm not gonna wait all day."

"Fuck this, fuck that," Dean muttered as he slid the blood covered pants off. "Is that the only fucking word you know?"

He lifted his shirt and stood before the mirror, staring at the crusted, puckered seam that the doctor had stitched an inch above his belly button. It seemed so long ago that he'd been stabbed on the street corner, but as he glanced at the clock he realized that since Sabrina had been taken, his whole world had come to a crawling halt. Time seemed to be barely moving and he realized at that moment he'd been wasting his life, letting it race past without stopping to appreciate the important things.

How could he have been so stupid? How could he have thought that time apart would allow Summer to come to grips with what had happened? There was more to it, and it was all too clear now. He'd never forget the look in Summer's eyes when she told him that Nate had found her crawling from that ditch. Dean shook his head, knowing that he'd been the one searching the city and countryside nonstop, praying that she'd be fine. Then lucky old Nate,

Dean's body tensed at the thought, had swooped in and become the hero—Summer's hero.

"Why couldn't it have been me? Why couldn't I have been the one to find Summer?" Dean shook his head. He knew that if he'd been the one to find Summer, then her life now would be different. She'd still love him and wouldn't be afraid of his touch.

Dean pulled on the fresh pair of pants and buttoned them hastily. "I'll bet she doesn't pull away from Nate, like she does me."

"Come on, Dean," Gavin yelled from downstairs. "Hurry the fuck up!"

Dean took one last look at his reflection in the mirror and agreed that his appearance did look better—at least his clothing did—but his face was still pale and shinny, looking dramatic against his dark head of curls.

He cinched up the belt and stuffed the gun in his waist band, beneath his shirt, grateful for the added insurance. When he reached the bottom of the stairs, he noticed Gavin was waiting impatiently at the front door for him.

"You don't have to come with me. Just drop me off at the office and I'll take the company van down to the station."

"Don't be silly, Dean. What kind of brother would I be if I let you go off by yourself in this condition?" Gavin smiled and grabbed Dean's arm, hurrying him to the car. "Besides, if Mother found out I let you go on your own looking like you might drop dead at any time, she'd kill me."

"Don't worry about her." Dean grinned. "I'm the one with the gun."

Gavin's face hardened. "You're bringing it with you? To the police station? Are you completely fucking mad!"

"What?" Dean pulled the prescription bottle from his front pocket and popped another pill in his mouth. "It's not like I'm going to pull it out and start shooting everybody."

Gavin ran around the car and climbed in. "You fucking better not!"

"What's your problem?" Dean opened the passenger's door and cautiously lowered himself inside. "You said your prints aren't on the gun."

"No, but if they confiscate it, they might just trace it back to some other job."

"Like what? What else are you messed up in?"

"Nothing. I'm just saying, I got it from a friend, but I can't guarantee that it's completely clean. He's usually pretty reliable, but I wouldn't bet my life on it." Gavin gave Dean a quick once over. "You on the other hand look like you could drop dead at any moment, so go ahead and bet. The odds aren't that high."

"Oh, thanks for the confidence." Dean placed a hand over the wound and the warmth felt good. "The doctors did a good job patching me up. Don't worry. I'll be fine."

When Gavin turned down Wellington Street, heading toward the police station, Dean couldn't believe the amount of vehicles around the station. There were media vans parked all throughout the parking lot and down the sides of the streets.

"That's a lot of fucking press for a kidnapping," Gavin said.

"Kidnapping, plus the jailing of John Scott. I guess they want to see that bastard locked away as much as I do."

Gavin laughed. "You don't get it, do you? Jail doesn't do that fucker justice, not after what he'd put Summer through—and you."

"Well, that's all we have so it's the best we can hope for."

Gavin pulled to the edge of the road behind the Chanel 9 news van. "Yeah, too bad we don't have the death penalty here, cause he'd be fried crispy in no time."

Dean climbed from the car, careful not to strain his abdomen muscles and stood on the side of the road, beside the bridge. His eyes followed the winding water as it twisted and turned along the downtown until it disappeared in the distance, around the bend at the park.

He shivered, feeling the morning sun on his back and was glad that the rain had stopped. In his current weakened condition, the last thing he wanted was to be soaking wet.

"Come on, Dean." Gavin glanced at his watch then crossed the road. "Let's ask around and see what's happening."

The last Percocet he'd taken was beginning to kick in. His head was spinning and his legs felt like rubber as he struggled to keep up to Gavin, who seemed to be on a mission. He had almost caught up when he recognized Ike Turner, the local news reporter standing at the back of the crowd of reporters, giving a sound bite for the camera.

Dean turned and headed straight for him. If anybody knew what was going on around here, it'd be Ike. But Dean didn't have to walk far. It seemed that Ike had recognized him, too, because he and his camera man were now racing across the parking lot toward him.

"Mr. Demure," Ike said, jockeying for position before the camera. "I thought you would still be in the hospital."

Dean forced a grin. "They let me out on good behaviour."

"I heard you were stabbed only hours ago. Is this true?"

Dean nodded. "What's going on here? Is all this because of Sabrina's kidnapping?"

Ike looked slightly confused. "Yes, the kidnapping, but also the ransom deadline is approaching and we're waiting for John Scott to be released."

"What the hell are you talking about!" Dean stumbled forward, grabbing Ike's shoulder. "There's a ransom for Sabrina?"

The outburst attracted the attention of the other reporters who, after a brief discussion, all must have decided that Dean's story was worth filling in the time as they gathered their equipment and raced toward them.

"Yes. You haven't heard?" Ike glared at the approaching competition. "Of course you haven't. You've just come from surgery. How stupid could I be? The kidnapper left a ransom note demanding that John Scott be released at ten o'clock this morning. Now, if you'll step into my van we can—"

Dean spotted Gavin talking to an officer beside the barricades and took off shoving his way through the sea of reporters as they inundated him with every question possible. But Dean couldn't be bothered with their questions, for he had a question of his own swirling around in his mind. One that he needed answered right now.

"Gavin," Dean grabbed him roughly by the shirt collar and pushed him through the two barricades, "did you know anything about the ransom to have that bastard released?"

The officer standing guard started to protest, then recognized Dean and stepped back, grabbing for his radio.

"How the fuck would I know something like that?" Gavin whispered.

Dean leaned in and lowered his voice. "Cause you already tried to have him killed."

"Not killed." Gavin broke free of Dean's grip. "Just messed up."

"How do I know you're not in on this?"

"Because I wanna see the fucker pay his price, not walk away free."

Dean wanted to believe him. He prayed that Gavin wasn't involved in this mess, but the evidence was piling up and even he couldn't look past all the coincidences.

"But why the hell would someone kidnap Sabrina just to get John Scott released from jail?" Dean muttered. "How the hell could they possibly plan to get away with it? Half the cops in the country will be on the lookout for them the minute Sabrina's released—unless they don't plan on releasing her."

The sight of Summer stepping out the front door of the station was enough to send Dean into a rage. He wanted answers and he wanted them right now. Dean stormed across the grass, glaring up at her as she stood on the edge of the steps, her face looking a mix between sorrow and happiness. Maybe it was the painkillers, but he swore she never looked as beautiful as she did right now. Her blond hair was blowing in the morning breeze, and for the first time in a long time there was a glow to her skin. He knew that if Sabrina was safe and sound, he'd run up the stairs, scoop Summer into his arms and take them as far away from this place as possible, because all he wanted right now was to get his family back and get things back to normal.

"Summer," Dean said, his anger fading with every step he took. "Why—" His words caught in his throat as Nate stepped out those same doors and placed his arm around Summer's shoulders, almost smothering her with his massive size. Dean had been right. She never pulled away from Nate's touch. Maybe Nate was the reason that she wanted a separation? Maybe he'd talked her into it, hoping to snatch her away while she was vulnerable?

Dean staggered up to the top step, holding his wound tightly, feeling the ripping pain inside. "Get your hands off my wife!"

Nate immediately removed his arm from Summer's shoulder. Probably not out of fear for Dean, but more fear of what the media would do with the story. "Sorry, Dean. I was only taking care of her."

"Dean, don't start," Summer whispered, stepping closer. "I'm in no mood to listen to your ranting about our relationship. Not now. Not with Sabrina missing."

Dean stood glaring up at Nate until his vision began to blur, then turned to Summer. "Why didn't you tell me about the ransom?"

"When? When could I?"

"At the hospital. You could've told me then."

"And what difference would it have made? It would've only ended up in another fight and you…" Summer smiled as the tears began flowing. "You stupid ass. Why aren't you in the hospital? You know you're in no shape to be out walking around."

"How can I just lie around when he has Sabrina? I never could when they took you, so what makes you think I could now." Dean reached out his hand to Summer, waiting to feel her touch. He didn't care how long it would take, he was willing to stand there forever until she took his hand. He watched her eyes move from his hand clenching the wound, to his tearful eyes, then to his outstretched hand quivering before her.

It took a few seconds, but her fingers reluctantly met his, sliding down over his palm and the warmth of her touch ignited his body.

Dean smiled. He felt complete for the first time since John Scott had entered their lives. "I just don't know where to start looking," he said, taking the last step up and standing beside Summer. "Help me. Give me a clue. Any direction and I'll go search for her."

"I wish I knew." Summer shook her head. "But nothing's surfaced. We're waiting for the chief to release John Scott, then hopefully the kidnapper releases Sabrina right away. Otherwise we'll tail John Scott and hope he leads us to the hideout."

Dean gave her hand a squeeze. "I don't like the thought of that bastard walking free. Not after what he's done to you."

Summer leaned closer and Dean could feel her warm breath on his cheek. "Don't worry. They won't let him get far. Nate's in charge of the tail and I promise he'll do everything in his power to stop them and get Sabrina back."

Dean looked past Summer, up at Nate who was busy scanning the crowd around the station. "I'm sorry for jumping all over you, Nate. I had no right taking my frustration out on you."

"I understand where you're coming from, but just don't make a habit of it." Nate tipped his chin to the crowd. "What the hell is Gavin Stone doing here?"

"Sorry, he came with me. I borrowed a change of clothing and he wanted to help."

"Help interfere in the investigation's more like it."

"What do you have against him?" Dean asked. "He's done his time, Nate. What else do you want from him?"

"I don't know. I just don't trust that guy." Nate looked Dean in the eyes. "For your own sake, keep a close eye on him and don't let him loose in that business."

Summer pulled her hand free and glanced at the time. "Nine fifty-eight. Shit, where is he?" She dug in her pocket, withdrew the cell phone and flipped it open, making sure it was on as Nate turned and disappeared inside the station, drawing the attention of all the reporters.

"What exactly did the ransom note say?" Dean asked.

Summer turned and peered through the glass doors. "To release John Scott at ten o'clock sharp, then to hand him my phone. I suspect the kidnapper's going to call him and make sure he's free before Sabrina's released."

Dean felt sick to his stomach with worry and didn't know how much more he could take today. "Do you really think he'll let Sabrina go?"

"He has to." Summer started shaking. "It's part of the deal."

"It just sounds sloppy to me. It's one of those, who lets who go first deal. The minute he releases Sabrina then he's lost his security and the minute we release John Scott then we've lost our bargaining power."

When the automatic doors whined into action, Dean placed his arm around Summer's waist, feeling the tremors that she was fighting to control. This was the first time he'd been able to hold Summer. And now, feeling this once strong warrior trembling in anticipation of the man who'd attacked her, he finally understood how damaged she really was. Despite how she tried to hide the fear from him, she was a complete mess inside. How could he have not seen the extent that John Scott had hurt her? How could he not have known that inside that frail petite body lives a growing fetus—their love child. Dean placed his other hand on the slight bulge beneath her shirt as John Scott stepped through the doorway and out into the bright sunlight. Or that bastard's child.

The shouts from the reporters grew louder and louder with every step John Scott took toward the stairs. Despite his battered appearance, he seemed to be getting the rock star greeting from the press who were all screaming their questions, trying to out shout their competition.

Chief Dickson followed John Scott to the edge of the top step and held up his hands to the sea of reporters. "Quiet down, please! Mr. Scott will be glad to take your questions one at a time, but only if you behave in an orderly fashion."

"Are you associated with the kidnapper?" One reporter bellowed over the rest. "And if so, how does he plan to release the hostage?"

John Scott held a hand above his eyes, blocking the glare of the sunlight. He didn't seem bothered by the mass of reporters or the amount of cameras trained on his battered face

"I'm an innocent man. The cops dropped all the charges." He scanned the crowd of cops standing in front of the station and smiled when he spotted Summer and Dean. "As far as what happened to Officer Demure, I'm sure she had it coming to her. I'm just sad I didn't get to be a part of it."

Dean couldn't believe the bastard had the balls to say something like that—and in front of all the reporters and cameras, too. He let go of Summer and took a step toward John Scott, feeling her latch onto his hand.

"No, Dean! Don't do it," Summer said. "That's… exactly what he wants."

"You son of a bitch!" Dean walked right up to him, seeing the flashes from cameras reflecting in the glass front of the station. "How dare you speak to my wife like that! I know you're guilty and I know you're behind Sabrina's kidnapping, too."

A phone began ringing in the distance, but Dean could barely hear it as the blood was pounding in his ears. He'd never been so mad as he was right now, standing inches from the bastard who'd ruined his life. He wanted to reach out and smack that stupid grin right off his face, but he knew he'd fall flat on his own face in his current condition if he even tried.

John Scott leaned in close to Dean and whispered, "What's the matter? She too loose for you now?"

Something snapped. He could feel his arm moving, but couldn't control it if his life depended on it. The pain in his stomach was excruciating as his fist connected with John Scott's swollen jaw, but it was worth it. The punch felt so satisfying, but he wished he wasn't injured so he could continue the fight until he'd ripped the bastard's head right off, but instead he'd lost his balance and toppled down to the concrete, doubled over in pain.

The feeling of satisfaction lasted only briefly. John Scott recovered and gave a swift kick to his stomach as Dean landed on the concrete. The shot felt a hundred times worse than any normal kick should have and the bright flashes of light behind his eyelids didn't seem right. Dean rolled onto his back, reeling in pain and felt the gun digging into him.

"Maybe your daughter will get the same treatment as your w—"

Dean opened his eyes and saw the last words from John Scott being cut off by the massive right hook from Nate. He was so grateful that Nate was there to defend Summer while he was down for the count.

Bracing himself on his elbow, Dean reached behind his back and pulled the gun from his waist band. He knew there was no way he could let John Scott walk away from here. Could never chance him getting his hands on Sabrina. He raised the gun in the mist of all the confusion and aimed it at John Scott's head.

The look on John Scott's face was priceless. It was as if he never expected to see Dean with a gun—let alone a gun trained between his eyes. There was a moment of satisfaction knowing that John Scott wasn't immune to fear. That he could be manipulated like the rest of mankind.

Every police officer drew their weapon, training them on Dean's body.

"Drop the gun, Dean!" Nate yelled, taking a step closer to where Dean was lying.

A phone continued to ring in the distance as Dean lined the sight up with John Scott's nose. He knew at this range, he'd never miss the shot and John Scott would be dead before his body hit the concrete.

"Drop the gun!"

"Dean," Summer said. "Put it down! It's not worth it."

Dean heard her voice, but couldn't look away from John Scott. He waited, giving John Scott a chance to say something about Sabrina again, because if he did, Dean was ready to put a bullet between his eyes.

"What the hell are you doing?" John Scott held his hands up to fend off the bullet. "You're crazy. You'll never get away with this."

Dean lowered the gun and Nate quickly grasped it, taking it away. "Dean, don't pull that shit. You know we need him alive."

"I'm sorry," Dean said, rolling to his side and attempting to get to the sitting position. "I lost my head when he started taking about—"

"No, he's here. He's free to go, but I want to talk to Sabrina," Summer glanced at Dean and Nate crouched on the ground before John Scott, "before he leaves."

She listened, her face hardening with each passing second. "No! I want to talk to her. How do I know you'll keep your word and let her go?"

A second later a smile filled her face and she dropped to her knees. "Oh, baby. I miss you so much. Are you—god damn it!" Summer glanced over at John Scott. "Yeah he's standing right here." Summer walked over and held out the phone to John Scott. "He wants to talk to you."

"I don't want anything to do with this. Tell him to go fuck himself." John Scott glared down at Dean. "Better yet, tell him to go fuck your little girl, too."

Dean tried to get to his feet, but Summer beat him to it. She slapped John Scott so fast that he didn't see it coming.

"That's more like it." A smile covered John Scott's face. "You like to play rough, don't you?"

A whistling noise tore through the air and suddenly John Scott's head exploded before Dean's eyes. It was unreal how he was standing there talking, then the next second, the back of his head was gone. Just exploded right off! Dean watched as John Scott's body collapsed to the ground at his feet, sprawled out like a puppet—a bloodied puppet at that.

The crowd was silenced for a second until they realized exactly what had happened, then as if everyone sensed the danger, they dispersed in a heated panic. The police stood guard, guns drawn, looking for the shooter, but there was nobody in sight.

CHAPTER 12

Summer stood with the phone in her hand, unable to comprehend what had just happened. She'd seen it all and doubted she'd ever forget the image of John Scott's skull exploding, showering his twisted, demented mind all over the glass doors. At first she thought Dean had pulled the trigger and she wouldn't have blamed him if he had, but that little handgun could never do the amount of damage that had occurred. It looked more like a sniper's bullet and sounded like it'd been fired from a long distance away.

She slowly walked behind John Scott's body, careful not to slip in the gooey brain matter and stared out into the distance where she thought the bullet had come from. She should've been afraid for her life. After all, a sniper had just sent a bullet into this exact location, but she wasn't scared. She was angry. Angry that someone had used her and used Sabrina's safety to silence this man. Summer knew that the shooter would be running for cover, evacuating the area as fast as he could, or if he had balls of steel he might be sitting there watching her through the scope of the gun, waiting for

123

the order to take her down. But there was no need to take her down and suddenly Summer wondered if the shooter was actually there to help her. There like a powerless super hero taking care of crime in the city.

"What was that!" The kidnapper's voice sounded high and shrill. "Was that a gunshot? You better hope for your daughter's sake that it wasn't aimed at John Scott."

Summer swallowed hard, fearing the worst was about to come. "It wasn't us. Someone sniped him right before our eyes."

"Fuck! I knew this would happen. I just knew it! They wanted him silenced and they did it. Fuck! What the hell am I supposed to do now?"

"First, let Sabrina go." Summer grabbed a pair of binoculars from Jones and scanned the countryside. "I've kept my part of the bargain. Now, it's time for you to keep your end."

"But he's dead!" the kidnapper began ranting. "You said so yourself. What good is he if he's dead? They'll kill me if I don't bring him back. I can't go back now. I've got to get away from here."

"Then let Sabrina go and leave. There's no harm done. We'll forget this whole thing ever happened."

There was muffled silence as the kidnapper seemed to be rolling with the changes, and Summer hoped he was smart enough to get out while he could.

"I'll need money. I'll have to lay low for a while. There's a change of plans."

"Mommy?"

Summer's heart leapt into overdrive. Every emotion was surging through her body simultaneously. The sound of Sabrina's voice was unbelievable.

"Put her on. Please, let me talk to her."

"Shut up and get back in the car!"

Summer heard a stifled cry then the sound of a car door slamming shut.

"Get me a hundred thousand." The connection broke up for a second. "And be ready to make a drop wherever I tell you."

"But we had a deal! You can't do this! This isn't fair." The line went dead and Summer couldn't believe her luck. She was so close. He'd brought Sabrina with him to make the drop and he was going to release her, just like he said he would.

Chief Dickson finished giving the orders to secure the area and search the countryside where the shot had come from, then rushed to Summer's side. "Where is he? What did he say?"

Summer folded the phone closed and met his gaze. "He's got her in a car." She swallowed the lump in her throat. "He was going to let her go. I was so close. So fucking close!"

Nate lifted Dean to his feet and held him in place.

"He wants a hundred thousand," Summer drew a deep breath, "and he wants me to drop it off when he calls."

"A hundred grand. By when?" Nate looked to the chief, knowing he would have to organize the money for the drop, even if it involved faking the bundles.

"He didn't say how long, only to have it ready for when he calls."

Nate looked bewildered at the kidnapper's lack of planning. "That could be anytime. An hour, five hours. What's he playing?"

"The shooting took him by surprise." Summer paced to the glass doors and back. "He thinks they'll kill him next if he doesn't disappear."

Gavin stepped up behind Dean, placing an arm around his waist and steadied him. "And he wants enough money to hold him over until the shit settles?"

Summer stared at Gavin standing next to Dean and realized for the first time that they had the same colour eyes, but somehow Dean's looked softer and more caring. She studied Gavin's face for a second and thought she could see real concern in his eyes. "Looks that way."

"Dean, we've got fifty in the company account and we can borrow the other fifty from the credit account if you want. It'll pretty much tap the fucking business out, but at least it'll satisfy the ransom and get Sabrina back."

"Go get it." Dean nodded. "And bring it back here. I'll call the bank and confirm the withdrawal."

"No, Dean, don't do it," Nate said. "There's no sense. This guy's an amateur. He's not thinking straight right now. Bring me ten thousand, tops, and we'll mix it with some counterfeit." Nate looked to Chief Dickson for approval. "I promise he'll never know the difference."

Gavin was standing, anxiously waiting to leave, hanging on Dean's decision.

"No." Dean shook his head. "It's only money. I won't risk Sabrina's safety by short changing him. Money means nothing if I don't get Sabrina back."

Summer couldn't believe Dean. He was risking everything he had to get Sabrina back. His health, his money and his business. What more could she want from him? He'd always been the perfect man for her and she'd pushed him away.

"A hundred then?" Gavin waited until Dean nodded, then ran down the steps and through the crowded parking lot, drawing attention from every reporter.

The second Gavin tore off, a second car came racing toward them. There was nervous excitement buzzing through the crowd, and after the shooting, they could only guess what kind of maniac would drive up to the police station like a madman.

"Shit," Chief Dickson said, shaking his head. "He's back."

Summer watched as Grimshaw pulled the car into the parking lot as far as he could, then jumped out. He was gripping an envelope tightly in his hand and Summer realized where he'd disappeared to after the altercation in the chief's office. He'd gone crying to Judge Lynch and pleaded his case. And by the look on his face and the death grip on that envelope, he'd gotten just what he'd set out for.

The crowd of reporters were throwing out question after question to the detective, but he was in no mood to answer any as he charged through the crowd, his eyes flickering between Chief Dickson and Nate.

When Summer looked over at Nate, he had a big satisfied grin plastered on his face. A stark contrast to the chief's tight lipped glare at the man who'd undermined his authority. She knew the chief could remain calm and keep his cool, but it was Nate she was worried about. He was waiting, praying for the moment to knock the detective down a notch.

It was when Grimshaw stepped between the lines of reporters, standing at the base of the stairs that his hard black eyes dropped from the chief's face, to the lifeless body at the top of the stairs. Instantly his glare was reduced to a look of shock. What had happened to John Scott seemed to be outside his realm of understanding. He looked completely dumbfounded at the prospect of all his hard work being destroyed in the time it'd taken him to get the court order.

"What the hell?" Grimshaw said, standing at the top of the stairs, gazing down at the huge crater where John Scott's brain and skull had been.

Chief Dickson plucked the papers from Grimshaw's hand while he was busy examining the scene. He unfolded them and gave a quick glance over while shaking his head. "You went to Judge Lynch. I can't believe he authorized this. What the hell are you trying to pull here, Grimshaw?"

"What am I trying to pull?" He glared up at the chief. The bulging jaw muscles and pencil lips showed just how pissed he was. More pissed than when Nate had almost snapped his wrist.

"I was trying to keep our prisoner safe until we could try him for the crimes that we both know he'd committed," Grimshaw said. "But *you* had to go and fuck it all up. Why couldn't you leave the police work to the professionals and keep your nose out of my business?"

"Why you insubordinate piece of shit!" Chief Dickson crumpled the paper and dropped it beside John Scott's body, then walked to the front doors.

"Chief," Nate said. "What are we going to do with the crime scene?"

"We're not going to do anything. It's not in our jurisdiction anymore. Detective Grimshaw has kindly taken Mr. Scott off our hands, thanks to his friend Judge Lynch."

Nate looked confused as he followed the chief into the station. "Our jurisdiction? But this whole city is our jurisdiction?"

Summer wanted no part in dealing with John Scott's murder and quickly stepped around the detective, who was already eyeballing everyone in the area, and took Dean by the arm, escorting him toward the entrance.

"Come inside, Dean." Summer tossed her hair back from her face as she stepped through the door. "You're starting to look worse than shit."

"Worse than shit? Is that possible?" Dean smiled. It was as if that perfect white smile had been hidden from her for years. She'd forgotten how the bottom front teeth were only the slightest bit askew. That littlest imperfection in his appearance reminded her that he was only human.

He stumbled and staggered from side to side as they headed toward the chief's office and Summer knew if Dean didn't take it easy, and soon, that he would pass out and have to be rushed back to the hospital. But that was the last place he would want to go. Even if he dropped unconscious here in the hallway, she knew the second he came to in the hospital that he'd make another break for it—and he'd be really pissed off, too.

"Come on," she said, pushing the door open and guiding him inside the large office. She led him to the black leather couch that Chief Dickson used as his own small break area and laid him down. His colour was bad and his cold sweat didn't make her feel any better about his chance of staying there.

"Have you eaten anything this morning?"

Dean lifted his right arm and motioned to the bruised area where he'd ripped the IV out. "They said it was liquefied bacon and eggs, but I think they were lying."

"Always the smart ass." Summer opened the small bar fridge, grabbed an orange juice and a chocolate bar from the chief's stash. "But never very smart."

"Smart enough not to stand behind that bastard out there."

"Yeah, I'm glad the shooter only had one person in mind." Summer shook her head. "Sorry. Is that wrong to think John Scott deserved to die out there?"

"If someone had to die today, I'm glad it was him." Dean downed half the juice and started nibbling on the chocolate. "You think it was planned?"

Summer gave him a curious look. "You think it was just a coincidence that someone snipped the man the minute he stepped out of jail. They already tried to kill him while he was inside, and when that didn't happen then they waited until he stepped outside and blew his head clean off his shoulders." She shuttered at the memory. "But why would they want him silenced. What did he do to piss them off that they wanted him dead?"

Dean finished his snack and the colour was starting to return to his face. "First, he harmed you. Then he got caught. Maybe they decided that he was a loose end that needed to be tied up? Maybe whoever he was working for didn't want to chance him copping a deal and incriminating them and figured he was dispensable?"

"So, if John Scott's boss had him killed, and the kidnapper thinks he might be next, then the kidnapper can't be working for the same guy that John Scott was." Summer smiled. "He might be more forgiving?"

Dean lifted his shirt, exposing his stitches. "I wouldn't count on it. He means business. He might not have the same ethics as John Scott, but he's somehow involved with him and that makes him just as dangerous."

The office doors burst open and Nate came rushing in behind the chief. He tossed a large canvas bag onto the back table then grabbed a handful of tissues and began blotting his bloodied knuckles, a sight Summer had seen often during their time together.

"That's not the way we work around here, Nate! You better start following procedures or you'll find your ass out on the street if you keep that shit up. Now, he's going to file a complaint and this isn't the first time they've been looking at you."

"Let him file all the complaints he wants. It'll never stick. He's already been booked for attacking John Scott in the cell. The bruises and blood must have come from that fight."

Chief Dickson dropped into his chair and motioned for Nate to take a seat. "This is the last time I'll cover your ass. If you let your temper get the better of you one more time, it'll be your last in that uniform. Is that understood?"

Nate bowed his head and agreed.

"Where'd you take off to?" Summer asked, laying Dean down on the couch and stepping across the room to the desk.

"Off the record," Chief Dickson glanced at Nate. "We paid Seth Millar a visit. Figured that with John Scott dead, he was the only other link we have."

Summer had wanted to pay Seth a visit herself, but there hadn't been a free moment to deal with him. "But I thought he wasn't talking?"

"Still isn't saying much. The same old routine about doing it for you, Summer." Nate flexed his hand. "I couldn't get him to change his story, no matter what I said."

"Thank you, Nate. I appreciate your help, but you better lie low for the rest of this one. I'd hate to come back and be shackled with Jones as a partner."

Nate never looked up, but she could tell he was grinning by the way his ears moved. He was definitely the best friend that she had. One who would risk everything to help her in any way she needed. She knew she could ask him to kill a man and he wouldn't think twice about doing it. Nate was exactly the muscle she needed during the money drop. The muscle that would ensure she got Sabrina back, but she knew she couldn't take him along. Knew that he'd become too emotionally involved in this case and his muscle would inhibit him from making the right choices.

The phone on Chief Dickson's desk rang, startling Summer and making her jump. She fought to catch her breath, wondering if it was the kidnapper on the other line. She watched the chief step to the side of the desk and slowly pluck the phone from the cradle. Summer prayed that it wasn't the kidnapper calling because she didn't know how long it would take Gavin to get the money and she didn't dare risk making the kidnapper angry. She'd already done it once today and she didn't know how much more it would take before he snapped.

The shakes began to creep back into her arms, slowly spreading into her chest, causing her to twitch and jerk uncontrollably. "Who is it!" she blurted, unable to control herself anymore.

Chief Dickson shook his head and pointed to Dean on the couch. "Just a minute." He covered the mouth piece, carried the phone across the room and handed it to Dean then turned to Summer. "It's Gavin. He's at the bank now making the withdrawal, but they need to confirm it with Dean first."

Summer let out her breath. "They'll let Dean have it, won't they?"

"Should? It's his money to spend, but I think they want to make sure Gavin's not cleaning out the business on him."

"Good call," Nate said, getting to his feet and slowly making his way to Summer's side. "I wouldn't trust him with a pack of gum."

Dean glared up at Nate as he spoke to the bank manager. His colour was getting brighter, but part of that may have been from Nate's comments. When he handed the phone back to the chief, Dean struggled into the sitting position. "You may not like Gavin, and sometimes I don't either, but he's still my brother so keep your opinions about him to yourself while I'm around."

Nate walked to the door and stared out through the small frosted window into the main station. "You honestly believe that he's turned his life around and is walking the straight and narrow?"

"I have to believe in him. That's what family's for."

"Mark my words, Dean. The only thing Gavin learned in prison is how to clean up his trail so not to get busted again."

"We'll see, Nate. Time will tell, and when that time comes, you'll be eating your words."

Nate turned and fixed Dean with a hard glare. "You just watch your step and make sure the shit doesn't stick to your feet, cause if he's dealing, you just might go down with him. We saved your ass the last time and stopped that shipment before it hit your property, but don't think we'll be able to do it every time."

"Nate!" Summer yelled. "This is not the place or time for your theories. You're entitled to your own opinions, but for right now, please shut the hell up."

"Fine!" Nate met her glare then opened the door. "I can't sit around here any longer. I'm going for a ride. Give me a call as soon as the kidnapper phones and I'll scout the location for the drop and try to find a hiding place."

Summer nodded as Nate disappeared out the door. Could she risk Sabrina's safety and let Nate try to ambush the kidnapper? She knew it wasn't a bad idea if only the hostage wasn't her daughter. If it was someone else's child she was sure that she would do the same thing as Nate, but how could she? How could she take the chance? The kidnapper had brought Sabrina along so he could release her, so why wouldn't he do it now that money was on the line?

CHAPTER 13

"Go! Get in your room!" he said, shoving Sabrina through the door and into the mudroom.

Sabrina stumbled through the room, fighting to stop the sobs as she disappeared through the kitchen and into her dungeon.

He'd made a promise not to yell and scream at her, but after what had just happened, he didn't care anymore. The whole plan was falling apart. It was supposed to be so simple. Free that sick fucker from jail then let the girl go. And he was all prepared to do just that, she was standing at his side, moments from freedom, when he heard the shot echo into the countryside.

He couldn't believe anybody would risk killing John Scott right in front of all the cops and reporters.

The phone began ringing, igniting his fears. Only one person would be calling and he knew the caller wouldn't be pleased with the turn of events. After peeking in the next room and checking that Sabrina was sitting calmly in the oversized chair, he pushed the button and answered the phone, but didn't dare say a word until spoken to.

"You stupid ass! Why wasn't the girl released?"

"They killed John Scott. I heard the gun shot and the woman confirmed it."

"I don't care. You know the deal. You know how it was supposed to go down."

"But they—"

"Shut up! I don't care if they'd cut him into a thousand pieces and begun serving his flesh to the mass of reporters there. We had a deal. Take the girl then release her after they let John Scott go."

"But—"

"If you say but one more time I'll personally come there and slit your throat wide open." The man on the phone paused as if daring him to say the wrong word. "Now, I'll say this only once. Release the child, then call the mother to come get her."

"But, how do I know they won't try to kill me like they did John Scott?"

"You don't, but I can guarantee you'll be dead by sundown if I don't see that girl reunited with her fucking mother!"

"What about the hundred grand I asked for? There's no sense in letting it go to waste."

"Do I need to remind you that you've already been paid for this job? Asking for a bonus like that will only hurt your chances of survival, so just let the girl go and the mother will think you got cold feet and ran away."

"I don't know?" he said, moving to the window and glancing out at the front entrance. "It doesn't feel right. That guy, John Scott, he trusted you to get him out of jail, but look at him, he's dead. You were supposed to protect him."

"Was I? Who said anything about protection? You've got a lot to learn about this business. I give an order and you follow it. There's no reason for you to be using that fucking pea brain of yours. I call the shots and I made it completely fucking clear what you were to provide. Your services were complete, but for some reason you seem to be lingering around the water cooler. So unless you want to risk your life playing around, let the girl go. Or better yet, tell me where you're hiding at and I'll send someone to pick her up."

"No—no need to do that." He let the curtain fall back in place. "I'll take care of it."

"Just so you know. I'm an impatient man. So make sure it happens, and fast."

CHAPTER 14

With Nate gone, Dean collapsed on the leather couch, and Chief Dickson coordinating the cleanup of the murder scene on the front steps of the station, Summer felt all alone while pacing back and forth inside the chief's office. She checked the phone repeatedly, making sure it was still turned on and prayed that the kidnapper wouldn't call until Gavin returned with the money.

Every time she passed the small frosted window, she glanced out, hoping to see Gavin's car pulling into the parking lot, but ended up silently cursing him instead. She looked at Dean, resting comfortably on the couch and knew he should be back in the hospital. He did look better now that he'd had a chance to eat and rest, but he would expel all that strength the moment she tried to leave without him. She could already picture him ranting about being Sabrina's father and coming with her on the drop, but none of that mattered if Gavin didn't get back soon.

Hearing the sound of a car tearing through the parking lot, Summer opened the door and caught the back end of the car disappearing around the side of the building. She had to give it to Gavin, at least he had the sense to use the back entrance. Taking one last look at Dean, she disappeared out into the buzzing main room, then down the side hall toward the back door.

She was surprised to see a smile on Gavin's face. After everything they'd been through, he didn't seem to be holding any grudges for her putting him away in prison. It was like she'd told Nate, he did the crime and had to pay the time. She'd tried to explain it to Nate that what happened between them eight years ago was cool. She was only doing her job and if Gavin hadn't been running on the wrong side, then he wouldn't have been caught.

And, Summer smiled, she wouldn't have met Dean at the courthouse during Gavin's conviction. He had been the complete opposite from Gavin. Everything from his mannerism to his appearance, and she had been shocked to find out that they shared the same mother.

"I got it," Gavin said, rushing down the hall and tossing the large envelope to Summer. "It's all there. A whole fucking shitload of cash."

"Thank you, Gavin. I really appreciate everything you've done for me and Dean."

"Hey, that's what family's for." Gavin glanced around the corner. "Speaking of family, where the fuck is Dean?"

Summer hurried to keep up with him as he rounded the corner. "He's resting in the chief's office. He's lost a lot of blood and probably shouldn't even be here."

"Tell me about it. I tried to talk him into returning to the hospital, but you know how fucking stubborn he can be. Especially when he's feeling helpless and vulnerable."

"Helpless is right." Summer knew the feeling well. She was completely helpless right now and there didn't seem to be anything to do. She was at the kidnapper's mercy and all she could do is sit and wait until the phone rang.

Summer stepped inside the office and saw Dean was still out cold, so she turned to Gavin. "What do you think I should do? Nate's planning to ambush the kidnapper at the drop location, but I'm not sure it's the best thing to do. What if the kidnapper spots him when he arrives? What do you think he'll do if he thinks he's been double crossed?"

"If it were me, I'd shoot the fucker down the minute I saw him, but that's just me." Gavin raised his eyebrows, wrinkling his forehead all the way to his shaved hair line. "But you said he sounded willing to let her go the last time, so why not trust him. Give him the cash and I'm sure he'll let Sabrina go. You have to believe he'll do the right thing."

Summer snatched the duffle bag from the side table and quickly stacked the piles of money inside, then zippered it closed. "I don't know what to believe anymore. I used to believe that people were genuinely good natured, but I'm finding that harder and harder to believe with each passing day." She shook her head. "Once they caught John Scott I thought I'd be able to move on with my life, but even with him lying dead out there, I still haven't taken a single step in that direction."

Gavin rounded the desk and plopped down in the chief's chair and Summer couldn't believe his lack of respect. How could he and Dean be born from the same womb? How could they have been raised by the same mother, but turned out so different?

"Gavin, I wouldn't sit—"

"Don't worry. Dickson won't mind one bit."

"Yeah, not a bit. A whole fucking lot."

"I was thinking," Gavin said, his brown eyes watching her carefully, "maybe you'd like me to make the drop?"

"No." Summer turned and leaned back against the table. "He specifically said it had to be me."

"But I'm sure if you mentioned it to him, making sure to tell him that I'm an ex-convict myself, that he'd be willing to allow us to switch places."

Summer shook her head and hoisted the bag onto her shoulder. "No. It has to be me. I have to be there when he lets Sabrina go."

"Well, how about I just tag along?" Gavin leaned forward onto the desk. "You know, in case something goes wrong and you can't handle it."

"Can't handle it?" Summer glared at him. "I'm a cop! You of all people should remember that. After all, I'm the one who sent you away for eight years."

She saw immediately that he did remember. The vein on the side of his bald head bulged with anger. She never should've egged him on, not after he'd agreed to drain the company fund for her and Sabrina.

"I'm sorry, Gavin. I should never have said that. It was wrong." She shook her head and looked down at the bag full of money. "I'm just so on edge right now waiting for him to call back."

Gavin glanced at Dean sleeping on the couch. "You know, for the first year in prison I wished that something terrible would happen to you. Every night I prayed that you'd be shot or run down while doing your job—that same job that put me inside that small cube of steel bars."

Summer glanced at Dean, wishing he was awake to hear this, but he was still out cold. She knew it was good for Gavin to express his anger at being locked away, but not now. Not while her whole world was turned upside down.

"Then when I heard the news that you were marrying my brother, I wanted to kill you myself. I couldn't believe you had the balls to stick me away then invade my personal life like that." Gavin closed his eyes and leaned back in the chair. "But when Dean came to visit me, we had a long talk and I realized that if you could enchant my brother and make his life so full and complete, then maybe I was just being an asshole, sour at being bested at my own game of corruption."

Gavin opened his eyes and leaned forward on the desk, tenting his fingers before his face. "For Dean's sake—and yours—I've spent the last four years of my sentence trying to turn my life around. Trying to right the wrongs that I've done in the past. It hasn't been easy, but with Dean taking me under his arm, I'm learning how to make an honest living now."

Summer didn't know what to say. She was happy to hear Gavin was committed to her side of the law, and in debt to Dean, but right now she only had one thing on her mind. "I'm happy to hear that, Gavin. And I'm glad there's no hard feeling between us."

"So, about me coming along?"

Summer shook her head and opened the door, leaving a speechless Gavin behind.

Hurrying around the corner and down the hall, she made her way into the locker room. She had the money and phone, but her Volvo was still out of commission and Dean's Mercedes was currently being processed for evidence. There was no way they'd let her take it from the shop for at least a few more days.

When the kidnapper calls, she'll need to be ready to move. That meant taking a cruiser to make the drop, but somehow she didn't think the kidnapper would appreciate the irony of her showing up with the lights blazing away. Instead she headed to Nate's locker, knowing that he would stash the keys to his Malibu inside, like always.

When Summer opened the door, she stumbled backwards as her eyes settled on the images inside. There was an instant swell in her stomach as it churned and threatened to unload its contents all over the locker room floor. She took a step back and sat on the bench, drawing cleansing breaths until the feeling passed.

"How could he do that?" She glanced up, hoping that it'd only been her imagination, but the two pictures were still there, side by side. A gross before and after of the woman she'd been, and the woman she'd become, thanks to the hands of the corpse outside. She started to look away, but forced herself to keep looking at the damage that John Scott had done to her.

Anger filled her body, replacing the nauseous feeling and bringing a bitter taste to her mouth. It was the taste of revenge not yet fulfilled. She realized at that moment why Nate kept that picture there. He wanted to be reminded daily of the injustice in the world. And knowing Nate, he wanted to fire himself up, and what better way than to look at the partner he'd lost due to his own misjudgement.

Summer knew Nate still held himself responsible for what had happened to her that day. Knew he felt like the older brother who'd let his kid sister get harmed while under his care, and she understood exactly where those feelings had come from. At first she'd blamed him for not being there to stop John Scott from drugging her and taking her away, but with time she realized that it wasn't his fault. If it was anybody's fault, it was her own.

Summer snatched the key chain from the side hook then ripped the after picture from the locker and stood studying the image. She looked like hell, worse than being in a high speed car crash, but, Summer glanced into the wall mirror, she was still alive—that's more than she could say for

John Scott—and her wounds have healed. At least her physical wounds have.

Grabbing her stomach, Summer felt a twitch from deep inside. It wasn't the usual muscle spasm, but more like a tiny foot kicking and suddenly she wondered if it could be Dean's child waiting to be born. Just yesterday she was content to have the child and give it away without ever seeing its face and never letting Dean know about it, but after everything that had happened in the last four hours, she was beginning to wonder if she'd been too distraught to make a clear decision. After all, why hadn't she run the tests? Why was she punishing Dean by not telling him about the chance that he may be the father of this child, but she knew that answer. Knew that she still held a deep-rooted grudge at him for never coming to her rescue in that farmhouse while John…

Summer shook her head, clearing the memory from her mind. She folded the after picture up and tucked it into her pocket. There was a feeling of anger that seemed to be driving her now and she suspected it was from facing her past—Facing everything she wanted so much to run and hide from. Maybe Nate had the right idea, infuriate yourself every day so as to focus your mind on the end result. And now that John Scott was dead, she only had one last hurdle to overcome. She moved to the supply locker, grabbed an ankle strap and cinched it on under her pant leg.

"Damn it, Nate, where's my god damned gun!"

Slamming the locker door shut, Summer stormed to the mirror and stood looking into those green eyes. They were focused, driven, but not yet commanding like they'd once been. She brushed back her tangled blond hair and drew a deep breath, preparing herself for the challenges that lie ahead. She knew that if things didn't go down smoothly, she would need to regain her old composure and take action.

She would need to do whatever it took to get Sabrina back—even kill if she had to.

Marching out into the hall, she slung the bag of money over her shoulder and headed for the back door where Nate had parked his car. She burst through the door, shoving her way through the rouge reporters who'd gather at the back after Gavin had returned, hoping to get the scoop from a different angle, and limped toward Nate's red Malibu. She placed the bag on the rear seat, tucked the cell phone in the holder and started the car. The parking lot was crammed full so she turned the wheel sharply then drove over the curb and tore off through the grass toward the roadway.

She drove with purpose, feeling settled behind the wheel and wondered where Nate was right now. Was he just driving around aimlessly throughout the countryside, trying to think like the kidnapper so he could find him hiding away in the corner of a back alley? Or, Summer knew she had a better hunch, was he at the farmhouse where she'd been held captive, searching for a clue as to who the kidnapper might be.

If she was a betting woman, she'd have slapped down the hundred grand in the bag, because she knew a sure thing when she heard it.

After checking the rearview mirror and finding no news vans giving chase, she cranked the wheel and raced down the street, zigzagging down back streets along the way, hoping to keep anybody from tailing her. The last thing she wanted was to have the news cameras showing up at the drop location, trying to capture footage of the hostage release.

Once she reached Bloomfield Road, she punched the accelerator to the floor, challenging the Malibu and herself at the same time. The car tore down the road, picking up speed until the blurring houses thinned and only a few farms dotted the countryside. She should've eased up on the pedal, but she had to prove to herself that she could handle the challenge of a fast pursuit. It wasn't until she saw the overpass racing upon her at a breakneck speed that she stomped on the brakes, sliding the car for fifty feet until it finally came to a complete stop on the road, facing toward the cut off.

She squinted up toward the hillside and tried to spot the old farmhouse she'd been held inside, but it was completely shrouded with trees, invisible to the naked eye. It was almost as if the house was a secret hideaway, dropped from the sky into the thick of trees.

Summer saw the flash of movement in the rearview mirror as a car pulled onto the roadway far behind. Quickly she sped onto the gravel back road before the approaching car could spot her. She drove past the cut through that she'd taken earlier, choosing to take the long way around, not risking getting trapped down in the valley again.

The little alcove where the Mercedes had been parked was all cordoned off with yellow tape, as was the worn out driveway—except there was a police cruiser wedged under the tape. She knew immediately that her hunch had been correct. Nate was here and he was inside searching for a clue that Stevens and Malroy might have missed. The same reason she'd come. To find answers when there was nothing else to do but sit and wait.

Summer pulled tight to the side of the alcove and got out. She tucked the bag of money under the seat then locked the car and headed around the bushes, ducking under the police line as she tried to hold onto her new found courage.

CHAPTER 15

The same feeling of dread filled the pit of Summer's stomach as she headed toward the farm house. She paused on what was left of the ancient concrete sidewalk to the front porch, staring up at the rotting structure. The place looked totally abandoned. Paint peeled in large strips from the window trim and siding, covering the leaf strewn ground in an array of white and grey. The cracked and shattered windows reminded her of an eerie haunted house, but ghosts and ghouls were no match for the real monster that had inhabited this place in the not so distant past.

How would John Scott have known about this place? Was there a connection between this house and his past, or was it merely a convenient place to do his bidding? Summer had hoped that Stephens and Malroy would've tracked down some information as to who the property belonged to, but seeing as they've left, she suspected that's exactly what they were doing now.

Summer took the first step onto the front porch stairs, feeling strong knowing that Nate was inside, but as she stepped into the shadow of the house, a shiver raced up her spine. She paused, glancing at the location where her badge had been placed, knowing that the kidnapper had stood exactly where she stood now.

Had John Scott told the kidnapper about this place and what to say about that night here, or was it someone else? Someone who took charge of them both? She wondered just how many people knew the truth and were keeping the secret. A secret that she pledged to flush out, and in doing so, bring everyone involved to justice.

"Nate?" Summer said, turning the handle and opening the door a crack. "Nate, are you in here?"

She heard footsteps on the floor above, but no response came back. It had to be Nate up there. That was his patrol car parked outside. She was sure of it. Summer let the door go and it swung wide open, thanks to the draft from the broken windows.

The hinges squealed slightly as it approached the inner wall, drawing a sudden halt to the footfalls. She bent down, reaching to the ankle holster strapped to her leg, then cursed Nate for not getting her gun like she'd asked.

"Nate," she whispered softly, knowing that the person upstairs had definitely heard the squeal of the hinge.

"Summer?" Nate leaned over the upper railing, gazing down upon her with a surprised look on his face. "What the hell are you doing here? I figured you'd be holding down the station until the kidnapper called."

The feeling of relief flooded her body, leaving her drained and weary. It felt so good seeing Nate that she rushed into the house, temporarily forgetting her inhibitions. "What are you doing here? I thought you were going for a ride."

"I did." Nate stepped to the upper landing. "I drove around, checked my hunches and came up empty handed.

So, I came here to see how Stephens and Malroy were making out."

"And?" Summer made it halfway up the creaky stairs before she caught the image of the room and stopped in her tracks. It'd been stripped down. Every item processed and tossed into a pile in the corner.

"They took samples from the bed. Dusted for prints all over the house. Found a fresh set, which we assume is yours. But other than that, the place looks fairly clean. They've found samples from when you—" Nate met her on the stairs. "But nothing much new. We've got his footprints from the dust and a few from the yard, plus the car tracks, but it looks like he was fairly clean. No prints, probably wore gloves when he dropped the ransom note off. The door knob, note and even your badge is spotless."

Summer racked her brain, trying to think of anything left unturned. "Tire strip he used on my car?"

"Standard issue police strip," Nate said, ushering her down the stairs. "Could've picked it up from pretty much any undesirable on the street corner."

Summer couldn't believe it. She was hoping it'd be harder to pick one of those up. Hoping that they could trace it back to a supplier. "They're that easy to get?"

"If you have the money and the connections, they're not that hard to find. You know as well as I do that there's a whole other world out there stewing just under the calm society that we pretend is the reality of our existence."

"Dean's cell phone?"

"Thousand pieces. It'd been run over a hundred times before we could recover it from the road. The last I've heard, the lab's only found minute traces of prints on the outer plastic case, but no enough to get any kind of match."

Nate led Summer into the main room, on the lower level, and slid one of the remaining unbroken chairs to her. "Sit down and rest."

She hated to be told what to do, especially when she was feeling down and out over the lack of evidence they had. The kidnapper had planned very thoroughly for this. It was evident in how he waited, hiding in the pile of trash for them to show up. He knew everything about them. She shivered remembering the way the light had glistened off the blade of the knife when he'd stabbed Dean.

"Wait!" She grabbed Nate by the shirt. "The keys! Dean's keys for his Mercedes."

Nate shook his head.

"The kidnapper wasn't wearing gloves when he stabbed Dean. I'm sure of it." Summer paced around the room, stirring up the layer of dust. "Then he slipped on the mask and climbed from the trash. I can't be a hundred percent sure, but I'm betting ninety that he wasn't wearing gloves when he picked the keys from the sidewalk."

Nate grabbed her shoulders as she passed by and directed her to the chair, but she refused to sit. "They're clean. He must have wiped them down before he left the car. Everything was wiped clean. Not a print, except yours. Not even Dean's. So you know what that means."

Summer did. He'd used a clean cloth to erase everything before she climbed into the car. "But what about the key itself."

Nate was looking more and more confused every second that passed. "I told you they're—"

"Clean. Yes, I know," Summer grinned, "but the sweat from his skin would've corroded the metal. Now, if they use the Bond technique and apply an electrical charge and a fine carbon powder to the metal of the key, it might just reveal a fingerprint."

"Does it work?"

"The hell if I know. I'm not one of the lab rats." Summer moved to the cracked picture window and looked through the filthy glass at the shroud of trees encircling the house. "But it's worth a shot."

"Damn right," Nate said. He quickly called in the request to the station, having them forward the information to the boys in the lab.

Summer turned back to Nate. "They're going to do it?"

"As we speak. Said it'll take some time for the prints to emerge if there are any, but if he used some kind of oil based cleaner on the rag when he cleaned the car, then there might not be anything to see."

"He's smart. I'll give him that, but somehow I don't think he's that smart."

The phone in her pocket vibrated, then began ringing. Summer felt her calm wash away in a surging tide as the reality of the situation hit home. She fumbled, digging the phone out then quickly flipped it open. "H—Hello?"

"Get in a car and start driving south from the city."

"South, where?"

"Anywhere. Just head out of the city and go south."

"I want to talk to Sabrina first."

"Can't do that. They may be tracing the call."

The line went dead and Summer felt like she'd been kicked in the stomach. She'd been counting on hearing Sabrina's voice one more time and didn't care if they were tracing the call or not. She craved hearing that sweet little voice like a drug addict craved another hit.

"South?" Nate said, already heading toward the door. "Let's go. I'll follow and hang back."

"No!" Summer stood her ground. "I told you I won't risk Sabrina's life by pissing him off. I'm going by myself and that's my final decision."

Nate stood inches away, glaring down at her. "There's no way in hell—"

"Gun!" Summer held out her hand and was disappointed to see it shaking. She had hoped her nerves had settled, but they hadn't healed completely, even with John Scott dead.

Nate reached for his sidearm.

"No, not yours." Summer tightened every muscle in her body, willing them to remain still, but she knew it'd only hold for a very short period of time before the twitches and shakes took over with vengeance. "Did you get my gun like I asked?"

Nate's eyes were barely more than slits as he fought to control his anger at being told he couldn't come out and play today, then reluctantly he bent down and unstrapped the holster from his leg and handed it to Summer.

"I'm sorry, Nate." Summer took the gun from the holster then tossed the holster in the corner and slid her brand new sidearm beneath her pant leg. "I really appreciate your help, but you have to understand why you can't come."

Nate nodded, but she didn't think he did understand. She knew revenge was rooted deep in his mind and if she didn't want him following, then she'd either have to shoot him or lose him.

"Oh, by the way," Summer smiled, realizing what a stubborn ass she was partnered with, "I borrowed your car."

Nate's face slackened.

"I hope you don't mind."

"Then... you saw the pictures?"

Summer nodded and fished the after photo from her pocket. "I have to admit, it does get your blood boiling."

"It's—"

"I understand." She raised an eyebrow. "After years of working beside you. I finally understand what drives you."

Summer headed to the door then turned back. "And don't worry, I'll take good care of your car."

Nate forced a smile. "One scratch and you'll be buying me a new one."

Summer nodded and stepped onto the porch. "Promise that you won't follow me."

Nate bit his lip and nodded.

"Out loud. I don't want any of this, just kidding shit."

"Fine! I promise." Nate kicked over the chair and followed her outside. "But if something goes wrong—"

"Don't worry, everything will be fine. I'll call you as soon as I have Sabrina." Summer stopped on the top step and turned back. "I promise, if anything goes wrong you've got my permission to destroy the entire country just to get that bastard."

"I'll kill him!" Nate clenched his jaw. "And I'm not kidding."

"I wouldn't expect anything less from you." Summer smiled. "That's what makes you such a good partner."

"Go on. Get out of here before I change my mind."

Summer ran to the car as fast as her sore foot would allow. Once inside, she started the engine and tore down the gravel road, heading in the direction of the highway.

"South? How far south does he want me to go?" Summer said, placing the phone back onto the holder. Was south the direction that they would make the swap, or was he only keeping her moving, watching from a safe distance to see if anybody was tailing her?

Summer leaned over and opened the glove box, then fumbled through the assortment of maps she knew Nate would have. He always had the cruiser organized and his car was the same. She dropped map after map to the floor until she found the Ontario map. Flipping it open on the passenger's seat, Summer glanced at it trying to pick an area that was secluded enough for him to feel safe about making the exchange.

There were plenty of small towns and flat farm land to the south, but nothing on the map jumped out at her for the perfect drop spot for the exchange. He'd want somewhere where he could see her coming for miles around, with enough access that he could make a getaway without being seen, but as hard as Summer tried to find a location, she couldn't. There just didn't seem to be an ideal spot to the south, because eventually you ended up at the edge of Lake Erie with no place to go.

"Maybe this is a ruse to keep me guessing? He's probably going to call back and switch direction anytime soon." She glanced at the phone, but it didn't ring, so she rounded the next corner and headed south-west toward a hill. A good spot for him to be sitting on top, watching for her to approach.

She slowed her approach, scanning the hillside when her phone rang, causing her to jump.

"Damn it!" Summer grabbed the phone and flipped it open. "What?"

"Where are you?"

"Middle Line Road, past Buxton." There was the distinct sound of paper rattling.

"Okay, continue down to Four Rod Road then head south again and turn left onto the Sixteenth Line."

"Just name your location and let's get this over with."

"In time. Just make sure you're all alone, because if I see one cop, I'm gone and you'll never see Sabrina again."

"Don't worry." Summer bit back her anger. "I'm all alone. I don't care about the money. Just give me my daughter."

"Then keep driving."

The phone went silent again. Summer flipped it closed and set it back down. After checking the map, she turned left at the next road and made her way down the Four Rod Road. She ran her finger down the path that he'd told her, but there still wasn't anything up ahead.

When Summer turned onto the Sixteenth Line, the phone rang again. She glanced across the empty farmer's fields, then in her rearview mirror for any sign of the kidnapper or anyone tailing her, but the countryside seemed so desolate that she felt all alone in the apocalyptic future.

"Drive down the road until you see the lone barn with the red X on the door. Once you're there, pull inside all the way to the back wall and turn off the car."

"Are you in the barn? Hello…" Summer tossed the phone down beside her. "God damn it! Stop hanging up on me!"

She drove down, past a few collapsed barns until she spotted the first standing structure. Her heart started racing as she pulled slowly onto the rutted, muddy laneway that led to the old barn. As she neared, she sighed at the sight of the fresh red paint on the partially open door.

There still was no sign of the kidnapper anywhere, but she followed the orders and pulled her car into the barn until her bumper was nearly touching the weathered old boards. Once she turned the car off, the sound of bats was unmistakable. They seemed agitated by the rumbling of the car engine, but soon fell silent as the seconds ticked by.

Summer waited for what seemed like an eternity, glancing repeatedly over each shoulder, anticipating the kidnapper's arrival, but the countryside was extremely quiet today and no cars dared go past the barn since she'd pulled in. It was almost as if she'd driven down an abandoned road.

The phone rang again and she quickly answered it.

"Get out of the car, place the money and car keys through the hole in the back wall, then wait inside the car for me to arrive. Once I have the money, I'll send Sabrina out to you. Follow my tracks and you'll find your car keys a short distance away. Understand?"

Summer understood perfectly. She'd have to trust this man to release Sabrina after she'd folded all her cards. "Fine."

After gathering the bag from the floor, Summer climbed out of the car and cautiously walked to the back wall where there was a large chunk of board missing. She glanced out the back and noticed a service lane extending out into the field, disappearing over the hill in the distance. He was probably sitting just on the other side, waiting for her to make the drop. She debated whether she should hide beside the wall and shoot him when he gets close, or if she should play it safe and trust he'll live up to his end of the bargain.

Playing it safe, Summer held the bag out the hole and let it fall onto the makeshift table below, then dropped the car keys on top of the bag. She wished she'd brought her own set of keys from the Volvo. He wouldn't know the difference between the two sets, then at least she'd be able to chase him if he double crossed her. But she didn't, so she returned to the car and waited, gazing through the cracks in the splintered wood for any sign of them approaching.

Two minutes later she saw the sun reflect off the truck's windshield as it cautiously climbed to the top of the hill, down on the service lane. Summer felt butterflies swirling in her stomach, a welcome change to the nagging feeling that she usually got when the stress level increased.

He's bringing Sabrina and he's gonna release her.

Summer could almost feel Sabrina in her arms right now.

He's… stopping?

Summer squinted, trying to make sense of what he was doing in the distance. The driver's door opened and it looked like he was aiming a rifle off into the distance.

Summer looked to her left and bobbed her head until she found a gap in the boards. A car was coming down the road—A police car. "Damn it, Nate! I told—"

The gun shot echoed through the barn, sending the bats fluttering around the rooftop. Summer ignored the flying rats and watched as Nate's cruiser veered off the roadway and came crashing to a halt in the muddy field beside the barn.

CHAPTER 16

The feeling in Dean's stomach was one of pure nauseousness. He'd been resting so comfortably in the chief's office until Gavin had woken him, insistent that they should go and look for the kidnapper.

Dean stared at the display, wondering what had happened to the tiny blimp they had been following across the countryside for the last fifteen minutes. He tapped the side of the unit but the tiny blimp never moved.

"Something's wrong with this thing. Why isn't it working?"

Gavin looked curiously at the display then grabbed it from Dean, anxiously fiddling with the screen. "What did you fucking do? It was working just a minute ago."

"Nothing." Dean grabbed it back. "It's stuck. It's just sitting there on that spot. Why would it stop working?"

"I don't know. Maybe she's stopped for a fucking break or maybe she tossed the bag out the fucking window. Just wait a few minutes and we'll get to that location and find out."

Dean drew a deep breath and stared out the window in the direction that the machine showed Summer was in. There wasn't much to see, only a hill in the distance. "What if she's up on top of that hill?"

"Then you'll have to use your fucking eyes for that one, Dean. The machine is only as good as your senses are. If you can't see shit, then it's as useless as tits on a bull."

Dean flipped the handheld tracking unit over, looking for a supplier name, but found none. "How often do you use this thing? And what the hell for?"

"It's for emergency situations. I got it from a security supplier a couple of months ago. It's part of a bigger package designed to track the delivery trucks across the country." Gavin gave a wink. "That way we always know exactly where the trucks are and what the drivers are up to."

"You want to spy on the delivery guys?"

"No." Gavin shrugged. "Well, yes. Is it that bad of an idea to know where your shipments are? If you get the whole package, you can track them minute for minute, making sure they're not screwing around—Or stopped at some warehouse filling the shipment with drugs and guns." Gavin waited until the point had sunk in. "They showed me what the system has done for other trucking companies and it looks impressive."

"And when were you going to run it past me?" Dean reclined the seat and slid his leg out, easing the pressure on his stomach. "Cause I don't think the guys would like it."

"They don't have to know." Gavin tapped the screen. "Summer has absolutely no idea she's being tracked either. The only time they'd know is when we drag them into the office and bust them for fucking around when we're paying them to work. And if they're fucking me around, then I don't care how they feel about the system because they'll be history."

Dean held the screen up. "Are you sure Summer doesn't know?"

"Hell, this is the first time I've used it. There might be something wrong with the transmitter. Maybe it got wet or the battery ran low. What do I look like, a fucking techie?"

"Or she found it stuck inside the bag and tossed it out the window."

"No." Gavin shook his head. "It's so small she'd never find it."

"Well, no matter what, it's not doing any good right now." Dean tapped the tracking unit against the dash.

"Don't do that. You're gonna fucking break it, then we'll be shit out of luck!"

Gavin reached for the unit but Dean pulled it away, studying it closely. "I think it moved a little. Not much. Not like before, but just a tiny bit."

"Maybe her car broke down and she's walking?" Gavin said. "That could be the difference between the movements."

"Maybe?" Dean had no idea. He only hoped for Summer's sake that she'd armed herself before going out to make the drop. He knew she wasn't supposed to carry a weapon, but being allowed and being stupid were two different things. The old Summer wouldn't be caught in a situation like this unarmed and vulnerable. She'd have packed an extra gun and enough ammunition to blow away half a small town.

Dean couldn't believe how far she'd come since this morning. Back then she'd been so terrified that she could barely function when Sabrina was first taken, but now after only a few hours, she was acting ever more like her old self. He hoped this boost of confidence would remain after they got Sabrina back, because he hated seeing Summer acting so pathetic.

"How could you let me drift off in the chief's office and allow Summer to leave without me?" Dean glanced over at Gavin. "What was she thinking? She knew I wanted to go with her, even if it was against the kidnapper's orders."

"I didn't let you drift off, you fell into a comatose state and I thought maybe you'd bit the dirt."

Dean shook his head and stared out at the approaching hill. "You think John Scott getting his head blown off, had anything to do with her taking off to make the drop all by herself?"

Gavin turned the corner then glanced at the screen, making sure he was heading in the right direction. "Trust me. I offered to go with her, but she turned me down flat."

"You? You wanted to go?"

"Don't be so surprised. Like you wouldn't do the same thing if you were in my shoes?"

Dean knew he would. Even though his relationship with Gavin hasn't been the best over the years, he knew he could never turn his back on flesh and blood. "You're right. I'd do anything I could to help."

"Awe," Gavin said, tousling Dean's hair. "If your mother was still around, she'd be so proud of you."

"Stop it." Dean tried to knock his hand away, but the pain was too much. "You know she wouldn't. She never really gave a shit about either of us, now did she?"

"Not really. She always seemed more interested in finding a new man to knock her up. I think she thought it was her fucking job to help populate the world one man at a time."

Dean felt a chill in his body at the mention of their mother. "Speaking of that. How long's it been since you saw your old man?"

"Years." Gavin shrugged. "Last time I saw him, he was running from the house as fast as he could while *your* mother threw every fucking thing she could get her hands on at his head."

Dean had to laugh at the image. "Yeah, could've been a hell of a ball player."

"If only they used ashtrays instead of baseballs."

"That was her favourite weapon, now wasn't it."

Gavin looked over with a huge grin on his face. "We've gotta track that bitch down this Christmas and send her a big fucking case of the ugliest ashtrays we can find."

"You're evil. Pure evil." Dean started laughing harder and harder until he doubled over in pain. "She'll go nuts when she opens the box, then start flinging those things all around the house."

"Yeah, imagine the surprise on the guy's face she's currently shacked up with, when the glass starts to shatter. It'd be priceless. He'd be lucky to escape alive."

"Maybe we shouldn't?" Dean wiped his eyes, still doubled over.

"Maybe we should deliver it in person and watch the excitement ourselves?"

They came to the end of the road and Gavin reached for the unit, taking it from Dean's hand. "Looks like a right turn then a left up ahead."

"Is Summer still in the same location?"

"Yeah, looks like it."

"Maybe it's the drop spot?" Dean said, straining to return to the sitting position. He stared over at the half brother he'd barely known, even though they'd grown up in the same dysfunctional house.

"You know what," Dean said, feeling the seriousness of the situation seeping back in. "I've been thinking these last few months, that if Summer ever got over what happened to her, that I'd sell the business and move across the country for a fresh start."

"And leave me all alone in this fucking place?"

"Seriously, if Summer ever came to her senses and I got her back, how could we stay? How could I risk her falling back into the way she is now? The best thing for her would be a nice clean slate to start with. Maybe she could get a different job—something behind a desk. Something nice and safe."

Gavin gave a long stare then shook his head. "Here I thought you were the smarter one of us. If Summer does pull through this shit the last thing she's gonna want is to be strapped to a desk, locked inside a building for eight hours a day. She's always been a fighter and she'll want nothing more than to get right back into the mix and throw her punches."

Gavin hesitated before continuing. "You remember how messed up I was after she arrested me."

Dean nodded. "You looked like the guards had just done a number on you with their nightsticks."

"I never told you this before, but those marks weren't from any stick or even from her bodyguard, Nate. She kicked the living shit out of me the night I got busted. I resisted and she literally beat the fucking crap out of me."

Dean couldn't believe it. Gavin had never acknowledged the physical abuse during his trial. He refused to accuse anybody of police brutality and suddenly Dean understood. "That's why you wouldn't go along with your lawyer's motion to press for police brutality." An uncontrollable grin filled his face. "You couldn't admit that such a petite woman had kicked your ass so badly that you found your front teeth two days later in the shitter."

Gavin's face was burning red with embarrassment. "I guess I did deserve the ass kicking." Gavin swallowed the lump in his throat and flexed his hands. "I underestimated her. I looked at her size and that pretty face and I thought she was only on the force for PR work, so I took a swing at her and that's the last thing I remember until I came to in the hospital."

"Wow," Dean said. "I'm glad she never lost her temper around me."

"Don't worry. I'm sure she has a rule about beating up pussies."

Dean started to protest, but realized that he wasn't the most macho person in the world. He did have more looks than brawn and thankfully that was what attracted Summer to him.

"You're right," Dean said, flipping his long curls back and giving Gavin his big white smile. "I'll take the looks, cause it's easier than getting women with muscle."

"But," Gavin flexed his biceps. "You've gotta have the muscle to keep the women."

CHAPTER 17

"Nate!" Summer screamed, jumping from the car and rushing out the doorway to the muddy field where the cruiser was sinking. She glanced back, seeing the truck with Sabrina inside, turning around on the laneway. She could see her tiny head twisting over the seat, gazing out the rear window.

Summer jumped from the laneway into the thick mud and struggled to make her way toward the car. The way the car had jumped off the road, she expected to see Nate's head exploded like John Scott's had been. She hurried through the mud to the side of the cruiser and gave a quick prayer when she saw Nate moving behind the wheel. Blood covered the back of the seat and tiny fragments of glass stuck in the wet fabric of his shirt. The bullet appeared to rip straight through his left shoulder, lodging into the seat backing. Nate was lucky. The kidnapper missed his shot, or maybe felt a little kind hearted.

"Are you all right?" Summer pulled his shoulder forward checking the wound.

"Fine." Nate bit his lip, grimacing in pain. "Just a little hole. N—Nothing serious. Did he drop Sabrina?"

"No."

Nate tried to open the door, but Summer held him back against the seat. "W—What are you waiting for? Go get her!"

Summer turned and watched the truck disappear over the hill. "Are you going to be all right?"

"I'm fine!" Nate knocked her hand away and turned his head, gazing at the hole in his shoulder. "I'll call for an ambulance and backup."

Summer took a step backwards then stopped in her tracks. "No backup. I can handle this."

Nate raised one eyebrow. "You sure?"

Nodding, Summer trudged through the mud, back to the Malibu before realizing that she'd dropped the keys out the hole, along with the money. Cursing, she ran to the back wall, stuck her arm through the hole and struggled to find the keys. They were there somewhere, they had to be. She felt the cold canvas bag but the keys were nowhere to be found.

"Damn it, I know he didn't have time to grab the keys before leaving." Summer stood on her tiptoes and peered through the gap in the boards. She lifted the bag carefully, praying that the keys wouldn't fall to the ground. And once the bag was off the wooden crate, she saw the glint of metal balanced on the end slat of the crate. Carefully Summer lifted the bag through the hole and dropped it to the ground, then reached out through the hole, her fingers inches away from the keys.

Summer glanced to the service laneway as her chest began tightening. She drew a cleansing breath, stepped onto the bag of money and heard a small popping sound as she stretched with everything she had, ignoring the pain in her arm as the slivers dug deeper and deeper into her flesh. Once her fingers touched the cold metal of the key ring, she hooked her finger through the hole and lifted them back inside.

One deep breath, then Summer snatched the bag of money and jumped behind the wheel. Blood from the gashes trickled down her arm, landing on the console. She ignored the stain and turned the key, bringing the car roaring to life. Summer slammed it in reverse and raced backwards. The Malibu hit the rut at the entrance of the barn, sending it bouncing to the side and smashing into the half open door, which shattered into pieces on top of Nate's car.

Once she was clear of the debris, she floored the pedal and the tires spun, flinging mud ten feet in the air as she made her way around the barn, careful not to slide down into the deep muddy field. She took a quick glance back at Nate and felt relieved that he was busy talking on the radio.

Hitting the top of the hill, she scanned the countryside for the truck and watched as it disappeared out of sight, down on the main roadway at the end of the service lane. She knew she had to keep close. She couldn't afford to let him get a huge lead otherwise Sabrina's life may be in jeopardy. If only Nate would've listened and stayed back at the farm house like he'd promised, then Sabrina would be sitting right beside her.

She pushed the Malibu harder than she normally would've, given the condition of the laneway. The car wasn't made for off-roading in the countryside, but it seemed to be holding its own just the same. The rutted, pitted laneway appeared to have been abused for years by large tractors, making it difficult to navigate the course.

It looked like he'd chosen this drop location after careful consideration. Even if someone tried to follow him, there was little chance of the police cars making good time following him across the countryside. The big truck tires were definitely designed for this type of environment.

Summer remembered the tire prints that were at the farm house. They belonged to a smaller vehicle, not a large truck. And the pattern, it was definitely different. There was no way he was driving this truck earlier, so where was he getting the vehicles from? He could be stealing them, she supposed, but why take a chance when you've already got the cops scouring the countryside for you. Maybe whoever the kidnapper was working for had set him up with the hiding place and the vehicles?

The car bounced wildly, the undercarriage coming crashing down on the roadway, bringing a jarring pain ripping through her head as it smashed against the head rest. Summer cranked the wheel, fighting to keep the car from bouncing off the lane into the death trap of mud as she approached the smooth paved road fifty feet away.

She could feel the anxiety building, just imagining how fast she could go once she reached that roadway. The left tire spun as the car sank deeper into the rut at the side of the lane, pulling her ever so close to the smooth pool of mud soup. Summer cranked the wheel toward the side of the road and instead of fighting the rut, she turned into it, gaining speed until she was dangerously close to sudden death, then cranked the wheel slightly and floored the pedal. The wheels grabbed, then spun as the muffler scrapped on the mixture of gravel and rocks beneath.

"Shit!" The car was slowing, being dragged down by the exhaust. She heard the sound of metal tearing apart and a second later the rear of the car flew up, catapulting over the muffler that had been ripped right from the vehicle, sending the car over it like a pole vaulter making the most important jump of his career.

The car came crashing down, bouncing a few times as the tires took advantage of the lack of friction and sent the car screaming up the rut, toward the blessed asphalt. With the muffler gone, the car roared down the final stretch sounding like a stock car on a Saturday night.

"Sorry, Nate," Summer muttered as the front wheels grabbed the welcomed flat surface, pulling the car easily from the muddy gravel that had helped give the kidnapper such a huge lead. She sped down the road, mud flinging from the tires as the last of the gravel pounded the wheel wells, challenging the roar of the open exhaust. She knew there was no way of sneaking up on the kidnapper now. Not with this thing screaming for miles away.

With the pedal pressed against the floor, Summer gripped the steering wheel so tight there was no way her hands could twitch. The roar of the engine was so loud, she doubted she'd be able to hear the phone ringing if the kidnapper called, so she tucked it under her leg, praying that it would vibrate and she'd get another chance to save Sabrina.

The road ended up ahead, splitting in two directions, one back toward the highway and the other down toward the cliff surrounding the lake. Summer had driven along the lake a few times, enough to know there were plenty of hiding places along the cliffs. Houses were built, perched on the ridge, overlooking the expanse of water, while others found their seclusion building their homes down in the valleys, hiding from view of passersby. He could be in any one of these homes, seeing how most were now empty with the approach of winter.

Summer turned left, down toward the lake, hoping she was using the same logic as the kidnapper. She had to stop thinking like a cop—or a mother—and start thinking like him.

"He needs a place to hide," Summer muttered. "And where better than in the valleys, along the lake."

The changing landscape blurred past in a rush of fall colours as the flat farm land began slowly rolling down toward the lake front. She glanced at the map, following her current course until the road she was travelling ended at the Talbot Trail Road, which ran along the edge of the lake.

Most of the homes were located along this stretch of road, allowing easy access to the city, but there were a few side streets that jogged down the steep cliff toward the water's edge. The houses on these streets were hidden from the view of the roadway, secluded from the rest of the world, making them the perfect hideout for the kidnapper. The only problem was there were so many side streets and homes, not to mention tiny boathouses along the water, plus tiny shacks everywhere that he might be held up in.

When the road ended at Talbot Trail, Summer sat for a second, glad that the roar of the exhaust had subsided temporarily as she gazed out over the cliff, across the seemingly endless body of water before her. It looked so beautiful as the sun glistened off the surface and she remembered how much Sabrina loved going to the beach. She loved building castles and playing in the breaking waves as they crashed ashore, and today the waves were crashing, easily eight feet high, dangerous for anyone playing in them.

Summer hopped out, limped before the car and examined the pavement, hoping for a sign. Maybe there was a minute drop of mud from the truck's tires as he rounded the corner, knocked free from the sideway's force of the turn, which would indicate the direction he'd gone? But finding no sign, she stepped onto the quiet highway, glancing in both directions, looking for a clue, but finding nothing.

"Damn it!" Summer screamed at the top of her lungs.

The ringing of the phone barely made it over the rumble of the exhaust, sending Summer running to the car and grabbing for the phone. "Where the hell are you!"

"Right where you left me," Nate said. "Waiting for an ambulance."

"Nate?" Summer leaned against the car. Her legs were weak and tired all of a sudden. "I can't talk to you. I can't tie up the phone."

"The l—lab called. They found the prints. Matched them to Percy Campbell." Nate paused for a second. "Stephens and Malroy are headed for his place right now."

"Any chance it's down by the lake?"

"No, just on the outskirts of Chatham… Summer?"

"Yeah."

"Be careful. He's done time at Fenbrook for drug and gun possession. We know he's armed and dangerous so if you find him, please wait for backup. I can't stand the thought of losing you again."

Summer could hear the wail of the ambulance siren in the background and it brought a feeling of relief, knowing that Nate would be all right now that help was arriving. "Nate, see if Percy has any ties to the lake. See if he owns any property down here."

"Don't worry, I—I'll get Stephens to check it out."

"If he finds anything, I want to be the first to know."

"Fine."

"Nate?"

"Yeah."

"Be nice to the paramedics and try not to be such an ass." Summer closed the phone and climbed back inside the car. She turned left, seeing the fingers of land creeping out to the lake and guessed the lower lands would be of more interest to the kidnapper than the high cliffs.

Each house she passed, she slowed, searching for fresh tire prints in the soft gravel leading up to the homes. The early morning rain was helpful, giving a tiny shred of hope at finding tracks that normally wouldn't be there, but snow, a light dusting of snow would be a saviour right now. But alas, luck seemed like something of the past. Something restricted from her life for good.

The road dipped down suddenly, rounding to the right, heading back toward the water. Summer squinted at the approaching dirt lane up ahead on the right. It was pitted and cratered with mud puddles and Summer felt a brief surge of excitement at seeing the glistening wet ring around the puddles. She pulled off to the side of the road, careful not to disturb the water and opened her door.

There was definite wetness surrounding the puddle, a dead giveaway that someone had disturbed the liquid not long ago, and seeing how traffic was all but dead this morning, she knew there was a good chance the kidnapper had come this way. She glanced down the dirt laneway, eyeing the thick overgrowth of trees and bushes as the land neared the open water of the lake, knowing that he could be hiding behind any one of these bushes with his rifle trained on her head.

Summer drove slow, keeping the rumble of the exhaust to a minimum as she scanned every worn, decrepit shack she passed. Any of these would make a perfect hiding place. They were in such disrepair that nobody would come looking inside. She hoped that Sabrina had been kept warm and safe, even if she was being held captive.

Creeping along, Summer saw how far the huge waves were breaking on the land, coming closer and closer to the laneway as the wind began intensifying off the lake. As she turned the corner, she saw the fresh tire tracks heading to the first liveable home up ahead and pulled to the soft shoulder, then killed the engine. The tire tracks led straight inside the single car garage, but the door was closed, keeping the vehicle's identity a secret.

Cautiously, Summer climbed from the car, reaching for her gun as she went. She knew she wasn't authorized to have a weapon until she was reinstated, but she didn't care. He was armed and definitely dangerous, and she wasn't stupid.

Stepping into the thick of the brush, Summer slowly made her way to the front corner of the garage, careful not to expose herself to the house. The garage door was closed and after reaching around and pulling on the handle with everything she had, she determined that it was also locked.

"Shit!" She tiptoed back around the side of the garage, peering in the backyard at the waves which were crashing against the retaining wall, splashing plumes of water high into the air, soaking the entire weed choked lawn.

There wasn't any sign of the kidnapper or of Sabrina in the windows, but somehow she didn't think they'd be sitting in the window, watching the waves crashing out back. He'd be busy formulating a plan or he'd be disposing—

Summer drew a deep breath, holding it as she darted across the slippery lawn until she was standing, pressed tightly against the house, beside the patio doors. As she peered around the frame, movement in the far corner of the room caught her eye. She froze, feeling her hand begin to shake. What if it was him? What if he was standing right inside that room? Could she pull the trigger? Could she gun him down right there before her daughter's eyes?

Summer shook her head.

She had to do it. She had no other choice but to eliminate him from the picture. Taking a second glance, she saw exactly what it was she'd seen. The black cat cautiously crept to the side of the door, curious to see who was outside the glass wall. Summer felt relieved, but silly at being caught off guard by the animal. She tensed when she heard the footsteps inside, moving toward the cat—and the door. They were heavy footfalls, not that of a child. Summer prepared herself to step to the side and take aim at the bastard's head and, if he so much as flinched, pull the trigger.

Just as she was about to step into the door opening, her phone rang, scaring the shit right out of her. She fell back against the house, the gun shaking uncontrollably in her hand as she dug in her pocket to silence the alarm. Once she retrieved the phone, she heard the lock on the door being thrown and the heavy glass pane sliding slowly open.

Summer took a step backwards and held the gun out, pointing it at the old man's head as he looked out with huge unblinking eyes. He looked as scared as Summer felt right now. His shirt was soiled and filthy, covered with stains and his hands reeked of fish, like he'd been busy cleaning his morning catch.

The old man grabbed the cat before it could slip out the door. "What's going on out here?"

"Just stay where you are!" Summer tightened her grip on the gun, careful not to squeeze the trigger and accidentally shoot the man. Suddenly she didn't think this was the kidnapper. There was no way this was the same person who'd knifed Dean, but Summer wasn't convinced that he wasn't involved.

"What?" She barked into the phone.

"Nate said you wanted to know first. We've run Percy through the registry and he's got a place he inherited from his grandmother out at the lake on Talbot Trail Road. 4479's the house number. Looks like it hasn't been lived in for a while. No record of power or water service."

"Thanks Stephens." Summer felt stupid standing there, holding her gun on an old man when the kidnapper was miles away. "I appreciate the information."

"No problem, but you understand I have to report it to the chief and the place will be swarming with cops in no time."

"I know. Thanks anyway." Summer flipped the phone closed and lowered her gun.

The old man let the cat lick his hands as he stepped back toward the patio door. "I don't know what you're looking after, but I couldn't help but overhear. Talbot Trail is back the other way, on the main road."

"Sorry, I thought you were someone else." She took a step back toward the side door on the garage and held her hand on the door knob. "Mind if I take a peek at your vehicle?"

The old man shrugged and tossed the cat back inside the house when it began nipping at his fingers. "Go ahead. Nothing to see but my old Buick." He grinned. "If you like it, I'd be willing to sell it for a couple grand."

Summer opened the door an inch and saw the old white car sitting in the middle of the garage. "Thanks, but I've already got a ride." She turned and stepped between the house and the garage. "Sorry about the intrusion. It's official police business."

Summer hurried back to the car, started it and raced back down the street, worried that the old man would pull out a shotgun, not believing that she was truly a cop and blow some rock salt in her ass. When she came to the main road, she turned left and raced back down the opposite direction like the old man had said, wondering just how long it'd take for the chief to get some cars out there.

CHAPTER 18

"What happened?" Dean said, scooting up in the seat and staring out into the direction where the dot had last transmitted from. "Where's the tracking dot?"

"Here, take the wheel." Gavin grabbed the unit from Dean and started adjusting the controls. "It seems to be working fine. So the question is, what the fuck happened to the transmitter?"

"You think she found it?"

"I still don't think that's possible unless someone tipped her off and she went searching for it. And we're the only ones who know about the transmitter, so it can't be that."

"Then what else?"

Gavin shrugged and handed the unit back to Dean. "Maybe she made the drop and the fucking kidnapper found it in the bag? He'd have reason to be searching for the device."

"And," Dean said, suddenly aware of the consequences of Gavin's stupidity, "if he found it then he'll think Summer placed it there so the cops could track him down and arrest him. He'll be pissed right off. Pissed enough at being double crossed to harm them."

"On second thought, this guy's a fucking amateur," Gavin said, shrugging his shoulders. "He won't even know what the fuck to look for. If he was organized, then he'd be able to pick up the electronic signal coming from the bag, but I doubt he'd be carrying that kind of fucking technology with him. He appears to be the grunt. Only told enough information to get him through the day. They wouldn't trust this guy with a fucking calculator."

"Since when are you such an expert on this kind of thing?"

"What do you think they talk about in prison? It's not all fucking licence plates and poems. They talk shop, and if you're smart, you fucking listen."

Dean zoomed in on the map, concentrating on the location where they'd last seen the blinking dot. He knew they were heading in the right direction, but with the amount of dirt roads and long laneways heading to farm houses and barns, there were a million places she could be. They could drive right past her if she was parked behind a barn or down in the middle of a farmer's field.

They continued on in the general direction for fifteen minutes until Dean heard the wail of an ambulance in the distance. He turned the radio off and opened his window, listening for the direction that the siren was coming from. "You hear that?"

Gavin nodded and glanced around, searching for the location. "It sounds like it's coming from over in that direction."

"Turn right at the next road." Dean pointed to the stop sign in the distance. "We haven't found shit wandering around like this, so let's hope Summer called the ambulance for the kidnapper."

Gavin nodded and turned down the next gravel roadway. It was quite a change from the smooth pavement and Dean could feel each and every pothole they hit. He propped himself off the seat with his arm, trying to ease the discomfort in his stomach and thought about popping another pain pill, but couldn't risk being tired and unresponsive when the time came to see Summer and Sabrina. He'd have to suck up the pain and try to use it to focus his mind.

When they were halfway to the next concession the ambulance flew past the approaching intersection, racing off into the countryside. Gavin sped up, flying down the washboard road toward the awaiting pavement ahead.

Dean bit his lip, trying to keep from crying out for Gavin to slow down. He knew if he asked, Gavin would obey and that was the last thing Dean wanted. They needed to stay close to the ambulance. It was their last shot at finding Summer.

Once the car was securely on the asphalt, Gavin pushed it to its limit, giving chase down the road. The siren was all but muted from the distance, but the flashing lights still beckoned from up ahead.

"Keep on it, Gavin. I've seen you drive faster than this before."

"I've got it to the floor!" Gavin pounded the steering wheel as the engine revved out of control. "This piece of shit is harder to get going than an eighty-year-old nun."

"Come on. Come on!" Dean leaned forward as they crest the next hill, gazing into the distance, looking for the ambulance up ahead, but it was gone. Nowhere in sight. "Shit, we've lost it!"

"No. Not yet."

Dean followed Gavin's gaze. The ambulance had turned down the next road and was beginning to slow to a stop. It was turning off the road, pulling onto a small laneway to the side.

Gavin slid the car around the corner, quickly following the ambulance's path. It wasn't until they were nearly upon the ambulance that they saw the police car in the muddy field, beside the laneway.

"Must have been a hell of a fucking ride," Gavin said, pulling to a stop beside the ambulance.

Dean recognized Nate immediately and wondered if he'd followed Summer out here, or if it'd been planned from the start for him to provide the back up. He hoped for the sake of their relationship, Summer had warned Nate not to follow like she had him.

After carefully climbing from the car, Dean stood leaning against the door, holding tight to the stitches in his stomach. He felt the sticky warn liquid on his fingers and knew even before he looked down that the wound was bleeding. "Damn it! Why can't this shit just stop?"

"What the fuck's wrong?" Gavin came around the car quickly and the look on his face said everything. "You really should be back at the fucking hospital."

"I'm fine."

"You don't look fine. You look like you might drop dead at anytime."

"Can I get a second opinion?"

"Okay, you're also ugly as fuck."

Dean shook his head and pushed off the car, stumbling around the front and avoiding Gavin's outstretched hands. "I don't need any help. It's just a little blood. Probably from you hitting every damn pothole down that road."

"And I wasn't even trying." Gavin smirked as he followed behind. "You just wait until the ride home. I'll drive the whole fucking way with two tires on the shoulder."

"I thought that's how you normally drove."

"You're hilarious when you're bleeding. Too bad you weren't a fucking woman. At least you'd be fun for four days a month."

"See." Dean stopped at the side of the lane, watching as the paramedics struggled in the mud to get Nate out of the car and onto the stretcher. "This is what I miss. Not your smiling face, or your shiny bald head, but your sick filthy mouth. What happened to you? Ever since you came to work for me you've been nothing like your old self, but now it comes back with vengeance."

"I didn't think you'd want me talking like that around the office."

"Not to customers, but it's okay around me. This is the Gavin that I remember growing up with. This is the sick fucker who'd gross me out so much I'd puke my guts out after dinner."

"Well, it's a pleasure to serve you again, master." Gavin took a step into the mud, watching as they placed Nate onto the stretcher. "Looks like he took a bullet to the chest. Must be up high or he wouldn't have survived for this long. The way he's moving around, I'd say more in the shoulder area."

"Lucky bastard," Dean said. "I just hope it wasn't Summer who'd shot him."

"Dean," Nate said as the paramedics trudged through the thick mud, dragging the stretcher closer to the laneway. "Summer's gone after him."

"Which way?" Dean felt the surge of adrenaline coursing through his veins just knowing that Summer was still on the move, getting closer to the kidnapper and Sabrina.

"Down toward the lake." Nate drew a sharp breath as the stretcher bounced when they set it down on the laneway. "He's driving a late model brown Silverado."

Dean turned and started back toward the car.

"And we've m—matched his prints from the car keys."

Dean stopped dead in his tracks. He knew if they had a match of the kidnapper's prints, then they'd also have a name for the bastard who'd stabbed him and sent his world careening out of control. And to have that name would make the kidnapper seem less powerful and more human.

"His name's Percy Campbell and he has some property down at the lake front. Inherited it from a grandmother, years ago. 4479 on the Talbot Trail." Nate sat up on the stretcher against the protesting hands of the paramedics. "Summer's g—gone there after him." Nate paused "Dean, he's got a rifle—and he's a pretty good s— shot from a long distance."

"You're a lucky man, Officer Long," the paramedic said. "A few inches to the side and we wouldn't be having this conversation."

Nate glared over at the young paramedic. "Ain't I lucky? Now, hold your tongue and give me a shot for the pain."

The paramedic took a step back from the stretcher, out of Nate's reach. "You just earned yourself a double shot of morphine."

Dean rounded the car, holding the fender as he went. "Which way did she go?"

Nate pointed behind the barn. "Down there, then right on the next concession. B—but she beat the hell out of my car going down there, so you'd better think about sticking to the main roads." Nate glanced at the bloodstain on Dean's shirt. "I'm guessing the bumps make you almost shit yourself."

"Something like that." Dean slowly slid back into the reclined seat and fought to close the door before Gavin backed out of the laneway. They followed Nate's directions down the road to the next corner, then turned left.

Dean lifted his hand and stared at his blood covered palm. "Nate looks like he should be all right."

Gavin glanced over at Dean's shirt. "Better than you."

CHAPTER 19

"Percy Campbell," Summer muttered. How could someone named Percy commit such terrible crimes? It just went against all the laws of logic. Percy was the name of a computer programmer, or an accountant. Not a kidnapper who'd tried to kill Dean and Nate.

Right now Summer wished she'd grabbed a cruiser instead of Nate's car. At least then she'd be able to pull up a photo of Percy on the computer and be able to recognize him if he drove by.

Summer continued on past the intersection, which she'd turned onto this road, and cursed at her decision to head east down to the old man's shack. It was a fifty-fifty chance and she'd come up empty. Nothing seemed to be going right today. Everything seemed to be falling apart, except for the prints from the keys. She couldn't believe it actually worked. She'd only read about the technique last month while flipping through a magazine, but it'd paid off big time. They had a name and hopefully Percy's hideout.

When Nate mentioned that Percy had done time up at Fenbrook, her mind was so caught up in finding Sabrina that it never really sunk in.

Fenbrook? That's where Gavin did his time. She knew the prison was huge, but she couldn't stop wondering if Gavin and Percy had known each other during their stay. If only she wasn't in such a rush to catch this bastard, she'd pull in Gavin and beat the truth out of him.

The road continued to climb higher with each mile she drove, as the trees thinned until she could see nothing but water down below the cliff. A few cars approached on the highway and Summer scanned the drivers and strained to see inside, wondering if Sabrina was hidden in the back.

Percy could've switched back to his first vehicle that he had stashed at the farm—the one they have a tire print from. It would only make sense, especially after she and Nate had both seen the truck. But that would mean Percy was on the run. No, he would've gone back to his hideout to lay low for a few days. But where on earth could he hope to go? The borders were all clamped down, looking for anybody with a child. So what was he going to do, sit and wait it out?

Summer glanced at the phone tucked beside her leg. Why hadn't he called yet? Why not take a chance and get the money he so desperately needed to get away from… from who?

"4479?" Summer said, wishing she had something to jot the number down on because she didn't trust her memory to keep it straight. She could easily mix up the digits and end up looking in the wrong area, potentially putting more people in danger.

She checked the number on the next mailbox as she soared past. 4563. At least she was heading in the right direction now. She was getting closer to Sabrina, she could feel it.

Summer glanced at the pistol on the seat beside. There was no way she could put it in her ankle holster for fear that Percy would be waiting to greet her when she arrived.

Just the thought of the gun gave her the boost she needed, and she had Nate to thank. Without him risking his job to retrieve the gun, she'd be walking into Percy's hideout like a lamb to the slaughter, begging him to take the money and release Sabrina.

The house numbers declined, growing close to Percy's hideout as the cliff grew to a dizzying height of over fifty feet. The view was magnificent, but the beach access left little to desire. As the land curved around, creating a slight cove, Summer saw the massive staircases the home owners had built down to the water's edge below. It seemed like a lot of work just to have access to the water for a quick dip, but she supposed if you paid the price for a beach front property, you wanted it any way you could get it.

Summer followed the curve of the road and slowed as the numbers counted closely down. She looked ahead and saw two homes on the far side of the treed lot and knew Percy's hideout was one of them.

Not risking being spotted driving past the house, Summer pulled across the roadway and tucked the car as far into the wooded lot as she could, praying that the rumble of the exhaust hadn't given away her arrival. After shutting off the car, she squinted at the closest house sign and realized that Percy's house should be on the far side of this home.

She paused with the door half open debating whether she should wait for backup, or if she should take the initiative and get Sabrina out of there before Percy goes nuts and does something she'll regret for the rest of her life.

When Summer glanced in the rearview mirror, she saw no flashing lights racing down the road in her direction and realized that she was all alone. It was her, or nobody.

She grabbed the gun and climbed from the car. There were no hiding places in the front yards. The homes were practically sitting right on the edge of the road, with a clear view of anybody approaching from either direction, so she turned and headed into the wooded lot beside.

As Summer made her way through the cloak of woods, she realized that she'd have to cut across the properties and approach Percy's hideout from the back, then hope to take him by surprise. When she stepped from the woods onto the manicured green grass, Summer heard the extent of the waves crashing below and hoped that it had been enough to mask the roar of the Malibu's broken exhaust.

She tried to put herself in Percy's shoes and figure out what his next move would be. He hasn't called since the botched drop off, so maybe he'd given up on getting the money, or maybe he decided to take off and disappear making ends meet another way? Or maybe he was waiting, staring through the sight of his rifle for me to come?

The first house appeared to be empty. Patio furniture had been stacked in the back corner beside the fence, next to the barbecue and every window covering had been drawn tightly closed to fend off the approaching winter winds. Keeping low, she moved across the back of the house until she came to the six-foot high fence separating this yard from the next, then followed the fence to the back of the property and the edge of the cliff. The owner had made his point. This fence was to keep the neighbours out as it stopped a foot short of falling off the edge of the cliff, leaving only a narrow, dangerous passageway into the next yard.

"If fences make good neighbours, then these guys should be best friends," Summer muttered, clinging to the fence post and peering carefully over the edge of the cliff. She felt her stomach flip at the sight of the fifty-foot drop, straight down to the sandy beach below and it made her realize just how much she hated heights.

At the far side of the yard, two huge cement pillars had been sunk deep in the ground with stairs attached to the upper landing. Her eyes followed the zigzagging levels down the side of the cliff until the stairs stopped beside the small boathouse.

A shutter filled her body as she stared down into the pit of churning water below. She holstered her gun, not willing to risk dropping it, then clamped her fingers onto the fencepost, clinging to it, praying that her stomach would stop flipping. It was a long ways down and she couldn't imagine braving those wooden steps in her life time.

The second she peered around the corner of the fence, she understood why the owner had erected such a large barrier. The house on the other side was like night and day. It looked totally rundown, beaten and battered by years of gusting wet winds coming off the lake. Of the two houses, this one screamed hideout if she'd ever seen one.

There was no mistaking that this was Percy's place. Besides being the right address, it reeked of being disregarded for years like the utility records showed.

With her fingernails dug into the wooden fence post, Summer closed her eyes and threw one leg around the fence, straddling the post and praying that she wouldn't slip and fall down the cliff. The sound of the waves crashing below combined with the pounding of her heart in her throat made her whole world spin like a top. It'd been years since she'd last fainted, but the way she felt right now, Summer didn't think fainting was far off.

She clamped her eyes so tight that the tears of fear couldn't even escape as she forced herself to move, dragging her right leg around the fence and collapsing to the ground, gasping for breath. Crawling to her knees, Summer swore she'd never do anything like that ever again in her lifetime. The fear of falling, arms flailing, to her death was too much to even comprehend. She guessed it was the feeling of no control as you sailed helplessly to your own demise, like what she'd felt with John Scott when he'd kept her hooded during the attacks. It was that same feeling of being in the dark, not knowing when death would come.

Summer wiped the tears from her face, squatted low behind the overgrown bushes next to the fence then withdrew her gun. She glanced inside every window on the back side of the house, but never saw any movement from the cracks in the drapes. If Percy was inside, he'd be busy watching for her to drive past, or at least approach from the front of the house. He would never expect her to know the exact location of his hideout, but she had outsmarted him.

The sound of a car approaching ignited fear that the backup was arriving as she waited, huddled down in the shadows. She couldn't stand the thought of being a witness to what was going to happen. She needed to be the cause and effect of the final outcome.

As the car soared past the house, continuing down the road, Summer took advantage of the distraction that would have old Percy running to the front windows, watching for the police to arrive, and dashed along the fence until she stood with her back against the house.

Peering in the first window, she saw the room was empty except for a dusty box lying in the centre of the room, overflowing with an assortment of old toys. Everything from dinky cars right up to a broken microscope sticking out the top. The layer of grime on the floors was enough to bring a tightening to her chest. With no fresh footprints in the room, she started to believe this wasn't his hideout after all.

Summer let her guard down and quickly moved to the next window. The old dining table was against the wall, tipped on its side and there was no indication that anybody had been here for years. The possibility of finding Sabrina here was dwindling with each second she spent gazing through the rotten old curtains.

Stepping to the back door, Summer tried the handle, but it was locked. She peered through the window and was willing to bet her life that nobody was home so she lifted her revolver and, after closing her eyes, tapped the butt of the gun on the thin glass window, shattering it into large fragments that fell noisily to the yellowed linoleum floor.

There was no screaming from inside. No footfalls racing to see what the noise was. There was nobody here. Not Percy and not Sabrina.

Reaching through the opening, Summer found the lock and quickly opened the door. Time was running out and she had to find Sabrina—and fast! She stepped quickly across the kitchen, scanning the front entrance floor for signs of visitors, but the floor was undisturbed.

Moving through the house at a dangerous speed, unconcerned about her own safety and well-being, Summer checked every room but came up empty handed. The house was vacant and it had been for a long time. Sabrina had never been here.

Maybe she was dealing with a smart man after all? He'd planned the whole kidnapping so thoroughly and seemed to be prepared for anything they threw at him, even smart enough not to use the obvious hideout. But where else would he go? He was definitely heading down to the lake front. But why would he settle for this rundown place when half the other cottages were sitting empty, packed up for the approaching winter weather? Why settle for a cold damp building with no running water? Why not find an empty cottage and invite yourself in for a little visit?

"Think like a criminal on the lam. If I had to hide out, I'd want somewhere where I could see the cops coming, and somewhere where I could see them checking my grandmother's place, knowing that they're getting close and knowing that it's time to get out of the area."

Summer cautiously stepped to the front window and glanced across the road at the empty field which stretched for miles and miles. There was no place comfortable across there. She moved back into the kitchen and glanced out the window on the end of the house.

She knew it the second she saw it. There down the road, partially hidden in a sloping valley was the ideal hideout. A large beach house sat perched on the edge of the cliff, equipped with a double car garage big enough to hide a brown Silverado and a car that would match the tire print back at the station.

Summer stepped to the side of the window, peering down at the beach house. There was movement inside the window, but from this distance she couldn't tell if it was from a man or child. She backed away, searching through the boxes on the floor for a pair of binoculars, but there was none. Only cheap old china and dusty blue drinking glasses filled the rotten cardboard.

"Looks like even he didn't want this shit." Summer moved down the hall and into the first room she'd glanced into. She remembered seeing the microscope sitting atop the old box and ran inside, dumping the contents onto the floor. She heard the glass crack as the microscope hit the hardwood floor, but fumbled to grasp the rolling telescope as it tumbled over the assorted toys.

"Bingo," Summer said, raising the kids telescope from the toys and peering quickly through the lens. "Dusty, but then again what isn't dusty in here?"

Moving quickly through the house, careful to stay out of sight, Summer rubbed the thick dusty grime from the glass lenses. The movement in the beach house was gone, but that was good. She'd hate to stick the telescope in the window and have the kidnapper see the sun reflect off the lens.

Summer tipped the telescope toward the window. The landscape bounced through the viewfinder, making her dizzy in the process. Trees passed by upside down and Summer looked away from the viewfinder, peered out the window then aimed the telescope in the right direction.

When she gazed back into the viewfinder, her breath caught in her throat. It was Sabrina inside that house. She was there. Right there! Inside that room. Summer scanned the rest of the house, peering into each window as she went, but there was no sign of Percy.

"Where the hell are you, Percy? Did you take off and leave Sabrina behind?" There was a quick flash of movement and a growing shadow on the inside wall. Summer quickly stepped to the side of the window and dropped the telescope to the floor.

It was time to go. Time to make her move and get Sabrina.

Summer stepped out the back door, tucking in close to the wall and hoping for her sake that Percy wasn't aiming binoculars in this direction. But he'll be watching out front for me to come down the road.

The empty field between this house and the beach house down in the valley was sparse and rocky, nothing like the wooded lot where she'd left the Malibu sitting. There was no way she'd be able to cross it without being spotted, and that was exactly why Percy had chosen it. It stood all alone with a clear view of the countryside in all directions. Every direction except beyond the cliff.

Summer scanned the backyard of the beach house and saw the familiar sight of the zigzagging stairs at the very edge of the cliff. It was identical to the staircase mounted at the back of the next door neighbours yard—the one she swore she'd never step foot on.

Summer's legs started shaking at the thought of scaling down the cliff side on that wooden deathtrap.

There has to be another way. Summer racked her brain, but knew unless she had the cloak of night, she was shit out of luck. It was either take the back way in, or take the risk of being gunned down in broad daylight.

She held her gun out, peering through the sight. She'd been one of the best shots on the force, but she knew a rifle always won for shooting distance. She had to get close. Close enough to take a clean shot at Percy's head, because if she took a shot and missed her mark, it would cost Sabrina's life.

"Damn it!" Summer moved quickly down the steps, hugging the back of the house as she made her way along the yard. When she met the fence, she climbed on the overturned flowerpot and jumped for the top of the high fence. Her hands ached gripping the cold wooden boards, but Summer concentrated on the task. She'd done obstacle courses in her past and nothing ever slowed her down. She could scale a fence like this at full speed and drop down before most had a chance to throw a foot over. So why was she having such a hard time now? She knew she should've been over it in five seconds flat, but here she was hanging onto the top board, grimacing in pain.

Summer knew her reluctance was only mental. She still had the same physical abilities as she did five months ago. Her body had healed. There was nothing wrong with it. She stared at her shaking hands clinging to the top board and wondered how deep the mental wounds had cut.

Dropping back on top of the flower pot, Summer stared at her uncooperative arms. The strength was still there, just forgotten, that's all. She thought about Sabrina over there in the next home and tried to picture Percy.

"John Scott's dead," Summer muttered. "He can't hurt you anymore. What he's done is passed, stripped away like his life before your eyes. He can't cause you any more harm." She clenched her hands, flexing the tightness from her joints. "He is dead."

Summer pictured Percy driving away in the Mercedes with Sabrina crying in the back seat. That rage of anger was returning to her body and it felt good. She concentrated hard on the look of fear in Sabrina's beautiful eyes until her body was shaking with fury.

Summer ran, stepped on the flowerpot and jumped to the top of the fence, landing with one leg over the top board. It wasn't her best, but it was good enough to get the job done. Dragging the other leg over, she fell to the soft ground with an awkward thud then got quickly to her feet, not letting her mind think about anything but Sabrina's cries for help.

Safe from Percy's sight, she ran through the backyard toward the upper landing of the wooden staircase. Once there, she clung to the railing and nervously looked over the edge. Down to her right sat a much larger boathouse, with a shorter staircase rising from the sand to the back of the beach house where Percy was holding Sabrina.

The house was beautiful. It must have cost a fortune to build something that size, and right on the edge of paradise.

Summer stepped out onto the landing, her hands still clamped to the top posts, reluctant to let go of the stable platform and trust in the craftsmanship of some stranger. Standing on the edge, she saw how large the waves were and how far up the shore they were crashing. The bottom landing of the staircase was already getting soaked from the constant spray of the crashing waves and they seemed to be growing with every second she stood there.

Drawing a huge breath and holding it, Summer let go of the post with one hand and quickly snatched the small wobbly railing along the exposed side of the cliff. She felt the whole structure sway with the shift in her weight and couldn't believe the owners actually used this contraption to get down to the water.

One foot after the other, she felt bile rising up her throat until it nearly choked her. When she reached the first landing, she bent over the railing, holding onto it with a death grip and hurled the contents of her stomach over the side, down to the soft wet sand below.

Summer wiped her mouth on her sleeve and gazed from the landing, up to the top of the staircase. She'd only travelled down ten steps, with about forty more to go, and even though she didn't want to navigate forty more, at least she was descending and not climbing.

Forcing herself to move, Summer turned on the landing and started down the next level of stairs. These ones seemed to be going better. Either she was becoming more comfortable with descending the wobbly stairs, or she was losing her mind and forgetting how much she hated heights. Either way it didn't matter. All that mattered was getting to the wet sand below, then safely across to where Sabrina was.

One step after another, Summer contemplated how she would get Sabrina out of the house alive, and everything came down to two options. One, she'd snatch Sabrina while Percy wasn't looking and rush her away to safety. Or two, she'd blow his fucking brains all over the modern artwork inside the beach house.

Halfway down, a large gust of wind slammed the staircase against the cliff side, knocking some sand and rocks loose, sending then falling to the platform below. Summer held tight to the railing and as soon as the stairs stopped rocking, she hurried down the remaining flights until her feet were standing on the solid wooden platform at the base of the stairs. She glanced up the cliff to where the earth met the sky and marvelled at how she'd conquered her greatest fear.

"Holly shit!" Summer stepped off the platform and onto the wet sand. "I'm so glad that's over." She hurried down the beach, dodging the waves as they crashed dangerously close to the base of the cliff.

Her legs felt like rubber as she half jogged, half limped down the beach, already nervously eyeing the staircase in the distance.

CHAPTER 20

The wind coming off the lake dropped the temperature five degrees, bringing a chill deep inside her body and numbness to her hands and feet. Summer hurried along the stretch of beach, ignoring the fact that her right foot was getting sorer and sorer with each step she took. She could feel the cut burning, flaring up and igniting the entire depth of the wound. Normally a cut like that wouldn't have bothered her if she'd gone home and rested it, but there was nothing normal about today. Nothing to say the least.

Once she reached the base platform for the stairs, Summer realized just how massive the boathouse was. It could easily house two twenty-footers and still have room for more. Not only that, but the front of the building was designed more like a guest house than a place to launch a boat from.

Summer turned her attention to the staircase reaching up the side of the cliff. It was built better than the last one, and the height of the cliff had dropped off considerably as they neared the valley, but the idea of climbing up it still terrified her.

"With all their money, you'd think they could afford an elevator," Summer muttered, stepping onto the lower platform and grasping the double railing. Each step she took, she breathed a sigh of relief at how much nicer this staircase was. Maybe it was the fact she was only climbing half the distance, or maybe she was just getting better at dealing with her fear of heights, but she was making good time and would soon be at the top of the stairs, gazing into Percy's hideout.

She paused, patting her leg and feeling the security of the pistol strapped there. It was quite a morale booster, but she knew even without it, she'd still be planning the same thing, only her chance of success would be near zero.

The wind gusts continued to grow in strength as she neared the top of the cliff. The air was crashing, surging up the side and lifting her shirt periodically, bringing an icy chill all the way up her back.

Climbing the last step to the final landing before exposing herself above the ridge of the cliff, Summer paused and withdrew her gun from the holster. She thought many times during the climb about getting her gun ready in case Percy was waiting at the top of the stairs, but in her current condition she didn't dare trust her hands not to drop the gun down to the sandy pit beneath. Now, holding the gun in her hand, her finger gripping the trigger tightly, grateful that the safety was on, Summer slowly climbed the remaining ten stairs, scrunching down as her head protruded over the top of the cement landing.

She kept low, scouring the windows for any sign of Percy or Sabrina, but the rooms were empty. Satisfied she could get safely off the stairs and make a mad dash to the garden shed at the back corner, Summer scurried up the remaining steps and ran, limping across the lawn, diving for cover behind the shed.

Squatting behind the shed with her right leg stretched outward, kneading her ankle with her free hand, Summer scouted the layout of the house and yard, contemplating what her best move would be. She'd seen Sabrina in the side window on the right and assumed she'd still be there waiting while Percy formulated another plan.

Summer pulled the phone from her pocket and glanced at the display, making sure it was still working and receiving a strong signal. The fact Percy hadn't tried calling since he took the shot at Nate, unnerved her. Maybe he thought the deal was too risky now that he'd tried to kill a police officer? If his time behind bars had taught him anything, it would be that cops don't take kindly to a cop killer—Or in Percy's case, an attempted kill.

Sliding to the edge of the shed, Summer peered through the patio doors, into the back sitting room which overlooked the scenic lake view. There was absolutely no movement from inside that room and by her calculations, Percy wouldn't be the least bit interested in watching from behind. He'd have no reason to believe the cops would place him in this house. The only thing linking him to this home was its vicinity to his grandmother's place, but even Percy would know it'd be a long shot for the cops to connect the places together, so he'd feel very secure sitting, peering between the blinds, watching the roadway.

Convinced of her theory, Summer moved quickly from the shed, keeping low as she went, sneaking toward the house. She kept large objects close in her path in case she saw even the slightest shadow move inside.

Summer dodged toward the iron patio furniture then paused, resting her burning legs. This was the most action she'd seen in many months and realized her previous training habits had fallen to the wayside for the last while. She cursed, knowing she should never have let her body deteriorate like she had. She should've kept up the regiment even if her heart and mind were breaking.

Standing tall, Summer felt the burn in her muscles and realized the feeling was more satisfying than any pill she'd popped down her throat. She dashed to the rear of the home feeling alive once again and wedged her back against the stucco wall beside the patio door. Her heart pounded so loudly in her ears, she swore she wouldn't be able to hear if Percy were standing right beside, talking to her.

The patio door was closed, so she reached out a finger and pushed with everything she had, but the door wouldn't budge. It was either locked, or heavier than she thought it should be. After taking a quick glance in the room, Summer stepped past the door and slid in behind the tall potted spruce on the other side. It made for good cover, allowing her to squat and peer through the house while still being hidden from sight.

From this angle she could see through this back room, into the large open kitchen and even the two doors on the far side. She knew Sabrina was located in one of those rooms, but couldn't be sure which one it was. She'd seen her sitting inside, and should've remembered which it was, but her emotions were running so high with relief that she couldn't be sure.

Summer couldn't decide what to do next. Should she round the side of the house and peer into the room where Sabrina was, then hope she could somehow get her out of the window without her screaming with joy, or for that fact, without Percy noticing the smashing of the glass. Maybe if Sabrina were a few years older, her reaction might be more predictable, but for now she had to assume the worst—that Sabrina would scream and cry and draw unwanted attention her way. Or, if all else failed, Summer could break the lock on the patio door, storm inside and gun Percy down on the ceramic tiled kitchen floor.

Five months ago it would've been no decision. She would've done just that without a second thought. She would've loved to see the look of terror in Percy's eyes when she appeared from nowhere, holding his pea brain in the sight of her gun until he surrendered.

With the lack of movement inside, Summer wondered if Percy had vacated the house while she'd been busy navigating the stairs and beach. Suddenly she had to know. Had to know if she was wasting precious time. She needed to take matters into her own hands and make things happen instead of waiting to react to the situation.

Summer ducked down below the window height and ran along the back of the house to the attached garage. Once there she stepped to the window and peered inside. The brown Silverado was there, closest to the window, while a white car occupied the remaining spot. Breathing a sigh of relief, she bent and plucked an iron garden stake from the flowerbed then held it before her eyes. The pointed end of the stake was perfect.

She dug the end of the stake into the meshing of the window screen, slicing it straight across the bottom of the window. After grasping the black netting, she yanked it loose from the frame in one quick motion.

After a sideways push on the glass, she realized the window was locked. Summer holstered her gun then used both hands to force the iron stake between the window and the frame. It took a few tries before she was able to wedge the stake securely between the two. She pried the window, watching as the plastic frame bowed and stretched. She swore the glass was about to break and shatter into a thousand pieces, but it held strong, keeping its tempered ability as the window opened with a light popping noise.

Pausing and listening for any sound from within, Summer held her breath and waited for a second longer, then dropped the stake to the ground and slid the window all the way open. Carefully she gripped the top of the window sash and lifted herself, throwing her right leg up and through the window opening. Once she was balanced on the lip of the window, she pulled her other leg through and dropped softly to the cement floor in the garage.

Running her hand quickly over the truck's hood, she confirmed her suspicion. The engine was still warm. She did the same thing as she passed the car, but got a different response this time. She paused at the front of the car then ducked between the two vehicles and started to unscrew the valve caps. Squatted down, she let the air out of both front tires at the same time, knowing that it wouldn't stop him from trying to get away in either vehicle, but it'd certainly slow him down quite a bit.

Summer stepped softly as she headed for the door to the house, but swore she could still hear each footfall echoing through the garage as she went. Over on the far wall was an assortment of tools and Summer eyed the pry bar, keeping it in mind in case the door was locked. She held her breath as she climbed the steps to the door, praying that she wouldn't need to use the pry bar to force the door open and lose the element of surprise. With the handle gripped tightly, she felt her hand begin to shake until the knob twisted slowly to the right.

The knob turned freely and a second later it stopped with her hand fully twisted. He'd left this door unlocked. Probably figured it was safe enough beings it was inside the garage. Pushing the door open a sliver, she peered inside the back entrance room. It was a huge mudroom separating the garage from the main living area.

Stepping quietly inside, Summer tiptoed across the room, standing paralysed at the door, listening for any sounds from within. There were footfalls in the room to her left.

Probably Percy pacing before the picture window, waiting to shoot her down the second she arrived.

She opened the closet door slowly, careful in case the hinges were noisy, then searched inside for anything that might help. There was little left in the house, only a pair of winter coats and boots in case the owners decided to come here for a Christmas dinner, but just behind the coats was something interesting. A cold air return mounted in the top of the closet. Summer stepped inside the closet and tipped her ear toward the metal grate. Percy rambled as he continued his pacing in the other room, but as hard as she tried, she couldn't make out a single word.

Stepping out of the closet, she opened the door to the kitchen and almost screamed out at the sight of Sabrina sitting in the room straight across from where she stood. The urge to run across the kitchen and scoop her into her arms was almost unbearable. Her heart ached just seeing her there, knowing she couldn't touch her.

The sound of Percy pacing in the other room was louder now, drifting through the swinging door that separated this end of the kitchen from the front room. His ranting seemed to be getting louder with each passing moment. He seemed to be losing it. Everything he'd tried today went wrong and it looked like the pressure was getting the better of him. She watched as his shadow cast upon the door, blocking the sunlight from passing under the base.

Summer opened the mudroom door wide, hoping that Sabrina would see her and come quietly across the kitchen to where she stood. The waiting was almost unbearable as Sabrina was totally engrossed in something in the other room. Something that was holding her attention even during the strenuous circumstances of today.

Waving her hands, Summer stepped from the mudroom and cautiously walked into the kitchen, between the counter and the island, making her way slowly across the room toward Sabrina. She gave up trying to catch Sabrina's attention and pulled her gun from the holster then held it trembling, pointed at the ground. She paused, hearing Percy's voice growing louder as he neared the end of the wall which separated the kitchen from the front room. His footsteps ended dangerously close to the corner and Summer raised the gun, watching it shake before her eyes.

She was all prepared to fire if Percy stepped around the corner. But instead, he muttered something then turned and paced back in the other direction. She felt weak with relief and stepped to the edge of the separation, waiting for a chance to dash into Sabrina's room. It took two more times of Percy pacing dangerously close to the kitchen before she built up enough courage to take the chance.

With her finger tight on the trigger, she waited for him to reach the turning point at the kitchen wall, then when he turned, she made her move. Stepping quickly from the kitchen wall, she raised the gun and quietly tiptoed across the opening and slid into Sabrina's room, placing her back to the wall.

Sabrina was glued to the television, totally engrossed in her favourite show which she watched every day at home. It was no wonder with everything that had happened today, she was more than willing to let her mind drift away from the horror, back to the world of fantasy for an escape.

Sabrina looked fine. Not a single mark was visible on her little face. Glancing around the room, Summer realized that Percy had taken good care of her. It was almost as if he was told to treat her nice.

Once Percy made another pass near the kitchen, Summer moved quickly behind Sabrina and scooped her up, covering her mouth in the process. Sabrina fought for a second then let up when she recognized whose arms she was in. It was almost like magic how fast she relaxed in Summer's arms and when she removed her hand from Sabrina's mouth, there was a huge smile waiting for her.

"Shh," Summer whispered into her ear, feeling the warmth of contentment spreading throughout her entire body. She smiled and placed a kiss on Sabrina's forehead as she carried her back against the wall. Anxiety was growing, replacing the feeling of contentment with each passing second. Summer wanted to get out of there—and fast. The sooner she was gone, the better.

Percy continued muttering his rant as he paced back toward the front room and Summer made her move. She hurried across the open expanse between the bedroom and the kitchen, chancing a look into the front room at Percy. His back was turned toward her as he slowly walked to the front window, gazing out the crack in the curtain. She felt good, like she was almost assured a quick speedy escape. She knew she'd have to brave the staircases again, but that was all right. At least now she had Sabrina to hold onto and that would definitely take her mind off the height.

Moving between the cabinets and the island, she watched the open mudroom door, anxiously anticipating her escape, but the moment she and Sabrina passed the swinging door, it burst open and Percy came rushing through, crashing hard into Summer's side, sending her and Sabrina sprawling to the floor.

Percy's eyes were full of rage and his fist was clenched into a tight massive rock. He charged at her, landing on top and knocking the gun from her hand, sending it skidding across the room toward the patio doors. Summer glanced at Sabrina, who was two feet away, climbing to her knees. The fear in her beautiful eyes nearly broke Summer's heart as she reached out her hands, begging for the man to stop.

Summer grasped toward the gun as it slid to a stop across the room, then gave up and turned just in time to see

Percy swatting Sabrina away, sending her crashing into the wall. He turned to face Summer and his eyes were bloodshot and wild as he climbed on top, positioning himself firmly in control. Percy drew back his fist as his face twisted into a horrible look of fear and anger. His first punch landed on her left cheek, sending an explosion of stars through her mind and pain surging through her jaw.

"Why couldn't you make this easy!" He sat up, drawing his arm back again. "Why did you have to get the cops to follow you?" He slammed another fist into her face and Summer could taste blood oozing inside her mouth and could hear Sabrina screaming at the top of her lungs.

"I didn't want to shoot him. It's all your fault for letting him follow."

Summer wanted to argue. She wanted to tell him that she had nothing to do with Nate following her, but she knew better. She knew her best chance of getting out of here alive was to play possum, so she closed her eyes and laid still on the floor, hoping that he would underestimate her pain tolerance and leave her be, passed out on the floor.

CHAPTER 21

Dean spotted Nate's red Malibu sitting off the roadway, hidden in the thick of trees. He'd been counting the house numbers, and Percy's would be on the other side of this one.

"That one!" He pointed to the decrepit grey house that looked in complete contrast to the house beside. "Right there."

Gavin glanced at the Malibu then back to the house Dean was pointing at. He didn't argue and sped toward the flaking grey clapboard house, sliding the car to a stop in the front yard. Gavin was the first one out and already running for the front door, leaving Dean behind, struggling to get out of the car.

"Remember what Nate said!" Dean screamed as loud as he could. "He's got a gun." He realized that it was too late, Gavin had already kicked down the front door and disappeared inside the dark mouth of the grey monster. Dean couldn't believe how determined Gavin was to get Sabrina back. He seemed willing to risk his life like a madman just to stop this Percy guy from hurting anybody else.

"God Damn it!" Dean said, standing and feeling the intense pain ripping through his stomach. With the medication wearing off, he could feel every muscle movement tugging at the stitches. Placing a hand over the wound, he could feel the warm, wet trickling of blood seeping from his body. He took a step toward the broken front door, sliding his hand down the hood of the car as he went, hopeful not to fall flat on his face.

The sound of waves crashing below the cliff brought a warm feeling to his heart. He remembered how excited Sabrina got every time they brought her to the beach. She loved playing in the sand and chasing the waves as they broke on the beach. But, today the waves sounded fierce, angry at the world. Normally they visited Rondeau Park where the beaches stretched on for miles, but at this location the water had a definite churning effect, driving the waves hard against the cliff.

Dean let go of the car and stumbled up the front steps, into the house. It left little to be desired. Everything was covered with dust and grime and falling apart. The footprints on the floor gave away Gavin's path as it appeared he'd ran throughout each room, searching for any sign of Summer and Sabrina, but it was the smaller set of prints in the room to his right that attracted Dean's attention. They were the perfect size of Summer's feet. He'd be able to identify them anywhere. He walked across the room and stopped, standing with his feet planted firmly where hers had been not long ago.

"She'd stood right here, looking out this window at something." He shuffled closer to the window, squinting into the distance, trying to decide what Summer had found so interesting, but there wasn't much to see, only an enormous home perched on the edge of the cliff down in the valley.

He turned away from the window and started toward the back door when his foot hit something. He glanced down, spotting the cylindrical object rolling toward the wall. Realizing what it was and where Summer had been standing, he quickly picked up the telescope and rushed back to the window.

"What were you looking at?" Dean muttered, aiming the telescope over the empty land, stopping when the house came into view.

Something out there had enticed her to leave this house and he intended to find out exactly what that might have been. He followed the roof top of the house, lowering the telescope carefully until he could see into the side window. Someone was home. There was definitely some movement going on inside that house, but he had a hard time keeping the telescope steady enough to make out anything other than dark shapes and rolling images.

Dean propped the telescope on the bottom edge of the windowsill then bent over, and ignoring the pain, focused the dial on the side window of the house. He saw the side room was empty, but just beyond the entrance to that room was some movement. He watched as a man came into the opening. His shirt was ripped and stained.

Dean held his breath. It appeared to be stained with blood. He waited, continuing to hold his breath and ground his teeth as the man pulled someone into the opening.

It was Summer!

Feeling his stomach lurch, he watched as the man held Summer by the neck, choking her before his eyes. Her blond hair was streaked with blood and her eye was swollen and split wide open.

Dropping the telescope to the ground and shattering the glass lens, Dean hurried back to the front entrance frantically looking for Gavin, but he was nowhere to be found. He tried to call out for him, but the pain was too intense, so instead he did the only thing he could think of. He hurried to the car and climbed behind the wheel. Once the car was started, he floored the pedal and tore ruts in the front lawn all the way to the road.

"He's going to kill her," Dean muttered. He never thought it would end like this. He wanted a happy ending like he deserved—not this. Not to find his wife strangled to death. And... Sabrina? What would that bastard do to Sabrina?

Dean didn't know how much longer Summer could survive before Percy would choke the life right out of her. He had to get there and stop it, but how, he wasn't in any shape to put up a fight. He knew, at best, he'd only be an annoyance to Percy, so Dean opted for a less conventional means of attack. He pressed the pedal all the way to the floor and felt the car surge down the decline in the road, awkwardly steering the car while holding the house in his sights as the speedometer steadily climbed.

He could picture Percy and Summer fighting just outside that room and turned the car sharply at the last moment, sending it screaming from the pavement onto the grass, sliding toward the side window. The car hit the incline of the raised, manicured lawn and became airborne for a second before crashing into the side of the house, beside the window.

The impact sent Dean smashing into the steering wheel, knocking the breath from his lungs. Even with debris crashing down all around, he could feel the car continuing to move through the room, finally coming to rest as the inside wall gave way, wedging the car under the weight of the collapsed structure.

Dust and plaster filled the air, slowly dissipating as the wind carried it out the gaping hole and off on the strong winds. Pushing his body away from the dash and clearing the shattered glass from his body, Dean grunted and groaned, feeling not only like he'd been stabbed, but beaten and battered by a heavyweight fighter.

All of a sudden Dean remembered why he was there, stuck inside the crumbling walls of this beach house. "S— ummer!"

He opened the door, slamming it into the shattered remains of a dresser, then fought to slide out the opening and onto the floor. As he got to his feet, he realized what a mess the house was in. He'd destroyed the entire side of the building and smashed down the wall—the wall where Percy had been killing Summer.

Holding onto the car, Dean made his way around the back of the car, toward the hole in the sloping wall where a door once had hung.

He let go of the crumpled car fender and lurched for the door opening, grasping onto the jamb and staring through into the kitchen. The sight of Summer lying motionless on the floor sent a wave of panic through his body. He staggered across the room, tripping on his own feet and falling hard to the ceramic tile beside Summer.

"Summer…" Dean whispered, lifting her head from the hard floor and placing his face in front of her mouth. "Please… be alive."

Her hot moist breath had never felt so good and he couldn't stop the smile from engulfing his face as a tear fell, landing on her chin. He couldn't stop the tears from falling. It'd been a long time since he'd felt this content. Dean stroked the blood soaked hair from her face and kissed her. It felt good.

Like magic, his touch brought her back to reality. Her one good eye snapped open and she looked around, taking in the whole situation.

"Sabrina?" Summer cried, struggling to get off the floor. "Where's Sabrina?"

Dean tried to match the speed she was moving with, but he couldn't. Suddenly he realized that he was in worse shape. The stitches had been ripped completely out, probably from the impact of the crash, and the blood was flowing pretty good. Summer was totally oblivious to his injury as she searched the house for any sign of Percy or Sabrina.

With Summer distracted, Dean headed for the kitchen counter and riffled through the contents of the drawers, searching for a cloth to plug the hole in his stomach. He had to stop the bleeding or he would drop soon and never get back up. The second drawer he opened, he found exactly what he needed, a small washcloth. He lifted his shirt and held it before the gaping hole, trying not to think of the pain he was about to endure, but it was impossible. He knew it would hurt—hurt like hell.

Summer limped across the room, stuck her head into the garage, then turned her attention to the open patio door. She muttered something about Percy going to the boathouse as she passed, totally oblivious to the fact that Dean was patching himself up.

Dean could barely make out her ramblings as she stepped through the patio doors and ran awkwardly toward the staircase at the back of the yard.

After catching his breath, Dean found some packing tape in the next drawer and began wrapping it tightly around his waist, sealing the washcloth inside his body and slowing the loss of blood. As he finished the roll off, he watched Summer hesitate briefly at the top of the stairs before cautiously disappearing over the edge.

He sighed at the sight of Summer, battered and beaten near death, charging after the person who'd hurt her. It was like she had not a care in the world about herself. She was more like her old self now than that cowering sack of flesh John Scott had left for dead, and it made him feel better knowing the old Summer was going after Sabrina.

Staggering toward the patio door, Dean eyed the black object under a chunk of plaster. He walked carefully around the damaged wall and bent slowly, then reconsidered and dug the object from the rubble with his foot. He recognized it immediately. It was Summer's gun. He didn't know how the hell she'd gotten her gun back, but it was definitely department issued.

Once the gun was free, Dean leaned over, feeling the tape tighten as he bent. He bit his lip as the pain spread throughout his entire stomach area, but continued stretching until his fingers felt the cold steel, then snatched the gun from the floor.

Standing and fighting to regain his breath, he held the gun before his eyes. The cold steel felt good in his hand. Suddenly Dean realized that if he had the gun, then that meant Summer didn't.

CHAPTER 22

With her left eye swollen almost completely shut, Summer found descending the stairs was even more difficult. Her fear of heights had been bad, but add the dizzying effect of losing one side of her vision and it made her almost sick to her stomach to take each step. But Summer couldn't slow down. She had to keep going after them, so she slid her hands down the railing, slipping and stumbling on steps that appeared to be closer than they actually were.

When the howling winds relented, she could hear the screams of a child sailing up the cliff side, stabbing her straight in the heart. Sabrina was down there and Percy was harming her.

Summer spit the taste of blood from her mouth, wondering what that sick fucker was doing to Sabrina right now and her head almost exploded with rage just thinking about it.

"Fuck the law!" Summer muttered, knowing Percy may have gotten the best of her back there, but only because he'd taken her by surprise. She felt her temper flare and had only one thing on her mind—Kill Percy!

"Fuck the trial by jury." She knew Percy was guilty and was about to enact her own brand of justice on him, saving the taxpayers the burden of supporting his sorry ass for a life sentence behind bars.

Pausing, she reached for the ankle holster then her waist band, but there was no gun. She tried to think back. Tried to remember where she'd dropped it. Then it hit her hard. She remembered fighting to scramble across the kitchen floor after it.

"Shit." Summer flung her blood soaked hair back from her good eye and hurried down the steps. She was almost to the bottom when she heard a sharp cry from within the boathouse. There was no mistaking it. It was Sabrina. She was crying from his hands. Hurt and scared enough to call for help.

"Don't worry, baby," Summer muttered, taking the steps two at a time. "Mommy's coming—and Mommy's gonna stop that son of a bitch!"

Leaping from the last few steps, she landed hard, feeling the pain shoot up her right leg, but fought the urge to accept the pain as real. It was nothing more than an annoyance to her right now. She could be running on a broken ankle for all she cared, because it wouldn't make any difference right now. Pain only meant she was still alive.

Summer ran across the wooden deck connecting the stairs to the large boathouse and lunged at the weathered wooden door. She threw herself full force, shoulder tightened for the impact, toward the handle side of the door. The impact jarred her body, but it felt great. Felt like the old days when she and Nate would argue about whose turn it was to force open a locked door during a chase.

Today she won the tossup and felt relieved, hearing the shattering of aged wood splintering into a hundred pieces. The door flung open, slamming against the inside wall with a loud crack. She stumbled a few steps inside before regaining her footing. Percy stood over Sabrina's tiny body, bounding her securely in tape, wrapping a final piece over her mouth. He stopped immediately, staring in shock at Summer.

"Let her go, you fucking son of a bitch!" Summer yelled, charging across the room straight at the man who'd caused her so much pain and anguish today. His eyes were wild, like a caged animal readying for the attack as he stood tall, holding Sabrina in his hands before him.

Summer cut the room in half when Percy launched Sabrina at her. The image of a bound child sailing across the room with no way of softening her impact was enough to stop Summer in her tracks. The terror on Sabrina's face was enough to split Summer's heart in two. She couldn't let her fall to the floor. She had to save her from another ounce of pain.

Diving forward, she reached out her arms, praying she'd make the distance in time. Her eyes were locked on Sabrina's and Summer wondered if she was strong enough to make the catch without dropping her.

The impact of the deadweight in her outstretched arms pulled Summer forward, causing her to lose momentum. Down she went, pulling Sabrina close, anticipating the impact. She crashed to the wooden floor with a bone jarring impact that knocked the wind from her lungs. Summer grasped wildly, feeling Sabrina bounce, and gripped her sides tight as they slid across the wooden planks.

After drawing her close, Summer never thought it would feel this good to hold her daughter again. She knew she would cherish this moment for the rest of her life.

214

Quickly she pulled the tape from Sabrina's mouth, and after scurrying to the sitting position, cradled her like a newborn.

"Oh, baby," Summer kissed her face, smearing traces of blood across her cheek. "You're okay." She began removing the tape from around her body. "I missed you so much, baby. I don't know what I would've done if I'd lost you."

There were tears in Sabrina's eyes as she raised her freed hand and gently touched Summer's swollen eye. Summer tried not to react to the touch, but she flinched with the pain. "He lied, Mommy. He said he would never hurt me. He said he would never hurt you."

"It's nothing. Just a little scratch." Summer finished unwrapping the tape, listening to the commotion in the boathouse as Percy was destroying the place, searching for something.

She set Sabrina down on the floor. "You stay right here. Mommy needs to have a little talk with him."

"No—don't go!" Sabrina stood, grabbing onto Summer's sleeve. "Don't leave me."

"I'll be right back. You stay right here. I need to make sure that bad man doesn't hurt anybody else. You wouldn't want him to hurt any of your friends, would you?"

Sabrina shook her head reluctantly.

"Go hide in the corner over there. And if he comes back before Mommy, then keep hiding until the police show up."

"Officer Nate?" Sabrina muttered while walking slowly toward the corner.

Summer nodded, even though she knew Nate wouldn't be coming to the rescue today. "Or another officer."

When Sabrina was safely in the corner, Summer ran to the door that Percy had disappeared through a few seconds ago. She stood searching the large dark room, listening for any sign of the bastard. It wasn't until something fell in the connecting room to the left that she ran to the door and threw it open.

Percy was standing at the side of the boat with the keys in his hand. The room had been ransacked, torn apart like a tornado as he searched for the keys to the getaway boat. The waves rolled under the boat launch door, lifting the boat high inside the stall making it almost impossible for Percy to gain entrance onto the vessel.

Summer charged across the wooden platform, racing straight for the large man who'd decided it was better to run away than face the consequences of a pissed off mother. His hands were grabbing onto the side ladder, pulling himself up off the platform when Summer slammed into him, knocking him against the boat and causing his left hand to slip from the ladder, flailing helplessly in the air.

Percy kicked wildly as he fought to regain his grasp on the ladder, connecting his right foot to Summer's ribs. The sharp pain exploded in her side, but she refused to stop. She stumbled backwards a step then lunged forward, grabbing his leg from the ladder and flinging it back, ducking down as it careened just above her head, missing by only a fraction of an inch. Summer waited until his leg had passed her head, then popped up and slammed her fist with everything she had into his groin.

His body crumbled with the impact, dropping down a rung on the ladder. Summer planted her feet and wound up a second time, landing a full blow to his balls and bringing him dropping to the platform like the catch of the day. She pounced on top of him, wrenching his head back, away from his chest, and began landing blow after blow to his face.

Summer landed a series of punches, bringing blood oozing from his flattened nose and thought the fight was about to be over when a large wave came splashing through the end door, racing under the platform and slashing up into her face, washing the blood from her forehead down into her eyes.

The mixture burned, blurring her vision.

Percy took advantage of the lapse in her attack, swung his massive arm, knocking her off to the side against the boat. Summer felt the surging boat sliding against her head and fought, gripping for the platform, trying to pull herself away from the massive boat before her head became trapped between the boat and the platform. The boat rose on the wave high in the stall, smashing against the hoist above and falling down hard against the platform as Summer rolled away. The impact rocked the platform, cracking a few boards where Summer's head had been a moment ago.

Summer hurried to her feet, watching as Percy tried to climb the ladder while holding onto his crotch like his balls might fall off at any moment. She bent down, gripped the cracked board and pulled with everything she had. The far end of the board came loose, but it remained secured with long bent nails at her feet. She kicked and cursed the board, wrenching it with everything she had.

Percy was halfway up the ladder when the board finally came loose. She stepped to the side, swinging the board with everything she had. It landed in his ribs, knocking the cell phone from his pocket, down to the side of the platform. With the air knocked from his lungs and his feet slipping from the rungs, Percy was left hanging from the top rung, struggling to keep from falling.

Summer took a step closer and wound up, but stopped, staring at the end of the board. The long bent nails were protruding from the back of the board, sticking out wildly. Clenching her jaw, she flipped the board over in her hands then swung with everything she had. The nails sunk to the bone in his side, bringing a howl of pain from Percy as he let go of the ladder, falling flat to the platform at her feet, grasping his side wildly in an effort to free himself from the excruciating pain.

Summer stepped behind, placed a foot on his butt and pulled back hard on the board. Percy squirmed and squealed like a pig in the slaughter house, wiggling back, trying to keep the nails from sinking deeper in his body.

"Who are you working for!" Summer relented on the board for a second, but Percy refused to answer so she continued her attack, pulling back with everything she had. "Who ordered you to kidnap my daughter!"

"No—Nobody. I—I did—"

Summer jerked the board back then twisted it sharply to the side, bringing another howl from Percy as he tried to buck her off his back. "Tell me who ordered this or I'll rip your fucking intestines from your body piece by fucking piece!"

"They'll…They'll k—kill me if I do."

Summer ripped the board with everything she had and the rusted nails sliced through his flesh, tearing his shirt wide open as the board came completely freed from his body, bringing an uncontrollable scream from Percy as he clenched his hand to the gaping hole in his side.

"I'll kill you myself if you don't tell me who the fuck it is!" Summer swung the board again, sinking the nails into his side just below where his blood soaked hand was clenched. He jumped with the impact, eyes snapping wide open and meeting hers. He seemed to understand at that moment just how serious she was.

"I didn't hurt her. I—I was nice."

Summer raked the nails through his side and stumbled backwards, staring at the chuck of flesh hanging from the nails. It brought a sickening feeling to her stomach. This

wasn't her style. She was the calm controlled cop. Nate—
Yeah, Nate could pull this shit off. But even after everything
she'd been through, slowly ripping the man to pieces was just
out of reach for her.

"Get up!" Summer held the board over her head,
ready to use it if need be.

"I—I can't." Percy curled into a ball, holding tight to
his side. "It hurts too much."

"You should've thought of that before you stabbed
my husband." Summer brought the board down enough to
sink the nails through the skin on his back.

"You should've thought about that before you
kidnapped my daughter." She stabbed him again in the back,
encouraging him to get to his feet.

"You should've thought of that before you gunned
down John Scott." One last poke and he slowly got to his
feet, standing, doubled over in pain.

"No—No that wasn't me. It was…"

"Who!" Summer sunk the nails into his shoulder,
hearing footsteps running down the platform leading to the
boathouse. She knew she was running out of time. Soon the
police would arrive and she wouldn't be able to strong arm
Percy for information anymore.

"I don't know his real name." The footsteps were
racing through the connecting room. "But I could…"

Gavin stepped into the room, gun raised then fired,
landing the bullet in the centre of Percy's forehead. The back
of his head exploded as the bullet whizzed dangerously past
Summer's head. She stood, frozen in place with the board
stuck in Percy's back as he gasped his final breath. It all
seemed too much of a coincidence that in the matter of a
few hours, two men had been shot dead because of her.

CHAPTER 23

The gunshot echoed throughout the boathouse, bringing a ringing to her ears which matched the roar of the waves crashing against the boat launch door. She couldn't believe what she'd just witnessed. Her chance to finally put her past to rest was blown away before her eyes. He was about to cooperate. Percy was going to say he could ID the man who'd orchestrated this whole charade when Gavin shot him dead.

"What the hell did you do that for!" Summer screamed over the roar of the crashing waves.

Gavin looked terrified standing there with the gun shaking in his hands. He stood like a statue, watching as Percy crumbled before him, pulling the board from Summer's hands as he fell.

"It—It's all right now, Summer." Gavin stepped over Percy's body and placed an arm loosely around her shoulder. "He can't hurt you anymore."

"Hurt me!" Summer shoved Gavin, stumbling back over Percy's body. "I was the one doing the hurting. What the hell were you thinking? I had everything under control. I was the one who was getting him to talk and you—you killed him!"

Gavin's nervousness turned to anger for a split second before he regained his composure. He looked around nervously and quickly tucked the gun in his waist band. "I—I came through the door and I—I thought he was hurting you. I'm sorry. I shouldn't have fired so fucking fast, but… I saw your bloodied face and just figured…"

"Well, you figured wrong." Summer flung her damp hair back, then bent down beside Percy and did the formalities of feeling for a pulse, but like she'd known, there wasn't any to be found. She started to stand when she spotted Percy's cell phone on the platform next to his body. After glancing at Gavin, who was busy checking to see if anybody was coming, Summer snatched the phone and slid it into her pocket.

"He had a gun," Gavin said, looking through the doorway into the next room. "Didn't he?"

"I don't know." Summer stood and stepped over Percy's body. "He did when he shot Nate. Had to be a rifle. Had to have a scope to make that kind of shot."

"So, you'll back me. Tell them that he was armed and dangerous."

"That wouldn't be lying," Summer said, trying to remain calm even though she knew Gavin had meant to kill Percy the second he saw him. Maybe it was his way of making up for his criminal past, wanting to right the wrong permanently? "Hell, Percy *was* very dangerous. He almost killed me up in that house."

Summer couldn't help but notice how nervous Gavin was acting right now, but he had just killed a man and she knew he wasn't in any hurry to return to prison. "Why don't you give me that gun so the cops don't accidentally shoot you when they arrive?"

"No! It's fine," Gavin snapped, then quickly changed his mood as he stepped into the next room. "Dean? Where the hell did you take off to?"

Summer raced to the doorway, watching as Dean entered the next room holding onto Sabrina's hand. The image was terrible. Dean was battered and bleeding, but the smile on his face—that smile—it filled her heart so completely. Something she thought would never be possible again in this lifetime. Dean looked like shit, teetering on the edge of his death bed, but he was there for Sabrina and her, even though he should be in the hospital.

"Went for a little joy ride, Gavin." He threw a wink in Summer's direction. "Sorry, couldn't wait for you."

Summer stepped into the room, blocking Dean and Sabrina's view of the carnage in the boat room. "You found her."

Dean tipped his head toward the doorway. "Is he…"

Summer nodded, bent down and hoisted Sabrina on her hip despite the incredible pain it caused. "Thanks to Gavin here. He saved my life in there."

"Wow, a real h—hero in the family." Dean reached out to slap Gavin on the shoulder, but fell into him instead.

Summer felt her world starting to disintegrate before her eyes. Dean didn't look good at all. He'd lost plenty of blood after the stabbing and as she looked at the blood soaked cloth taped to his side, she didn't know how much more he could take.

"Shit, he's still bleeding. Get him in the other room and lay him down." Summer rushed through the boathouse and stood staring around at the chairs, but there was no place to lay Dean down. "Better yet, let's get him up to the main house. It'll save time when the ambulance arrives."

"That's not a good idea," Gavin said. "We shouldn't move him."

"What the hell do you suggest? We leave him down here to…" Summer gave Sabrina a squeeze and hoisted her higher on her hip, then glared at Gavin. "Take him up to the house and put him in the back room. We'll follow right behind."

Gavin hesitated momentarily before slinging Dean's arm over his shoulder and dragging his staggering body from the boathouse. "He's lost a fucking shitload of blood already and he'll lose even more trying to climb those stairs."

"Then I suggest you carry him." Summer followed behind Gavin and Dean, watching the trail of blood droplets that were splattered on the wooden planks. "That is, if you're capable."

"I'm capable. Don't you worry about that?" Gavin scooped up Dean when they reached the bottom of the stairs and stumbled to get his balance, then started up the steps toward the beach house.

Summer stopped on the first landing and shifted Sabrina to her other side, refusing to let her go for any reason—even excruciating pain and exhaustion. Summer stared at Sabrina's image against the backdrop of the turbulent waves racing to the shore. She saw the glimmer in her beautiful tea coloured eyes and it brought such joy to her heart. She hadn't noticed it for the last months, but it'd always been there. Summer didn't think she'd ever be able to let Sabrina go again in her lifetime. She had been there for Sabrina in body, but not totally there in her heart. But after such a trying experience today, she realized how precious Sabrina was. Glancing at the slumping form in Gavin's arms, she knew Dean truly did care about Sabrina—and her, too.

The way Gavin was struggling up the last few steps, Summer wasn't sure if he'd be able to make it to the house at all. His breathing was laboured and his legs were quivering with each step he took. When Gavin stepped onto the upper platform, he dropped to his knees, setting Dean on the cold hard cement.

"I… I can't… anymore."

Summer knew exactly how Gavin felt, her legs were throbbing from carrying Sabrina and they felt like rubber, ready to bend and fold to the ground at any moment.

"That's okay, just leave him there for a minute and rest." Summer set Sabrina down and held tight to her hand, nudging her away from the side of the cliff.

There was a distant wail of sirens every time the wind relented, bringing a nervous anxiety to her body, wondering if the ambulance would arrive in time. Summer bent beside Dean and noticed he was still conscious and breathing. The bleeding had slowed since they'd set him down, but she still wanted him inside the house, that much closer to the ambulance.

"Gavin…" Summer said, turning around and seeing the top of his head disappear down the staircase. "Where the hell are you going?"

Gavin didn't stop or even take the time to respond. He continued down the stairs toward the boathouse—and Percy's body.

Summer let go of Sabrina's hand. "Hold onto Mommy's coat and don't let go for anything." She hoisted Dean's arm over her shoulder and strained to lift him from the ground. It took everything she had, but she managed to get him back to his feet. She could hear the wail of the ambulance growing louder with each step she took as they struggled toward the patio doors. The warmth of blood coated her side and she realized that she was only making Dean's injury worse, but she had no choice. She had to keep him moving. She couldn't sit like a duck, waiting to be rescued.

Ten feet from the patio doors and Summer felt her stomach churn. The ambulance had arrived, but not at this house. It was over at Percy's grandmother's place. She could see the lights flashing on the hilltop just off the road.

"Damn it!" She stepped through the doorway and dropped Dean to the ceramic tiled floor, then rummaged through her pocket for the cell phone she'd confiscated from Percy. She opened it and was about to dial 911 when she saw the last number dialled was still displayed. She pressed down on the selection button, highlighting the number, then pressed the connect button.

The phone rang, but not just in her ear. She heard the receiving phone ringing somewhere over the edge of the cliff.

"Gavin? Gavin's behind all this?" The ringing stopped, cut short by the receiving phone. He must have gone down there looking for Percy's phone. The only thing tying him to the crime. But now he knows I'm onto him— and he's still got the gun.

Hurrying, Summer dragged Dean across the floor, smearing blood in his wake toward the side garage door. She had to get out. Had to get away from Gavin. It wasn't until they were halfway to the mudroom that her gun slipped free from Dean's waistband. It sat there in the middle of the bloodstained floor like a treasure waiting to be taken by the worthy.

Summer hit the redial button a second time and heard the ringing even louder as Gavin raced up the last steps onto the top platform. His face was red with anger. His brown eyes narrowed and beady as he stared right at Summer.

"Couldn't fucking leave it alone?" He stood bent over, gasping for breath. "Couldn't fucking walk away and let it be, now could you!"

"Run Sabrina! Go through the garage. Get out of the house!"

"Mommy, I can't. I don't want to—"

"Go! Now!"

Sabrina ran through the mudroom into the garage and a moment later Summer heard the garage door open. She felt better knowing that at least her little girl would survive this day.

"I was only trying to help you, Summer. They ordered a hit on John Scott and I was more than willing to take the job. It should've been easy. Should've been all taken care of in the jail, but no, your buddies decided to break up the fight before Seth could finish the job. Honest, I was only trying to help you."

Summer took a step toward the patio doors. "You hired Percy to kill Dean?"

"I did what had to be done to get John Scott out in the open. Besides, Percy was a total fuckup. He was only supposed to get Dean out of the way." Gavin forced a smile and tried his best to look happy. "Summer, don't you feel better knowing that John Scott finally paid the price for what he did to you?"

"Don't give me that shit. Percy knew where John Scott had held me." Summer took another step toward the patio door. "That means you did, too. You know who's behind this."

"No—No. You got this all wrong. They gave me the information with the orders." Gavin stood and started walking slowly toward the house. "The deal was simple. Silence John Scott and collect the money."

"Money! Is that what all this is about? Money!" Summer couldn't believe her ears. Dean's own flesh and blood was willing to sacrifice Dean's life just to make a profit. "Why not let Sabrina go after you had John Scott killed?"

"That's what was supposed to happen until Percy went all rouge on me, but now I'm stuck cleaning up his fucking mess." Gavin glanced over at the ambulance on the hill. "I hate to do this. Well, not really hate. You did put me away for eight years of my life, so I do owe you something. I just never thought it'd cost you so much."

Summer saw the gun twitch and knew what was coming. She dropped to the ground as the bullet ripped past her head, slamming into the wall behind. She sprang toward the gun on the floor, grasping it quickly between her fingers like she'd practised so many times on the firing range and rolled, taking aim as she stopped, then fired every last bullet in the clip.

CHAPTER 24

Summer counted all fifteen bullets as they zipped through the air, striking Gavin's body with such intensity that he staggered backwards with each impact. He stood there against the bright blue sky, weaving to and fro in the gusting wind as blood began appearing in patches all across his chest. He staggered a few steps toward the house before collapsing to his knees and dropping the gun. His mouth was moving, but no sound came out as he appeared to be choking on his own blood.

Summer quickly clambered to her feet then ran out the doorway, straight to Gavin. She knew by the amount of shots that had ripped through his body that he wouldn't make it to the hospital—and she had to find out what he was trying to say. If Gavin thought he was dying, he might be more willing to name names than he was before.

Collapsing to the side, Gavin landed with his fingers inches away from the gun, but Summer wasn't concerned. She knew with his injuries that he'd never be able to pick the gun from the ground, let alone lift it and fire a shot, because she'd hit each mark she'd aimed for, not missing one shot.

"Gavin," Summer said, dropping to his side and lifting his head, hopeful that she would divert the blood away from his windpipe long enough to get him to answer a few questions. "Who put you up to this? Who ordered my attack?"

"Eight years. Eight… fucking years I waited." Gavin took a huge breath and the blood gurgled in his throat, causing him to choke. He spit a mouthful of blood down his chest, then clenched his eyes tightly closed. "Dean's… a lucky man. You… you were good that night. "

Summer pulled back, letting Gavin's head drop to the ground as he drew his last breath before falling silent. She felt dirty, so dirty after trusting this man to be so close to her family. She heard the sirens as loud as ever and turned to see the paramedics racing around the side of the house, pushing the stretcher toward her.

"No! Inside the house." She turned back to Gavin and shook her head. "It's too late for him."

Immediately the paramedics ran inside the back room and began lifting Dean onto the stretcher. Summer walked slowly back to the house, fearing the worst with every step. It wasn't until she stepped inside the doorway that she drew a full breath. She didn't know what she'd do if Dean didn't make it through this. If he died right here, surviving John Scott would've been for nothing.

"Dean?" She apprehensively approached the paramedics, fearing the worst. "Dean, can you hear me?"

"He's alive—barely. He's lost a lot of blood, but his vitals are still strong." The paramedic turned to Summer. "What the hell happened to him?"

"He came for me." Summer felt her chest heave and realized that Dean had never given up on her. Never forgot about her for a split second. "And he saved me… this time."

Dean's eyes flickered open and met Summer's, and she was never so happy to see those chocolate eyes gazing at her. It was almost as if everything bad that had happened between them was gone. How could she have been so stupid to force him away from her life—and Sabrina's?

"Sabrina," Summer said, dashing out the mudroom door, into the garage. "Sabrina!"

"Settle down there, partner," Nate said, holding tight to Sabrina's hand. "Anybody know who this angel belongs to?"

"Nate? But… how?"

Nate bent down and lifted Sabrina in his good arm. "You know how hard it is to find an ambulance out here? Shit, I had to wait a half hour for this one. And besides, there's no way I'd leave you all by yourself with that maniac on the loose."

Summer walked to Nate's side and kissed his cheek, then plucked Sabrina from his arm. "Thanks. I knew I could count on you."

"So, where's that bastard at?" Nate pulled his gun out and walked ahead of Summer. "Cause if you didn't kill him, then I will."

"Percy's already dead."

"Makes the trial a lot shorter that way."

"Gavin killed him."

"Son of a bitch! I never should've told them where you were headed."

"It's okay, Nate. He would've found him sooner or later. Percy was working for him."

Nate stopped and spun around on her. "That little fucker! What did I tell you?"

"Gavin's dead, too."

Nate placed his good arm around her shoulder and escorted her into the garage. "I'm sorry. I knew he was dirty, but I would never have suspected that he'd be in this deep."

"Me neither." Summer stepped through the mudroom and into the kitchen where Dean was being hooked up to an IV drip. His colour was returning and he was starting to look a little better.

"Gavin admitted to contracting out John Scott's hit and he was behind the kidnapping too."

"But why?" Nate furrowed his brow and shook his head. "Why his own flesh and blood?"

"He was bad." Summer set Sabrina down on the side of the stretcher and watched as she touched Dean's cheek, bringing a bright smile to both their faces. "Bad enough to sacrifice his family to get ahead in life."

Nate tipped his head to the dark shape outside on the walkway. "That Gavin?"

Summer nodded and watched as Nate followed the bloodstained pathway to the lifeless body. He bent before him, feeling for a pulse—a nasty habit that cops and paramedics couldn't break even when they knew there would be no chance of survival—then searched through Gavin's pockets, retrieving his phone and wallet.

She knew what would happen next and wasn't disappointed when the phone vibrated in her pocket, then began to ring. The ringing stopped almost as fast as it had started. Nate punched a few more buttons on the phone, then dropped it into his pocket and made his way back into the kitchen.

"That's some nice shooting you did there."

"Not really. I never should've shot to kill. I should've aimed for the arms and legs."

"You know that's not procedure. He was armed."
Nate glanced at the hole in the wall behind Summer. "And
your life was in danger. You did the right thing. Eliminate
the threat and protect yourself. That's the first rule of
survival. I would've hated to come here and find you lying in
a pool of blood all because you wanted to try to rehabilitate
him. Gavin's already had eight years in prison, plenty of time
to rehabilitate himself. If after eight years he hasn't changed
his direction in life then no amount of time would do it."

Nate grabbed Summer's hand, pulling her away from
the stretcher and out into the bright sunlight of the back
yard. "You might not like what I'm about to tell you and you
might want to shoot me in the balls, but I don't care what
your reaction is. I think you deserve to know the truth."

"What the hell are you talking about?" Summer pulled
free of his grip and stood staring him directly in the eye.
"You know something that I don't?"

"No." Nate held out his hands. "Nothing like that."

"Then what? What could you possibly know that's so
important you had to pull me away from my daughter?"

"Remember Detective Grimshaw said he'd run John
Scott's DNA earlier?"

Summer nodded.

"Well, I took a peek at that report and couldn't help
but wonder if he was the father of your child, so I searched
your medical reports and had the lab—"

"You bastard! You had no right to! You—"

"He's not a match. There's no way he could be the
father. Even without running a full DNA match, we know he
isn't the father."

"And Dean?"

"I'd say it's a good chance."

Summer balled up her fist then raised it, looking at Nate's bandaged shoulder. "If you weren't already hurt, then I'd hurt you myself."

"That's some gratitude. Besides, I still have a good arm."

Summer raised an eyebrow and slugged him in his good arm as hard as she could, barely moving the big lug. "Thank you, Nate. But if I ever catch you digging into my personal business again, I'll kick you straight in the balls."

Nate smirked and nodded. "Understood." He placed his arm around her shoulder and led Summer inside the house to where the paramedics stood, sneaking glances at them.

Dean pulled his shaky hand from Sabrina and set it down on Summer's hand. "You... did it. You got Sabrina back. That's all that matters."

Summer blinked away a tear at the pained look on Dean's face. "No, that's not all that matters. Keeping you alive long enough to see our daughter grow up is what matters."

Dean's hand slid from Summer's, landing against the slight bulge under her shirt. "B—oth our children."

She couldn't tell if the tears in his eyes were tears of happiness or sadness, but either way he was willing to accept this child inside her as his own, no matter if it was his or not. "You really think it's ours?"

Dean nodded as the paramedics pulled his hand from her stomach and strapped his arms down. "Time to roll," the paramedic said, kicking off the brake and wheeling the stretcher out the patio doors.

Nate snatched Sabrina from Summer's arms as they passed and carried her to the back of the ambulance. A minute later the stretcher was loaded inside and Summer took Sabrina back, then waited to climb inside.

"You coming?" Summer asked, seeing Nate take a step back from the ambulance.

"No. You go on ahead. I'll wait and catch a ride back with Jones." Nate glanced at his watch. "He should be here soon. But, then again, he might have gotten lost like usual."

"Come on, Nate," Summer begged. "There's plenty of room."

"No, I'm fine. The bleeding's stopped and besides, you need some family time. I think it'll do you a world of good right about now." Nate waited until they were inside, then slammed the door closed. "Don't worry," he yelled. "I'll stop at the hospital for my tetanus shot when we get back!"

CHAPTER 25

With the bright sunlight streaming through the tinted windows, bringing a warmth to Summer's chilled body, she watched outside as a police cruiser soared past, racing to the scene of the shooting. She couldn't help but wonder what could've driven Gavin to orchestrate such a destructive plan just to get revenge. It wasn't like he'd sold his soul to the devil for eternal life. He'd risked his brother's life and his own niece's safety in the process, with little risk involved for him.

Summer closed her eyes and saw all the pieces falling into place. It all seemed so easy to read now that it was over. Gavin's dying words—those last muttered syllables he'd croaked out before dying—those words she would've missed if she hadn't gone to his side. It'd been him that night. John Scott had only been a means of distracting her from her real attacker who'd sat beside her husband in that office as if he was a concerned sibling.

Summer fought to control a shiver that snaked through her body. Nate had been right all along about Gavin.

Maybe she was too naive? Maybe that was one of her faults, looking for the good in people instead of damning them to Hell, like old Nate. She opened her eyes and saw the smiles on Dean and Sabrina's faces and knew she had nothing to regret about her way of thinking. She'd hate to go through life always suspicious and always looking for the bad side of everyone.

Summer caught Dean's wink and realized that even though his eyes were so similar to Gavin's, there was nothing but good inside those chocolate eyes. She knew Dean would never be capable of anything bad in his entire life because even when she'd lost confidence in him, he continued to give until she came back around.

The smile faded from Dean's face. "Gavin's dead?"

Summer nodded and felt the tears fighting to get free. They weren't tears for Gavin, but for Dean's loss of his only sibling. "He was behind the whole thing. Your attack. The kidnapping. John Scott's murder."

"But why?" Dean tried to shrug his shoulders but stopped immediately, winching in pain. "Why would he do it? It makes absolutely no sense."

Summer knew if she said Gavin had done everything as revenge for putting him behind bars then Dean wouldn't ask another question, but she didn't think she could say those words—that Gavin was the person who'd abused her that night. That knowledge would surely eat away at Dean for the rest of his life knowing that he trusted Gavin and that trust was broken.

"Gavin said he did it for money. There was a contract on John Scott's head and he took the job for the money."

"But who would put a contract out on John Scott?"

Summer shrugged her shoulders and pulled Sabrina close. "There are some questions that may never be answered."

She wondered what would've happened if John Scott had never been picked up last night. Would things have continued on like clockwork, like it had for the last five months with Gavin hiding the truth while she died a little more each day? Or would he have eventually let the secret slip out one day? Summer knew there wasn't much chance of that. She knew Gavin planned to take the secret to his grave seeing how he wanted John Scott silenced, eliminating any chance of the truth coming out.

There was no way John Scott would take the fall for kidnapping, rape and assault of a police officer. He would've spilled the beans when the prosecution started counting out the years he'd be looking at for the crimes, and he would've quickly spill everything he knew.

"Don't worry, Mrs. Demure," the paramedic said, breaking the tension in the ambulance. "Your husband will be fine. *And* if he stays in the hospital for a few days, without sneaking out, I'm sure he'll be home in no time."

Dean shook his head. "No we don't—"

"Honey, if he says you'll be fine, then let it go." Summer bent forward and placed a finger on Dean's lips. "He always likes to argue. Can never accept that everything will be back to normal in no time."

"You mean." Dean struggled to swallow. "We can go back to how it used to be?"

Summer nodded and felt a warmth spreading in her chest, knowing that he still loved her no matter what she'd put him through these past months. "Like they say, what's past is past. I don't want to even think about what happened. All that's important is that we enjoy the rest of our lives together."

Sabrina slid off the seat and locked her arms around Dean's head, smothering his entire face. "Can Daddy come home and live with us, like a family?"

Summer nodded and loosened Sabrina's death grip on his face. "Yes, baby. Just like before."

"And can we go to the zoo tomorrow like Daddy promised?"

Summer pulled Sabrina into her arms and squeezed her tight again. She never thought holding her daughter would bring such pleasure as it did right now. "Not tomorrow. Daddy's going to need to rest for a few days, but yes, we can go sometime soon."

Dean smirked. "I thought you said the animals would all be hibernating?"

"Don't even start with me, Dean Demure. You're the one who put that notion in her mind. Just watch your mouth or I'll make you take her to the zoo tomorrow like she wants."

"Wouldn't be the first time I walked around all day feeling like a zombie?"

"No, I don't suppose it would be." Summer slid forward in the seat and narrowed her eyes on Dean's smiling face. "You realize how close you came to crushing me when you crashed through the side of that house? You could've killed me, not to mention Sabrina."

Reaching out a trembling hand, Dean gripped Summer's shirt and pulled her down until their lips touched. "Just shut up and kiss me."

Summer relaxed as her swollen lips met Dean's and she swore she felt a little charge surge through her body at his touch. It wasn't anything like that awful feeling she had been getting for the last while, but more like the spark of energy that lovers shared. Dean's touch brought a calm to her racing mind and heat to her entire body. She opened her eyes and saw his chocolate eyes gazing up at her and knew at that moment everything was going to be fine. She could tell from that one kiss that Dean was her knight in shining armour who'd come to her rescue.

"You know," Summer said, feeling the hot tears filling her eyes, "I never doubted you. I knew you'd come for me."

"I never gave up before and I never would as long as I have a shred of life left in this body."

Summer smiled, gazing into his beautiful eyes. "You came close to using it all up, but I'm glad you never gave up. I'm glad you came for me."

"I wasn't a lot of help."

"But you were there at the right moment and that's what counts."

Summer slid back on the bench and stared out the window as the hills gave way to the flat farmlands of the countryside. The strenuous day had taken more from her body than she'd thought as every muscle tingled with exhaustion. She wished they were at home so they could all curl up on the bed and fall asleep knowing that they were safe once again, but that wish would have to wait—at least for a few more days until Dean recovered from his injuries.

"Oh," Summer gasped, grasping her stomach.

Dean turned quickly, his eyes full of concern. "Are you alright?"

"Yeah, it's nothing." Summer forced a smile. "It's just the baby kicking."

"It's kicking already. Isn't it a little early for that?"

"I don't think Sabrina started kicking until she was six or seven months along." Summer grinned doing the math and realized that maybe this was Dean's baby after all. Maybe she would be able to look at this child and not think about that night of terror at the hands of Gavin.

"I told you it was mine. You doubted me, but I never lost faith that we'd complete our family." Dean reached out and took Summer's hand. "Maybe this time the baby will look more like you."

"Maybe it might." Summer grinned lopsidedly. "Maybe it just might."

Please be kind and leave a review on Amazon.com

ENJOY A FREE SAMPLE OF:
WAMPUS SPRINGS
Mark of the Wolf

Prologue
— Four Years Earlier —

Lori Foster sat slouched in her chair, mesmerized by the leaves dancing on the playground. At 12 years-old, she wasn't the only student in Miss Hopkin's class who found the world outside much more interesting than math lessons. Her eyes darted quickly to the wall clock then back to the leaves, waiting for the wind to whisk them high into a funnel, only to return them to their partners a moment later.

As the sunlight retreated from the angry clouds, an eerie darkness descended upon the schoolyard. It was the darkness of dusk, thick and heavy, covering every crevasse under a blanket of grey. Even though the classroom lights reflected off the dark windows, Lori noticed movement in the distance, near the edge of the woods. She squint her eyes as a fluffy white and brown bunny hopped from the woods and nibbled on a patch of tall grass.

A flash of lightning sliced through the dark sky, forking off into the distance. The overhead lights flickered, sending the classroom into temporary darkness. It was at that moment Lori saw them—two faint red dots staring out from the blackness of the woods. She blinked fast, trying to adjust her eyes, but as the classroom lights came back to full brilliance, the red dots disappeared, leaving Lori to wonder if she'd actually seen them or if it'd only been the lightning playing a trick on her eyes.

"So class, it looks like we're in for a good storm," Miss Hopkin said, turning from the chalkboard with a nervous look on her face. "I hope that's the last of the lightning. I'd hate for everyone to miss their lunch recess."

Lori glanced from her teacher, back out into the darkness of the playground. She couldn't spot the bunny anywhere.

"Lori... Lori!" She turned back to face the front of the class. "I know you'd rather be out playing, but please, let's just finish up." As if on cue, the lunch bell rang and immediately the students began to fidget.

"All right, fine. Eat your lunches then go outside." Miss Hopkin plopped into her chair and opened her desk drawer. "But if you get your shoes wet and muddy, don't even think about wearing them back in my classroom."

After retrieving her lunch sack and dumping it onto her desk, Lori dangled the plastic bag before Cindy. "Tuna. Wanna trade?"

"Tuna again." Cindy tossed her peanut butter and jam sandwich onto Lori's desk then snatched the offering. "How many cans does she have?"

"Too many." Lori ripped open the bag and took a bite. "Eat fast, cause I saw a cute bunny out by the woods. Maybe if we're fast, we can catch it. If my mom won't let me keep it, maybe yours will."

"My mom won't even let me have goldfish, let alone a rabbit." Cindy took a bite of the tuna sandwich then lifted the top piece of bread and gazed inside. "But yeah, we can see if it's still out there."

Lori pulled on the gold chain, fishing the half pendant from beneath her shirt. It had been a birthday gift from Cindy and one she absolutely cherished. Lori held her half of the pendant out, dangling it before Cindy, waiting for it to be completed.

Without hesitating, Cindy fished her pendant out and like two superheroes activating their magic power, they whispered the phrase in unison as they connected the two halves. "Best friends forever."

When the second bell rang, Lori and Cindy quickly cleared off their desks, dashed from the classroom, down the hall to the glass door. The door had barely started to close when Max and Randy stepped into their path.

"Hey, where's the fire?" Max asked, trying hard to even out his lopsided grin. "You two almost knocked us down."

"Yeah," Randy made kissing noises and shoved Max into Lori, "like you wouldn't want your girlfriend to fall on top of you, so you can suck her face off."

"Shut up!" Max grunted, returning the shove. "She's not my girlfriend. We're just friends."

"Sure, lover boy." Randy rolled his eyes then smiled at Cindy. "Where you guys going in such a hurry, anyways?"

"To the woods, to look for a bunny," Cindy said shyly. "Why, do you guys wanna come?"

"Sure, you girls might need our help catching it."

"But, if we get caught?" Max looked around nervously. "We'll be in detention all week."

"Someday, Max, you'll have to take your mother's tit out of your mouth and stop being such a baby. I'm going!" Randy started toward the back of the schoolyard. "You coming?"

"Um…" Max waited until they were a few feet away then made up his mind. "Okay, but if anything happens—"

"Don't say I didn't warn you," all three mocked in chorus.

Max shook his head, running to keep up. "You guys are the babies."

As they reached the tree line, Lori headed straight to the patch of tall grass where she'd last spotted the bunny, but it was nowhere in sight. After stepping around the bushes she spotted faint bunny tracks in the soft earth and followed the trail behind the first row of Maples. Randy and Cindy were right behind, but Max paused, peering nervously around for any sign of Miss Hopkin.

"Hey, guys. I think the old bag went inside to find the Janitor." Max snickered. "She's probably helping him mop the floor with her dress."

"You're just disgusting!" Lori said, rolling her eyes, unsure at that moment why she was actually friends with Max, but when a rustling sound captured her attention, she forgot all about him. Slowly she turned, listening and judging where the sound had come from.

"Over this way! Walk really careful so you don't scare her." Lori led the way, followed by Cindy then the two boys. They made their way down the small path, through the brush, and around more Maple trees. The woods thickened and darkened with each step they took. It was as if the trees were crowding closer, huddling against the frightening darkness. They were twenty feet from the forest edge when

Max came rushing past, almost knocking Lori off the pathway as he sprinted on ahead.

Lori saw the white patch of fur flash across the path and watched, surprised at Max's sudden burst of bravery. He seemed to be suddenly sparked with life, a welcome change from his normally nervous behaviour.

For a moment, Max disappeared behind a stand of high weeds, emerging, panting for breath, holding a struggling bunny by the scuff of the neck.

"You're a fast little bastard." Max raised the bunny to his face, staring into its eyes. "But you're no match for me." The bunny tried to run but its feet only stirred the air. "Hey, I caught him!"

"It's not a him. It's a her." Lori carefully stepped off the path and into the deep greenery. "And I'm going to name her Rosy and keep her in my garage, and—"

The forest was suddenly lit, every tree and crevasse instantly illuminated in an eye-startling flash of lightning from overhead. Momentarily every shadow retreated to its hiding place, only to escape a few seconds later, growing stronger and darker in anticipation of the attack of thunder that was due. Lori heard a few startled screams from the playground, but they were muted when a deafening roar of thunder assaulted her ears, shaking the ground and her body, too.

She glanced at Cindy and was surprised to see her shaking uncontrollably. Her eyes were glued to something just over Lori's shoulder. As a shiver raced through Lori's body, she slowly turned to see what Cindy was staring at.

There, only a few feet behind, stood Max. The bunny was no longer in his hand, but hung, swinging back and forth, its teeth pierced through both of Max's nostrils. Hands shaking, eyes crossed and wide, he stared down at the bunny. Instantly it dropped with a dull thud, scrambled to its feet then dashed away into the shadows. Instinctively Max cupped his shaking hand over his nose as the blood began to flow.

Now that the storm was overhead, the forest was as dark as night. A steady rain began to fall, pattering on the canopy above, releasing an array of multicoloured leaves, which fluttered down all around them. Lori reached out and grasped Max's free hand then hurried him back to the pathway, past Randy and a pale looking Cindy. All Lori could think about was what Miss Hopkin would say when she found out they were playing in the woods.

"I knew…bad idea." Max fought Lori's help. He struggled, pulling free of her grip. "Never should've listened."

"Come on, Max! Hurry!" Lori looked out through the clearing at the empty schoolyard. The last few stragglers were running for the door, heading for cover. Just then, a scent drifted on the wind. It was horrible, like that of rotting garbage, but worse—much worse. She turned back to Max, who was sitting on a decaying tree stump, trying to catch his breath. Maybe the smell had come from the stump?

"Tell Miss Hopkin that it happened behind the…" Her words trailed off seeing the dark shapes on the pathway behind. What were they waiting for? Didn't they realize how much trouble they were going to be in? "Cindy, Rrr…"

Two faint red dots appeared from the darkness where Cindy and Randy had been. The sight triggered the memory from earlier when she thought the lightning had played a trick on her eyes. She'd dismissed it as nothing, but now, *Nothing*, was standing over a dark lump on the pathway.

"What? What's the matter?" Max asked, struggling to get to his feet.

Lori ignored the question. She took a step toward the glowing red eyes in the darkness, wondering what was back there. It wasn't until another flash of lighting pulsed across the sky, filtering through the small gaps in the branches, that Lori saw exactly what stood guard over the fallen body.

She gasped seeing its blood-soaked muzzle inches from Cindy's mangled neck, while Randy meanwhile stood to the side, watching and waiting.

It all happened so quickly that Lori couldn't get a warning out. The beast sprang from Cindy's lifeless body and in one quick motion sank its teeth into Randy's neck, ripping out his throat. Then it silently started back into the woods—even before Randy's body began crumpling to the soft leaf-covered pathway.

"No!" Lori screamed, unable to stop herself. She froze in terror as the beast stopped. Its massive head jerked around in her direction, eyes glaring, burning like embers in a fire.

Lori felt a tremor erupt throughout her body. They had been safe. It was going away, leaving her and Max to survive, but because she couldn't control her emotions, it was watching—No, coming for them!

Lori turned and grasped Max's blood-covered hand then sprinted, pulling him down the path to the schoolyard. She didn't dare look back, afraid that the beast would be nipping at their heels. Instead, she forced Max to run faster, but he stumbled and tripped on everything, finding it hard to keep up.

When they made the edge of the woods, Max tripped on a tree root, falling flat on his face in the soft mud. Lori stopped. She pleaded for him to get back to his feet and continue running, but he looked tired and defeated. His nose was still gushing blood, bright red against his ash-white face. She glanced back into the darkness of the trees and saw the red eyes closing in fast. Max turned to see what they had been running from and when his eyes fell on the charging monster, he scrambled to get to his feet.

"Go!" he yelled.

Lori obeyed. She turned her back on the approaching killer and ran as fast as she could toward the school—and help. Her only chance to live was to out run it. She was one of the fastest kids at school, but could she outrun a killing machine?

Twenty feet from the tree line, she heard the first shriek from behind. Her body shook. She couldn't help it. She pictured Max back there and could only imagine what that thing was doing to him. He'd always been so timid and reserved, and now he was sacrificing himself so she could get away. She felt ashamed at leaving a friend behind. Felt torn about whether to flee or to fight. Lori remembered how easily that thing had finished both Cindy and Randy and realized that there was no way to win a fight against it. Her only chance was to run for help.

Another shriek came, this one more like an animal cry than a human. Legs trembling, unable to continue, she stopped and glanced back. Just past the trees, in the long grass, Max lay clinging to the rear leg of the beast. It continued on, struggling three legged to resume the chase, clearly angered at Max's actions.

Lori couldn't believe it. Max was still fighting for her. He was doing everything he could to save her, but she was stopped, watching and wasting precious time.

"Run, Lori!" Max screamed as the beast turned its attention to the parasite on its body. Max snatched a loose rock from the ground and slammed it into the approaching muzzle. It connected, splitting the beast's lips wide open. The animal paused a moment, taken by surprise, and Lori prayed that it would change its mind and retreat from the attack. But after lapping at the gushing blood, it snarled, then in a fevered frenzy repaid the effort. Max's grip loosened then his hands fell, twitching onto the damp leaves.

The beast stepped away from Max's body and stood tall on all four legs. It was at that moment Lori saw exactly what she'd been running from—a wolf! But not an ordinary wolf. This wolf was huge. Its muscular body rippled under the tattered, matted fur as it slowly stepped toward her. There was something seriously wrong with this thing. Lori felt the tremble rack her body again. The colour of its eyes told her everything—it was pure evil!

The sky let loose as if at the command of the beast and the rain plummeted to the earth, stripping leaves from the trees. The roar of the downpour filled her ears, blocking the sound of the beast's footfalls as it advanced toward her.

Lori spun, sprinting full out toward the school. Her legs burned. Her lungs ached. She knew that if she didn't get to the school—and fast—she would die right here in the playground.

The pouring rain pasted her clothing to her skin, making it hard to get full strides. She couldn't tell how much lead she had and didn't dare glance back to check, fearing she might slow slightly. The glass door of the school was twenty feet away, illuminated in the darkness of the storm. She prayed for someone to be there to open it, allowing her to dive inside, but it remained deserted.

A flicker of red reflected off the glass door sending a shiver up Lori's spine. It was right behind, chasing her down like an animal.

Five feet away—the rain fell like a waterfall, cascading down her face and into her mouth as she gasped for breath. The red eyes reflected high in the glass door—it was launching itself at her for the finish! There was no way it was going to let her escape.

Lori's fingers wrapped around the cold steel of the door handle. She watched the red eyes grow larger and larger as the wolf sailed toward her back. Every movement slowed to a crawl. She pulled the door, which seemed to weigh a ton. Slowly it began moving on the hinges as the rancid breath of the beast filled the air.

The door was half-open, but the reflection in the glass was enough to make her stomach turn. The beast's jaws were wide open. A mixture of saliva, puss and blood strung from the mangled lips, down to the darkness. Lori was on the threshold, trying to squeeze through the half-opened door, when its teeth pierced her flesh and the blood began to flow. Her left hand snapped protectively to the side of her neck and Lori released an ear-piercing scream…

CHAPTER 1

Lori bolted upright in bed, screaming at the top of her lungs, her hand clasping the scar tissue at the side of her neck.

"Wolf!" she screamed. "Help!" Then as she became fully awake and realized she was safe in her own room, hundreds of miles and four years away from the horror in the school ground, she broke down sobbing.

After a few minutes the tears stopped flowing and she was able to catch her breath. As her finger slid over the raised scar tissue, she whispered, "So lucky. So damn, lucky!"

She had after all gotten away. The wolf had taken a chunk out of her neck, but as it bit down, she'd slipped on the wet entrance mat and lost her footing, sending the wolf crashing over her head, into the brick wall. Then while it was dazed, Lori had jerked open the door and squeezed inside.

"So lucky to even be alive," she said, but then her heart twisted with guilt. Cindy, Randy and Max weren't so lucky. How could that have happened? Killed by a wolf in this day and age?

Lori glanced at the clock on the nightstand. 7:30. "Shit, I'm gonna be late for school." She swung her feet onto the floor, hurried and gathered clothes then dashed to the adjoining bathroom.

Standing in front of the bathroom mirror, Lori held the pendants from both necklaces together between her trembling fingers. The gold plating had worn off years ago, leaving the words looking old and tarnished. But, it didn't matter because every time she rubbed the two words between her fingers, Lori felt somewhat closer to Cindy. It was, after all, the last thing Cindy had given her.

Lori wondered why the memory had resurfaced now. It had been years since the last time she'd woken up like that. Why now? Why the hell, now? She could still see Max holding onto the wolf's leg—giving his life for hers.

Tears filled her eyes. She clenched them shut, praying that the image would disappear. With shaking hands, she reached for her prescription bottle of tranquillizers, popped the cap and swallowed two. Quickly she showered, dressed, then descended the stairs to the kitchen for breakfast.

"Hi, Mom." Lori avoided her mother's gaze. "How are you this morning?"

Her mother finished pouring the glass of orange juice then set it on the table. "Never mind me, I heard you scream. Was it the same nightmare?"

Lori nodded her head, dropping into the chair. "It was the same one I had back in Wampus Springs, before we moved here."

"But it's been—"

"Years. Yes, I know how long it's been."

"I could give Sara Parker a call. Maybe she can get you in to see Dr. Bruce this afternoon. He might be able to help sort out these nightmares."

"This one's not a nightmare, Mom—it's a memory! It's exactly what happened! It's like I was right back there." Lori saw the hurt look on her mother's face. "I'm sorry, I shouldn't take it out on you... But, Mom, it felt so real. Like I was really there again, back at the school." Lori took a sip of juice. "I swear I could reach out and touch the others. I could even taste the rancid breath on that thing as it lunged for my neck." Tears blurred her vision. "Those eyes, those red eyes...they seemed to bore straight inside me."

Her mother stepped behind, placing her hands on Lori's shoulders then whispered that everything would be all right and that they'd get through this together.

Pulling away, Lori looked up, meeting her mother's gaze. "Mom... I still miss Dad." Lori swallowed the lump that was stuck in her throat. "Why wouldn't he come with us?"

"I wish I knew." The tears were welling in her mother's eyes but she blinked them away quickly. "I really wish I knew."

After eating enough breakfast to satisfy her mother, Lori grabbed her purse and school bag then headed out the front door. Reaching the end of the crushed stone driveway, she glanced back. The old Victorian home was picture perfect, barely visible behind the shroud of mature oak trees. Lori could just make out the large hanging swing on the front porch. The one place she could really relax and think.

Four years ago they moved here, to Ridgeway, Ontario, a small town nestled in the countryside, on the edge of Lake Erie. With its sandy beaches and crystal-clear bay, it was an easy choice. But the true selling point was the fact that it was far enough away to settle a hysteric young girl who felt her attacker was lurking in every shadow, waiting to pounce when no one was around.

Lori swung her school bag over her shoulder then headed off down Hillcrest Street. She walked with her head down, watching the sidewalk while her mind replayed that horrible memory. The guilt of seeing Max sacrifice his life for her was gnawing at her stomach.

"Lori... Lori!" Jessica shouted from in front of the school, casting a scowl at anybody else who dared look her way. "Over here."

Lori crossed the street, walking straight to Jessica. She didn't feel much like talking right now, but Jessica wasn't the type to let her alone to sulk. "Hi, Jessica. Were you waiting for me?"

"Of course I was, I'm always waiting for you," Jessica said, raising Lori's chin with one finger. "I've been watching you since you turned the corner down the street. You must've had a bad night, cause you look like shit."

"Yeah, I had trouble sleeping." Lori lowered her voice. "I had a nightmare."

"So, you've had that same nightmare for the last three weeks. What was it this time, wandering through the woods or the farmer's fields?"

"No, not that one!" Lori stepped away from the crowd, lowering her voice. "The other one I used to have."

"The one where you were attacked?" Jessica whispered.

Lori nodded. "It's been years, but it was exactly the same. Nothing's changed. Nothing's even faded with time."

"Wow," Jessica raised a manicured eyebrow, "I have trouble remembering last week, let alone years ago. But why would you have it now, unless—"

"It has something to do with my regular nightmares."

The bell rang.

Jessica grabbed Lori's arm and escorted her inside. "You know you're gonna have to get a hold of this thing before it destroys you. One day they're gonna find you dead in your bed, with a scream stuck on your face."

"I know. Dr. Bruce says it's all in my head, but I'm still scared. What if it comes back for me? And what if something happens to you, like it did to my other friends?"

"Don't worry. Nothing will happen to me. Nothing I don't want to happen. Besides, you don't think I can kick some ass?" Lori followed Jessica's gaze. It was directed at Jessica's ex-boyfriend, Marcus and Crystal, the most popular girl in school. "Remember what I did to her last year?"

"I still can't believe you broke her nose, and what for?" Lori said. "Because your stupid boyfriend was talking to her."

"Talking?" Jessica laughed. "Half an inch closer to that bitch and they would've been tonguing each other. It serves that slut right for messing with my man."

Raising an eyebrow, Lori said, "Well, you got the last laugh. You dumped him, right?"

"Um… right." Jessica shook her head and stormed down the hall as Lori ran to catch up. "He's a typical boy, follows his dick like a divining rod."

"Well, I'm just glad you're my friend," Lori ran right into Jessica as she stopped suddenly, "and not my enemy."

"Watch where you're going." Jessica drew a long ragged breath then exhaled deeply before turning to Lori. "Did you ask your mother about the dance Friday?"

"Let's just say we had a long discussion about boys, sex and drugs. I didn't think she was gonna give in and let me go, but after thinking it over for a few hours, she finally agreed."

"That's great cause Kirk just got his car running again. You know, the Buick, the one with the big back seat?"

"No, I wouldn't know about that, but I'm sure you've checked it out many times." Lori fell behind a step. "But I don't even have a date. Who's gonna want to go with me?"

"Don't worry your pretty little head about that. I'm working on it."

As they approached their lockers, Jessica suddenly stopped dead in her tracks so Lori almost stumbled into her. "Why is he always there?" Jessica complained, gesturing toward Douglas, who had the locker to the left of Jessica's. "You have to trade me lockers, Lori. I can't take it any longer. Every time I get something from my locker, that dork, Douglas is there. How come I had to get stuck beside him?"

"Look at the bright spot." Lori smirked. "At least you've got me on the other side to balance things out."

"If you trade with me, I'll do all your homework for the rest of the year."

Lori rolled her eyes, nudging Jessica along. "Nice try Jessica, but I do want to pass."

"Anything," Jessica begged dramatically. "Just name it."

"All right I'll trade, but only if you agree to go on a date with Doug."

"Bitch!" Jessica whispered. "Fine, let's get it over with."

"You know why he spends so much time at his locker?"

"Because he's a moron?"

"No, because he likes you. That's why he pretends to get stuff from his locker, just so he can wait for you to show up."

"That's just gross! The thought of that little dweeb thinking he could score with me." Jessica shook off the thought. "He's never even been with a girl before. For all I know, he might be gay. You know, I read once that all gay guys are obsessed with neatness. Take one look at his locker and you have to agree he's a candidate for a Butt-surfer award."

Lori shook her head. "Don't even start with that. You never read anything."

"That's not true. I read it in one of the smut magazines at Kirk's house."

"You reading smutty articles? No way."

"Hi Jessica," Doug said, his face turning a brilliant shade of red.

Jessica ignored his salutation and moved past to her locker. She glanced repeatedly from the corner of her eye, waiting for him to leave. Then after fifteen seconds and no success, she pasted a big smile on her face and poked her head into his locker. "Hey Doug, you got any tampons in here? If not, how bout a pad? Mine's all bloody. You know how it gets on the heavy days."

The colour drained from Doug's face and a cold sweat broke out on his forehead. "Um... No. Um... I don't... Why would I?"

"It was a long shot, but I think mine's full. You know, I think my panties are getting full of blood too." Jessica reached inside and fumbled through his gym sack. She pulled out a sock first then finally found what she was searching for. "Can I borrow your spare undies, just in case I leak?"

Doug couldn't take any more. After ripping his underwear from her hands, he tucked them back into his sack, slammed the locker door and turned toward the classroom.

"But Doug, I promise not to wash them!" Jessica yelled as he ducked into the classroom to avoid all the stares. "You can wear them after I'm done!"

"You're so mean Jessica," Lori said, unable to hold back the smile. "I still think you guys would be great together."

"If he's so nice, then why don't you date him?"

Lori opened her locker, stuffed her bag inside then grabbed a binder. "Cause he clearly likes you. He couldn't take his eyes off you the whole time."

Jessica shoved Lori toward the classroom door. "I never thought I'd say this, but let's get to class so you'll shut the hell up."

The rest of the day went by like clockwork. Lori attended her classes but found it hard to concentrate. Her mind kept drifting back to the images of the wolf attack and to the question of why it had resurfaced now, after weeks of being haunted by the other nightmares. She prayed they weren't connected, but deep down inside she suspected what was happening and it scared her—scared her to hell.

After school, Lori hurried down the hallway, anxious to escape. She nearly made the door before Crystal, Monica, and the latest addition to their group, Tanya, noticed her passing. Lori could feel their eyes following her every step and braced for the insults, which were bound to come.

"Wolfie. Come here, Wolfie," Tanya called. For being new in town, she seemed to adapt to her position as bully pretty quick. The fact that she towered over most the girls—and some of the boys, combined with the fact that her father was the latest recruit on the police force, made her pretty much invincible. She took advantage of her position beside Crystal, and Monica—the English teacher's daughter—to dish out an extra dose of punishment.

"Wolfie want a—" Tanya stopped when a classroom door opened and Mr. Schafer stepped out. He glared at Tanya and point down the hall, toward the principal's office. Without a word, Tanya shrugged her massive shoulders and shook her head before plowing through the crowd toward the office.

Lori turned, giving Crystal and Monica a big smirk before stepping through the door. It felt great seeing the stupid look on Tanya's face at being caught red-handed, but Lori knew it would only infuriate Tanya and the next time she'd be more careful *and* more relentless.

Once outside, Lori scanned the crowd and found Jessica and Kirk propped against the wall, making tongue babies. Normally she'd wait until they tired and broke apart, but today she found herself impatient.

"You coming?" Lori said, stepping behind Jessica. "Or are you gonna try to get your gum back?"

"Yeah, I'm coming." Jessica broke free of Kirk's groping hands. "It's not like another few minutes would've killed you."

"No, but if the principal releases Tanya, then she just might try."

A big grin filled Jessica's face. She hated Tanya more than anybody else in the school. Not just because she was bigger and stronger than she was, it was the fact that her father, the cop, had been spending too much time around her mother's coffee shop, getting too close to her personal life.

"Why what happened?"

Lori recounted Tanya's run in with Mr. Schafer, and described the look on Tanya's face when he'd stepped out into the hall. The news seemed to make Jessica's day, bringing her to full-blown laughter. It wasn't until they turned the corner and were clearly out of sight of anyone at school that Lori tagged Jessica then sprinted down the sidewalk. Jessica would give chase—she always did.

Lori couldn't believe how easy it was to out run Jessica today. Normally they were neck and neck, but today her feet seemed to glide over the sidewalk, hardly landing before pushing off again. She thought it might be the rush of hormones inherited from her first menstrual cycle. The extra little push she'd been missing for the last years. Other *normal* girls had suffered and complained for years about the pain and mess, but Lori had been immune from the whole deal, that was, until last month when it finally came. She'd been half relieved, half scared to death of it. Her mother said she was lucky not to have dealt with it at a young age, but Lori could tell its absence had worried her mother a great deal, too.

Reaching her driveway, Lori glanced back, spotting Jessica a block behind, holding her stomach and gasping for breath.

"Come on, Jessica! Let's get you in the house so you can rest." Lori jogged back, bouncing on her toes and grabbed Jessica's arm. "You want me to help you the rest of the way, Grandma?"

"Ha, ha, you're so funny." Jessica shrugged off the offered hand.

Lori's mother was standing just inside the front door when they entered. Her face relaxed the moment Lori stepped across the threshold and Lori wondered if her mother had moved from that spot at all during the day, or if she'd stayed there waiting, unable to proceed with her life until she knew her baby was safe at home.

"Hi, Mrs. Foster," Jessica said, trying to hide the fact that she was tired and out of breath.

"Hello, Jessica." She smiled and turned to Lori. "And how was school today?"

"Oh, the same as always," Lori dropped her school bag onto the hall table, "boring."

Jessica jabbed Lori in the ribs. "Hey, what about Sex Ed class?"

Lori felt her heart race. Jessica had a way of turning the ordinary into the extraordinary. She shook her head, praying that Jessica would hold her tongue, but knew her prayer would go unanswered.

"They showed slides of diseased penises." Jessica smirked at Lori. "Now you can't tell me you were bored looking at penises?"

Lori's mother nervously moved the school bag then arranged the magazines on the table. "That's enough, Jessica." She shook her head. "You must drive your mother crazy."

"I try." She grinned. "I think it's my duty as a teenager to make her ponder her decision to reproduce."

"Oh, I'm sure she ponders often." Lori's mother turned and headed to the den. "Supper will be ready shortly. Don't spoil your appetites with junk food."

Lori led the way into the kitchen and rummaged through the cupboard for a snack. After plucking a bag of cookies from the shelf, she turned to Jessica. "Nobody's gonna ask me to the dance. They're all scared of me. They think I'm some kind of freak and this scar proves it."

"Scar? You can hardly see it." Jessica ripped the bag from Lori's hand and set it on the counter. She closed her eyes and rubbed her temples. "I can see a young man who's interested in your body. Nice looking boy, dark hair, full lips, tight butt. Oh… Oh… but wait—

Wait a minute. I see it! Yes, I can see it! Oh…" Jessica opened her eyes and shook her head. "Too bad, he has a small cock. But hey, you're still a virgin, so you won't know the difference."

Lori glanced around, making sure her mother wasn't near. "I'm proud to be a virgin."

"Spoken like someone who's never had sex."

Lori exhaled heavily. "Who is he? And how do you know he likes me? And why didn't you tell me before?"

"Slow down." Jessica closed her eyes and reached for her temples only to have Lori restrain her arms.

"Just tell me without all the crap!"

"It's Josh Hughes."

"From English class?"

Jessica pulled her arms free of Lori's tightening grip. "Yes, Josh. He's always staring at your ass when you go to the blackboard."

Lori glanced out the doorway. "He's nice, right?"

"He'll do." Jessica grabbed the cookies from the counter and popped one in her mouth. "Too quiet for me. But Kirk kinda knows him and he mentioned you're looking for some action."

Lori shoved Jessica back. "He didn't!"

"Who knows what they talked about?" Jessica skirted around Lori and settled in at the table. "The important thing is, Josh is interested in taking you. Kirk's gonna call tomorrow and find out for sure."

"And what exactly is he expecting?"

"I don't know. Probably what every boy's looking for. But don't worry, just tell him Aunt Flow's in town. That turns them off fast."

"It might not be a lie. It's been three weeks since my first period so it could start any time." Lori grabbed two pops from the fridge and sat down at the table, then took a cookie from the bag. "Hell, if I was three years late, it might not come back for another six months."

After dinner, the rest of the night slid by with the usual routine of television and gossip. When eleven o'clock rolled by, Jessica headed home before her mother started calling.

With Jessica gone, the house seemed too quiet. Lori peered into the den and saw her mother sound asleep on the couch, the book she was reading still clutched in her hands.

Lori fought away a yawn as she made her way up the stairs. She was almost to her bedroom door when she paused to gaze at the old family photo hanging in the hallway. There she was, four years old, hoisted on her mother and father's shoulders as they posed before the colourful backdrop of the carnival. She found herself drawn to the picture like a magnet, probably because they all seemed so happy that day, something they'd been missing for many years now.

Breaking free from the picture, she continued on to her bedroom. There she changed into her nightshirt then crossed the room to the window. The sky was clear with only the brightest stars shining through the glow of the streetlights. Lori scanned the darkness, examining every hiding place, but there was no wolf lurking in the shadows waiting for her to leave the safety of her home.

She bent down, opened the lid of the window seat then lifted her sweaters and dug deeper until she found what she was looking for. Her diary.

After opening the diary to the last entry and reading it, she stared out into the night, thinking. Then finally...

Dear Diary — Friday

Mother's finally letting me go on a date. I know how hard it is for her to let go and watch me grow up. I can still see the fear in her eyes whenever I leave the house.

Jessica's getting Kirk to set up a double date for the dance. She told me that Josh had been asking about me a lot. Who would have thought that Josh liked me? Sure, we share a few classes and I have caught him looking at me. But here I just thought he was looking at me and thinking 'There's one messed up girl' but he wasn't. He actually likes me and by the way, he is cute and he does have a nice butt, just like Jessica said.

I was starting to wonder if I'd ever have a boyfriend. They all seem so scared of me. It doesn't help that Crystal and her new recruit Tanya spread all those stories about me.

Lori felt her blood pressure rise just thinking about that latest rumour. The previous one was bad enough, but to spread a rumour that she was the one who'd killed her best friends, then turned the knife on herself in a botched attempt at suicide. That crossed the line from being bitches to slandering bitches.

Lori sighed.

Maybe Josh is different. Maybe he won't care what Crystal says about him dating me. Besides, this could be the turning point in my life, going from such a screwed up childhood, to some kind of normal life.

It could be the beginning of a real relationship. Something that I thought this scar on my neck would prevent from happening. But now I'm getting carried away. We might not have anything in common, or he might change his mind and cancel before Friday. Oh well, no sense in worrying about it, I'll find out soon enough.

Gotta go

Lori closed the diary then placed it back inside the window seat. With her sweaters hiding her thoughts, she turned off the lights and climbed under the covers. The thought of Josh taking her to the dance caused her body to tingle with excitement. It was a welcome change to the dread that she normally felt, worrying about the nightmares and memories that would inhabit her sleep.

CHAPTER 2

The sun was high overhead as Lori walked the two blocks to Jessica's house. Her mind was reeling from the memory of the dream she'd had last night. But at least it'd only been one of her usual dreams. She dreaded reliving that memory of the wolf attack at the schoolyard. The mere thought of seeing her friends being killed all over again sent her stomach churning. She hoped she would never see that image ever again for the rest of her life.

Just as she stepped onto the sidewalk, heading up to Jessica's house, the front door opened and out ran Jessica. She grabbed Lori's hand and pulled her quickly down the road.

"What's the matter?" Lori asked. "Your mother hounding you to work at the coffee shop today?"

"No, it's her new *boyfriend!*" Jessica's jaw muscles were bulging. "She finally let it slip who he is."

Lori wanted to ask, but waited until Jessica finally spilled it.

"Ken Parry! I should've guessed. He's new to town and—"

"Ken Parry—As in Officer Ken Parry. The same man who fathered Tanya, the Sasquatch?"

Jessica nodded. Her face looked long and pale. "I should've known it was him. They've only been here for less than a month and I should've known it was someone new by the way she was acting. But, how could she find him the least bit suitable? Just look at his offspring. It looks like he mated with a fucking Bigfoot. What's going to happen if they get along? What if they get married?"

"Then the fucking Bigfoot will be sharing a room with you."

Jessica slowed to a walk when they were a safe distance away. "As if. I'd rather move out and live on the street."

"Did Kirk call yet?" Lori asked, thinking she'd change the topic before Jessica got into full melodrama mode.

"Call who?" Jessica shrugged her shoulders. "I don't know what you're talking about."

Lori gave her a playful shove, sending her stumbling to the grass.

After regaining her footing, Jessica gave Lori a long careful look. "Kirk said he'd call him sometime today."

Lori dropped her gaze to the sidewalk. She felt her hope fading fast. After all, it had all been too easy. To think Josh would actually want to be seen out in public with the girl who was rumoured to have murdered her childhood friends then blamed it all on a wolf attack, was preposterous.

"Hey." Jessica put her arm around Lori's shoulder. "If Kirk doesn't call by suppertime then I'll make him call. You've gotta understand, it's not easy for a guy to ask another guy something like that. They have all these macho hang-ups about being cool. And nagging another guy just ain't cool."

"It's just that I'm so excited. Last night I couldn't stop thinking about Josh and the dance. But, what if he changes his mind and doesn't want to go with me?"

"Then I'll go over there and kick his ass until he changes his mind." Jessica gave her shoulder a squeeze. "Don't worry. I'll take care of you."

They continued down two more blocks then turned right at Len's Corner Store. Once they rounded the curve in the road, shimmering water danced between the gaps in the trees. At the far end of the road, a pathway had been sliced through the thick grove of pines, carved with care to form a perfect walkway. The branches were pruned high above their heads, forming a peaked ceiling. No matter how many times they took this path, it always seemed like they were following a secret pathway to some strange and mysterious land far away.

The air seemed to drop ten degrees as they entered the shade of the tree line. With each step taken, the aroma of pine intensified as their feet stirred the fallen needles. They followed the pathway for five minutes then the cool darkness gave way to blinding sunlight reflecting off the clear blue water of the bay.

The beach was unusually barren for this time of year. Usually a dozen kids or more would be swimming in the water or playing football at the edge, but the cool spring had kept the water cold, forcing the sun worshippers to pray for enlightenment on the beach instead. Off in the distance only a few kids dared each other to go in the water, but they were lucky to make it waist deep, before running back to the warmth of the sand.

Lori and Jessica strolled along the beach for twenty minutes, stopping occasionally to pick up a stone and skip it through the waves, as they headed down toward the pier. The ancient wooden structure creaked and moaned with each step they took. When the boards up ahead looked too rotten to support their weight, they plopped down on the edge and dangled their feet inches from the water's surface as brightly coloured sunfish gathered, circling below their feet, imitating Piranha readying for a quick snack.

Removing her top, Jessica revealed the bikini beneath then readjusted her contents as she lay back on the wooden platform.

"When I called Kirk last night he mentioned that Josh has been asking all kinds of questions about you."

"He has?" Lori felt warmth stirring deep inside at the thought. "Like what?"

"Well, he asked if you put out on the first date."

"He did not!" Lori felt the heat in her cheeks and knew her face would be bright red. "He wouldn't say anything like that. Would he?"

"I'm just messing with you, but apparently he has been asking if you have a boyfriend, and if you date and you know, guy stuff. It sounded like he was interested in asking you out anyways, so we'll just get Kirk to give him a little shove in your direction."

"This will be great. You know," Lori closed her eyes against the bright sun, drinking in the warm touch, "the more I think about it, I have noticed him looking at me in class. But I thought he took Monica Jones to the last dance?"

"He did. I remember seeing her plump little body squeezed into that purple dress. You really should've come. It was great. She looked like a fat grape ready to explode."

"Then why would Josh ask me to the dance? Why not take Monica again?"

"Just look at her. There's no contest between the two of you."

"Stop."

"No, really. Josh would be an idiot not to pick you. I think the only reason he took Monica is that he wanted to get a good mark in Miss Jones's English class. You watch, if he dumps Miss Jones's little baby and takes you instead, his mark will nosedive."

"Come to think about it, Josh was looking at me yesterday in class. Maybe if I hadn't ignored him, he might have asked me to the dance then."

Jessica turned on her side and faced Lori. "See. I told you he liked you—or just wants to get in your pants."

Lori turned, slapping Jessica's thigh hard. A red handprint rose immediately.

"Hey," Jessica rubbed away the sting. "That's gonna leave a mark."

Lori raised an eyebrow and smirked. "From what I've heard, Kirk spanks your ass harder than that."

"Yeah, but my ass has more padding. And besides it makes me really horny when he does that." Jessica spanked her ass then let out a long exaggerated cry of pleasure. "Just think. We'll be going on our first double date Friday night. Me and Kirk, and you and Josh. Hey, maybe Josh might give you a little spanking in the back seat then we'll hear you moaning and groaning."

"Oh, stop it." Lori shook her head. "Like I'd put out on the first date. I'm not you."

"Yeah, you couldn't handle being me." She rolled on her stomach and propped herself up on her elbows. "Hey, since when do you sleep past seven? At first, I thought your mother was trying to get rid of me when I called this morning. I thought there's no way you could still be in bed at ten o'clock."

"Um… I didn't sleep so well last night. I… I woke up during the night and, um…"

"And what?" Jessica sat up and looked Lori in the eye. "Another nightmare. Which was it this time, the school attack, or the other?"

"It was the other. I was wandering through the woods again. It feels so real like I'm actually there, but…" Lori swallowed hard. She remembered how dirty she felt when she finally realized what had happened last night and she still couldn't get over the embarrassment of it. "When I woke from the nightmare, I was… naked."

Jessica shrugged her shoulders. "So we're all naked sometimes. Hell, I sleep in the nude all the time. One time I got up and started downstairs for breakfast. I was halfway down the stairs when I realized that there was a breeze in the valley below."

Lori shook her head. "No, it wasn't the fact that I was naked, but that when the nightmare ended and I finally woke up, I was standing in front of the window."

"Exhibitionist," Jessica gasped. "Now that's what boys like. Me, I've never tried that, but hey—"

"I felt so dirty standing there in front of the window. I couldn't believe that I'd stripped down and stood there for... for god only knows how long."

"Was the light off?"

"Yeah, but what—"

"Well, the most anybody walking by would see is the outline of your body. It might be enough to horn up the old man who walks his dog late at night—or freak him out. Either way I don't think you have to worry about pictures being posted on the internet or anything like that."

"But why would I do it? I've never done it before."

"What's different this time?"

"Nothing—Just the nightmare the other night of when I was bitten. That was the first time I'd had it since I moved here four years ago. I used to wake every night after the attack from that exact nightmare, but then we moved here and it disappeared. It was like the distance severed the tie to it."

"More likely you just relaxed, not having to worry about the wolf around every corner."

"Or the distance broke the control the wolf had over me?"

"Don't say that again. You've told me what happened, and yes, I'll admit it's pretty fucked up, but I doubt there was anything special about that one pissed off wolf. You guys probably stepped into its territory and disturbed its den or something like that."

Lori knew Jessica's viewpoint on the wolf attack and knew there was no way to change her mind, but if only she'd seen what Lori had seen then there wouldn't be any problem convincing her. "Maybe you're right Jessica. I guess I'll just have to pin the drapes shut tonight. I can't stand the thought of waking up naked in front of the window again."

"Just in case, I'll call Josh and send him over. What time should I tell him?"

Lori smacked Jessica's thigh again but Jessica just laughed and lay back on the dock, watching the clouds float slowly by. "So, what do you think you're searching for in all your nightmares?" she asked.

Lori shifted on the rough wooden planks then sat up, hugging her knees to her chest. "I don't know, all I can remember is walking around searching, but I don't think I ever found what I was looking for." Lori's eyes blurred with tears. She sat there staring off into the bay while the images replayed through her mind.

"So what do you think it means, Lori?"

"I don't know. Maybe it means that I'm looking for happiness—friendship—something?"

"But you've found both of those things. I'm your best friend and obviously you're mine. And how can you say you're not happy with your life? You're beautiful. You live in a nice house and your mother's a nurse who makes lots of money. Oh yeah and the best thing is—if I haven't already mentioned it—you have me." With that, Jessica sat up and wrapped her arms around Lori.

Lori continued hugging her knees. Her eyes burned with fresh hot tears. She felt the warmth from Jessica's body and her arms felt strong and supportive holding her tight, but there was still a chill racing down her spine at the memory of the nightmares. She feared that no matter how far away she ran, there would always be a tiny chance that the wolf would someday return and finish the job it started four years ago.

"I know it's been hard, Lori, but it's all behind you now. From here on in it's you and me, okay? You just let me know what will make you happy and we'll do it."

Sometimes Jessica could be such a pain in the ass, but at times like this, she made up for it tenfold. Lori smiled and was only able to nod in agreement as a few more tears overflowed, following the trails down her cheeks.

Jessica released her hug and sat back smiling. "Now, if you could do anything you wanted to today, what would it be?"

"Why don't we just sit here?" Lori said. She knew that Jessica would rather head to the mall or even to the schoolyard to see if the boys were playing a game of football today, but she didn't think she could stand either place right now. Her mind felt all mixed up and the best place for her to think things through and sort out her feelings was right here, listening to the water lapping at the wooden pillars under her feet. There was something calming about the water. Maybe it was the rhythmic sound it created or maybe it was the fact that life survived both above and below the water's glassy surface.

"I guess I could work on evening out my tan lines." Jessica dropped back, lying down on the pier then removed her bikini top.

"I don't know how you can do that." Lori wiped the tears from her cheeks and settled down beside Jessica. "Aren't you embarrassed that someone will see you?"

"What's wrong? They're only tits. Hell, you've got the same thing under there, too. Besides half the old men have bigger man-boobs than both of us. Who cares if it gets them worked up? Hell, it's half the fun trying to get them to walk around with a boner in their swimsuits."

"I don't know, Jessica, I don't think I could ever do that."

Jessica turned her head and shaded her eyes, meeting Lori's gaze. "From what you told me you've already shown the whole package in your window."

"That's different. I don't have—"

"I'm just kidding." Jessica rolled her eyes. "Don't worry about it. You're beautiful. Don't be afraid to show it off."

"Yeah, beautiful," Lori scoffed. "Beautiful girls don't have to have someone find a date for them."

Wampus Springs is available at: www.amazon.com